Seconds BEFORE Sunrise

By: Shannon A. Thompson

Seconds Before Sunrise
Copyright ©2015 Shannon Thompson
All rights reserved.

ISBN:978-1-63422-086-6
Cover Design by: Marya Heiman
Typography by: Courtney Nuckels
Editing by: Kelly Risser

For more information about our content disclosure,
please utilize the QR code above with your smart phone
or visit us at

www.CleanTeenPublishing.com.

To Calone – for showing me light in the darkest of times.

ONE

Jessica

IT WAS A HUMID NIGHT IN AUGUST, AND THE RIVER TRICKLED PAST us as if most of the water had disintegrated during the previous months. It skimmed over the rocks, and I hesitated to add to the collection by tossing pebbles across the already waning surface. The darkness was enough.

"Isn't it beautiful?" Crystal leaned against my arm, and I nodded because it was.

The park was secluded, hanging onto the edge of Hayworth, but it seemed to stretch for miles, past Hayworth, past Kansas, and past wherever my thoughts could take me.

"I knew you'd like it, Jess," Robb said, plopping down next to me. "Too bad we can't come here all the time."

I wanted to ask why, but I already knew the answer.

Trespassing signs littered the sidewalks surrounding the park. I understood the legal ramifications, but it seemed pointless to contain such a consoling place to a single family—the Welborns.

"I'm surprised more kids don't break in," I admitted.

"I'm not," Crystal said, pointing her thumb over her shoulder. The forest was a cluster of shadows behind her. "That's where she did it."

"Where who did what?"

Crystal's bottom lip puckered, but she didn't speak. Robb straightened up, cleared his throat, and explained instead.

"Welborn's mom," he said. "She killed herself in there."

My eyes shot over Crystal's bleached hair and focused on the looming trees. They were dark, but they weren't eerie. They swayed like any trees would do, but I felt as if I'd seen this forest before.

Goose bumps cascaded over my body, and I jumped to my feet, rubbing my arms. I stepped away from my friends, but I didn't move forward. I should've wanted to run away, but I didn't. I wanted to go toward it.

"Creepy, isn't it?" Robb's voice crawled over the back of my neck as I turned to him. When I met his eyes, he ran a hand through his hair. "We used to dare one another to spend the night in there," he continued. "I did it once. It about killed me."

Crystal sprung up and smacked his arm, waltzing past us. "You big baby," she said, smirking as she caught my eye. "Zac and him didn't even stay in there for an entire night. They ran out crying."

"We were seven," Robb argued.

Crystal giggled. "And afraid of the dark."

He folded his arms across his plaid shirt. "I'm not afraid of the dark," he grumbled as if he were stuck in his childhood. He wouldn't meet our eyes, and his confident demeanor had shattered.

Crystal ignored him as she stretched her palm out. "Give me the keys," she ordered, and Robb, without question, gave up his Suburban's keys. It was dark, and we had school in the morning. Summer vacation was over, and our parents would want us home.

"I'll pull it up to the sidewalk," Crystal said, walking along the river. "You guys better be ready in ten minutes," she shouted, knowing the car was yards away. She disappeared around the corner before Robb spoke again.

"Here's to the summer." He chucked a rock at the river. It splashed, ripples waving against the riverbank, and I cringed. The water moved tiny twigs and shifted the dirt, covering patches of grass with brown dew. The ripples were more like tidal waves against the shore, violent and fast.

"Jess?" Robb's thick, brown hair looked black in the night's shadows. "Are you okay?"

"Yeah," I breathed, hesitating to pull my eyes away from him to stare at the river. My gut was contorting with nerves. I glanced to the forest, to the river, and back to the forest again. Everything looked familiar.

"We should probably start walking," Robb said, heading toward the sidewalk, but I held him back.

"Are there any other rumors about the forest?" I asked. "Other than the suicide, I mean."

Robb didn't move. "What's bothering you, Jess?"

I held my hands in front of me and dug my nails into my palms. "I feel like I've been here before," I admitted.

He chuckled. "Come on, Jess."

"I'm serious, Robb." I waved my hands around. "It's too familiar."

His laughter was replaced with a grimace. "Are you sure it wasn't a different park, somewhere you used to live?" he suggested.

I hugged myself. He could be right. It'd only been eight months since I moved to Hayworth, and it was impossible that I'd walked into the park by myself. Crystal, Robb, and I went everywhere together.

"You're probably right," I sighed, and he started walking again. I followed him past the river and ignored my nostalgic feelings until we reached the river's guardrail.

I froze, gripping the cooling metal, and my blood turned to chilled water within my veins. I stared at my shivering hands and slowly brought my eyes up to the forest. The entrance was right in front of me, opening to darkened brush and thickened ground. I only saw shadows, but I believed I could see more. A figure lingered in my memory, a vanishing outline in the darkness, even though no one was there. I fought the urge to shout at the trees.

Robb touched my shoulder, and I jumped. He stepped back, his eyes widened, and Crystal honked from the street.

"Jess?"

"I'm fine," I repeated, brushing him off as I rushed past him. I didn't want him to see my face. I felt like I was crumbling, and I didn't want my friends, or anyone, to know it. My confusion was mine, even if it was bordering on insanity.

2

Jessica

"RUN."

The sudden voice was barely audible. My heart was racing as fast as my legs were. I leapt over torn up brush and twisted past trees at speeds I couldn't comprehend. The darkness blended together.

The ground was rigid beneath my feet, and I stumbled as I looked over my shoulder. They were after us. I could feel them, their heat and their strength. The suffocating air was filled with electricity, and it burned against my exposed flesh. As suddenly as it touched me, it was around my neck.

Her black eyes were boundless, and I lost myself in them before she tossed my body. I flew over her shoulder, easily and helplessly, and collided with wet leaves. My limbs splayed, and I clawed at the ground, attempting to stop my momentum—but it was too late.

My head cracked against a rock, and the sound shuddered through my body. Light consumed my vision before it was replaced with blackness, and then I was awake again.

I saw his eyes first, crystal-blue but clouded with concern. When he met my gaze, he dropped the cold rag he had brushed across my face. The condensation awoke my consciousness.

I gasped, trying to sit up, but his hand pressed my shoulders down. My body reacted to his touch, and his fingers lingered as if he couldn't let go.

He spoke, but I didn't hear him, and time blurred like the night had moments before. He moved too quickly, and I couldn't follow him. He was by the window, and my legs burned as if I'd stood moments before. But I was still in bed, and he spoke by the window.

I couldn't hear him, but I knew what was happening. He was leaving, and he wouldn't be back. He disappeared in a cloud of smoke, and I screamed.

———◆———

My shout echoed against my bedroom walls as I sat up, clutching my blanket. My chest was pounding, but it felt like my entire body. I gasped, surveying my empty bedroom, and shuddered when my eyes flew over to my window. No one stood in front of me.

It was only a dream.

I climbed out of my bed and walked over to the window. Moving the blinds, I gazed across our front yard. It was nighttime, but the road glistened from the streetlamps. I pressed my heated forehead against the glass and breathed. Despite the dream, my head felt as if it had smacked into the rock, and it wasn't the only part of my body that hurt.

Everything did. My arms, my legs, my chest. It burned and shook, but my unscathed skin proved the lack of reality. I was perfectly fine.

"It was just a nightmare, Jess," I whispered to myself, turning away. I snatched up my blanket, wrapped it around my shoulders, and walked downstairs. I needed to get out of my room, even if it were only for a minute.

I walked past my parents' room and went downstairs. The house was quiet, and lingering nighttime comforted my sudden fears. I'd always been a night person, but it felt more essential to my wellbeing tonight than any other night. The shadows felt right.

I twisted through the kitchen, the living room, and into my father's study. The computer buzzed, revealing my father's late night of work, and I turned it off. It shut down, and the only light dissipated.

Breathing was easier now, and the nightmare was beginning to make sense. It'd only been hours since I'd been in the forest with Robb and Crystal. Even if it were just a cluster of trees with a dark history, I'd dreamt I was almost killed in it.

"Jessie?"

I spun around, facing the high-pitched voice that broke through my train of thought. After turning on a light, my mother, who was dressed in a pink robe, fiddled with her blonde ponytail.

"Mom," I exhaled, praying my adrenaline would calm down. "What are you doing up?" Unlike me, she was a morning person.

She smirked as she sat down in the computer chair, rotating it to face me. "I could ask you the same thing," she said. "You have school in the morning."

"I know," I said, tightening my blanket's embrace. "I'll go back to bed soon."

Her round face tilted. "Are you all right, sweetie?"

"I'm fine." The words were beginning to feel repetitively empty. "I had a nightmare," I elaborated, knowing she would ask more questions.

She crossed her legs and placed her hands in her lap. "What was it about?" she asked.

I pressed my toes against the wooden floor. "I don't really know," I admitted, hoping to forget the scene as quickly as it came, but it echoed through me, refusing to leave. "It was just a dream."

"If it was, you would've stayed in bed." She raised her thin eyebrows. "You used to have really bad nightmares as a child."

"I did?" I couldn't remember.

"All the time, but you grew out of them." Her face tilted to the other side, and her ponytail waved over her shoulder. "They were really confusing for you."

"Why?"

She bobbed her foot up and down. "You thought they

were real."

I couldn't breathe.

"I thought it was entirely probable they were caused from trauma—"

She stopped because she didn't have to explain.

"They were fleeing, you know," I said, recalling the newspaper article about my biological parents' untimely death.

"I wish you wouldn't take Crystal so seriously, Jessie," she said in a scornful tone. We had this conversation numerous times during the summer, but she wasn't budging. "She doesn't know any more than the police do."

I bit my lip and looked away. The lack of information had been the most aggravating part of my adoption. Even with months of researching, I couldn't find my extended family. It was as if my biological parents had only existed to bring me into the world, nothing more. I couldn't even find people who remembered them, and residents rarely left Hayworth. It seemed impossible, but it was the truth, and I didn't like it.

"Is that what you're dreaming about?" my mother guessed. "The car wreck?"

"No," I said, fighting the flashing forest as it burned into my mind like a memory.

She ignored my answer. "What's done is done, Jessie," she said. "There's no worth in losing sleep over it."

"They were my parents," I argued quietly.

"And they still are," she agreed. "But death doesn't mean they aren't around you."

I groaned. "You sound like a Disney movie."

"I'm old. I'm allowed to," she said, standing up to approach me. She opened her arms, and I fell into her embrace, closing my eyes. She smelt like lavender. "Get some sleep. You have school in the morning," she whispered.

I stepped away. "Thanks for the reminder."

"Goodnight," she said. "I love you."

"Love you, too, Mom," I said.

She left the room, her robe dragging behind, and disappeared around the corner. I collapsed in her chair, unable to settle down. While some of her words had been comforting, the others disturbed me. As a child, I thought my dreams were real, and despite the illogical notion, I saw the truth in it.

My dream had felt more like living than my current life did. Every part of me wanted it as a memory instead of a nightmare.

3

Eric

I SHOVED MY HEAD INTO MY LOCKER AND BREATHED HOARSELY. IT was the first day of school and sitting next to Jessica was already killing me. I wanted to talk to her, hold her, be with her—anything really—but I couldn't. If the Light realized who or what we were, she'd be killed, and there was nothing I could do except stay away.

"You okay?" Jonathon asked, his voice squeaking through the slits of my locker.

I leaned back to stare at the partially blind artist. I wouldn't believe he was Pierce, a powerful shade, if I hadn't known his two identities myself.

"I'm dealing," I grumbled, unable to keep eye contact as Jessica passed us.

She flipped her brunette curls as she playfully hit Robb McLain's arm. Robb McLain with his sparkling teeth, gelled hair, and playboy personality was the perfect jerk.

Robb slipped his arm over Jessica's petite shoulders, and I gripped my locker.

"I am this close to killing him."

Jonathon chuckled. "I'd like to see that."

"This isn't funny."

Jonathon's hands stuck straight up. "No. No. Of course not." He tried to smother his laughter. "Not funny at all."

I ignored his humor and uncurled my hand from the

locker. "This is a lot harder than I thought it'd be," I said.

Jonathon gestured to the bent door I'd practically destroyed. "I can tell."

I pushed it back into place, cringing at the sharp noise.

"You have other things you should fix, too," he said, pointing to my face.

I knew what had happened. My eyes were ice blue, not green.

I rubbed the partial transformation away. "Great," I muttered. I couldn't even control myself during the day.

"Why don't you go home already?" Jonathon knew my schedule better than most. Homeroom was over and so was my day at school, but I hadn't gone straight to my car. I was too aggravated to drive.

"Are they dating?" I asked Jonathon, pointing my thumb over my shoulder. I knew Jessica and Robb hadn't moved. I could still hear her giggles, and I knew Jonathon was more in tune with gossip than I'd ever be.

"Would it matter?"

I glared. "Are they, Jonathon?"

"No."

"Good," I said. "I'd have to kill him twice if that were the case."

Jonathon sighed. "Jessica warned you this might happen," he said, attempting to be the angel on my shoulder. "You can't expect a seventeen-year-old girl to be single for long."

"Thanks for that," I snarled, swinging my bag over my shoulder. "I'm going home," I said, snapping my headphones on before he could speak again. I brushed past him, but his voice telepathically pushed through the tunes.

"Take some of that anger out in training," he said. *"You only have four months."*

I didn't respond. Instead, I waved my hand over my shoulder and shut our telepathic line. He couldn't continue the conversation even if he wanted to. I was done, and I wanted everyone else to be, too.

————◆————

The doorbell rang, and I knew it was Camille before I heard her voice.

"Hello, sir," Teresa—my guard, Camille, in her human form—said, and my father's grumble drowned her out. She'd started using the front door ever since I hadn't bothered to hide my strange comings and goings. I'd be in my room one minute, and then I'd transform to leave. I never used the front door, and my stepfamily was starting to notice.

"They aren't here," my father dismissed Teresa's concerns. "But they'll be back soon."

"Is Eric—"

"In his room," he answered.

Teresa tapped her foot against the wood floor. "He's not taking this very well." She didn't bother dropping her voice since she knew I was listening.

"Did you bring him home?"

"He drove."

I turned over, staring at my car keys on my desk. I hadn't bothered hanging them up. I hadn't bothered doing much. My room was a mess, and two of the light bulbs were broken. My room, aside from the nightlight beneath my desk, was dark, and I liked it that way.

"I should've figured," my father sighed. "He hasn't left his bedroom since he got home."

"He saw Jessica today," she said. The house creaked, and the couch squeaked as someone fell into it. I could practically see what they were doing.

"I shouldn't have told him about Jess, Camille," he said, using her Dark name. Apparently, the confusion with double identities was genetic. My father couldn't stand using human names any more than I could. "We should've kept it from both of them."

I knew what he was talking about. My life was destined for a successful battle by killing another, and Jessica was my only weakness. I was in love with her, and she was in love with me, but our relationship —our identities—would kill us both if the Light figured out who she was and used her against me. She could be absorbed, whatever that meant, and my battle's outcome would flip. I would lose, and everyone in the Dark would lose their powers. I couldn't see her, and I hadn't since Independence Day. Not until I saw her at school.

"With all due respect, sir," Camille began, quiet enough that even I, with my heightened hearing, could barely hear. "They found out on their own."

"Not about the destiny."

"Yet it happened," she said, and her nails tapped against the stairwell. "Do you know how Jess is?"

His jacket rustled, signaling a shrug. "I followed her around yesterday with her guard-to-be. She seemed normal enough."

I sat up. Jessica getting a guard was news to me.

"I'm going to speak with him," Camille said, but my father didn't respond.

I listened as Camille walked upstairs. She passed the kitchen, turning into the hallway, and soon her hand was on my doorknob. It twisted, clinking against the lock, and she breathed against the wood.

"I know you heard me," she said, but I didn't move. I listened to the metal lock release, and she opened the door. Her eyes were black, a sign of her power, and then they flickered back to blue.

"Why didn't I know about the guard?" I asked.

She stepped inside, supporting herself against the doorframe. Her pixie cut had grown to her shoulders. "Maybe if you talked to someone, you would've been told."

I flinched. "I don't feel like it."

"Quit the bullshit, Shoman." She threw her hands into the air. "It's incredibly frustrating, and it isn't helping anyone."

"I wasn't trying to help anyone," I said, standing up from my bed. I wasn't trying to be bitter. I was only trying to stay away. I knew my duties, and I didn't need everyone in my face

13

about it. I'd get it done, especially if it meant saving Jessica's life.

"So, what now?" Camille asked quietly, rocking from foot to foot. I knew what she was thinking. I only had four months before it was done. Darthon or I would be dead, and talking about it didn't change the circumstances.

"I train," I said, but she shook her head. Apparently, I didn't know what she was talking about. I was too caught up my own worries to think straight.

"Let's go out," she said. "Go for a flight—"

"No."

Air seethed through her teeth. "Why not?"

I didn't answer.

"Eric." Her rant came without a breath. "Do you know how much your stress is affecting everyone? They think you're worried. They think you won't succeed—"

I was in her face before she knew it. I was a shade, transformed by anger, and I'd transported inches away from her. "Do you think this is easy, Camille? Is that it?" I was glaring, and my body was heated with darkness. "Because it isn't. And it was never meant to be."

The nightlight beneath my desk exploded, and Camille stepped back, paling. I had never raised my voice to her.

"What's going on?" my father asked, rushing upstairs.

I gripped the doorway to keep myself from yelling at him, too. "Just losing my shit again," I grumbled.

Camille bit her lip, reminding me of Jessica, who always did that. I closed my eyes.

"It's entirely possible that you're reacting to Jessica's absence," my father said.

I forced myself to face him. "Meaning?"

He cleared his throat, pulling at the ends of his suit jacket. He was surely meeting the elders later. "Meaning, your energies have already mixed," he said, refusing to say the truth. Just by kissing, we'd become physically attached. My Dark side— Shoman—was adjusted to her existence. "Without her ability to transform, her energy doesn't exist," he continued. "It could cause a haywire in your control."

This was why she was my weakness. She affected me, even when she was absent. My hands threaded through my hair as I started to sizzle back into my human form. I could feel my hair curling. "That's good news," I murmured, but no one responded, and I kicked off the wall. "I'm going to the shelter."

"You should relax," my father called after me. "Urte is planning a rigorous day for you tomorrow."

"I don't have time to relax," I said, disappearing before they tempted me to forget my responsibilities for a single night.

4

"YOU HAVE TO HANDLE THE PAIN," URTE SAID, KNOTTING THE straps around my wrists and feet. My blood circulation was halted.

"This is ridiculous," I said, skimming the machine I was attached to. My father wasn't joking when he said Urte had rigorous training in mind. Urte was testing my pain resistance with a machine designed for shade torture. As soon as Urte pressed the *On* button, floods of Light energy would enter my body, and I would be left to deal with it.

"You need to be able to withstand all kinds of pain," he said as I squirmed against his touch like a child at the dentist. "You need to be able to handle torture."

"When the hell am I going to be tortured, Urte?" My question strained against my throat straps. A needle would pierce my jugular vein directly.

"You never know, Shoman."

"Actually, I do," I argued. "The prophecy states a battle, not a torture frenzy."

"And your wit isn't going to solve either one."

"You aren't the one being put into a torture machine," I pointed out, remaining still. The last thing I wanted was to start the pain early.

Urte couldn't meet my eyes. "I'm the teacher, you're the student."

"Like that's a reasonable explanation for your actions."

He tightened the last strap on my knee. "You don't have a choice."

I glared at his back as he fiddled with dials. At any moment, the pain would begin. "What if I were Pierce?" I asked.

Urte's wrinkles contorted around his frown. "Don't play that card, Shoman."

"I'll play any card I can to get out of this," I retorted, fumbling. I wasn't getting out of this one. "I'm Brenthan and Pierce at the same time."

Urte slouched onto the machine's controls, careful not to push any of them. "This is part of the lesson plan the elders created," he said, ignoring the mention of his sons.

I gritted my teeth. "I can guarantee which elder offered this."

"We all did," he said.

My lip curled. "Luthicer did, right?"

Urte refused to meet my eyes, and I fumed. Luthicer, the only half-breed elder, always pushed my limits. "I hate him," I growled.

Urte placed his fingers on the lever that I assumed would begin everything. "He saved your life," he said, reminding me of the spells Luthicer had singlehandedly removed from my blood. "Twice."

"And now he's trying to kill me."

"Torture isn't killing, Shoman."

"You're right," I grumbled. "Killing is more humane."

Urte shook his head from side to side. "Are you ready?" he asked.

I stared at his calloused fingertips. "No."

"Are you ready?" he repeated.

I clenched my teeth, preparing myself for every amount of pain I could fathom. "As ready as I'll ever be," I managed, and Urte pulled the lever down.

———◆———

I winced when my bedroom door opened, and my father appeared. I would've used my powers to keep him out if I had any energy left to do so.

"How was training?" My father's thick voice broke through my ringing ears.

"What do you think?" Using a wrap, I compressed my injured elbow. I had strained it against the restraints along with every other part of my body. I was burning from the inside out.

My father cringed at my tone. "George told me."

"You mean, Urte, right?" I asked loudly, hoping Mindy or Noah would hear.

"Don't start that." My father's eyes turned to slits. "You know they're home."

"I'm sorry." My sarcasm defeated the fake apology. "My mind isn't exactly on them. It's on the fact that the elders—including you—agreed to torture me."

"It's for your own good."

"You get in that machine before you tell me it's for my own good," I wheezed. "I can barely move."

"You'll be healed by morning, Eric," he said.

I knew it was true. Once I got the strength to transform again, my body would entirely heal. But I wasn't strong enough yet, and it felt as if I would never be.

It was rare for injuries from my shade identity to linger in my human body, but it was happening due to the extremities. Generally, our identities were separate. As a human, I could be out of shape, but my shade self would be fit. My faces were different, and I knew my bone structure in both. As a human, I had green eyes, brown hair, and soft cheeks. I looked young and vulnerable—an average teenager—but everything was different when I transformed. My shoulders were broad, and my jawline was structured. I was muscular, fit, and capable in all respects. It was almost painful to be different. That was the only reason I couldn't fathom Jonathon as Pierce. His identities were stark opposites, but he accepted them better than I could ever accept my own.

"I still can't believe this," I said, wondering whether I was referring to training or Jessica.

"I'm sorry, son, but we need to take as many precautions as possible," he said it as if he were simply grounding me, with a monotone suggesting a lack of concern.

"I'll make sure to thank you once Darthon captures me and sticks me in a torture machine for information."

My father exhaled noisily, moving back into the hall. Obviously, he no longer wanted to discuss my fate. "Get some rest, Eric," he said, turning off my light as he shut my door. "I'll see you in the morning."

My bedroom wasn't enveloped in darkness as I had expected it to be. A warm, red light spread across the carpet, and I traced it to the source. A new nightlight replaced the one I broke the night before. Twelve years had passed since my mother committed suicide, and my father involved himself with the symbolic light. He'd replaced the nightlight without a word, and I couldn't take my eyes off it. For once, it seemed I wasn't the only one wanting her to return home.

5

Jessica

THE WIND WAS BENEATH MY FEET, AND THE TOWN WAS MILES BE-
low. Lights twinkled through the mist of Hayworth, and
purple sparkles clung to the atmosphere, shining against
the moon's dim light. I could barely breathe, but I was alive,
and I couldn't deny the reality of flight. It was too real to be a
dream. Only by expressing myself through art could I subdue
my confusion.

My art class was an arrangement of seniors, chatting quietly as I sketched a loop of wires. I'd paint the sparkles across
the sky once I began, but I couldn't continue yet. My depic-
tion of the dream I'd had the night before wasn't even close.
The sketch was too innocent and held no emotion. The dream
wasn't a nightmare, but it lingered more than the one about the
forest. The comfort was peculiarly chilling.

"Nice painting."

I jumped in my seat and turned around to meet a class-
mate's eyes. While one was fogged over, the other was clear, but
both appeared focused on my work.

"I haven't even started painting yet," I said, recognizing the
boy. Jonathon Stone was the best painter in the school, but I
hadn't talked to him before now. I couldn't recall seeing him
talk to anyone but teachers.

His fingers hovered over the loops I had lightly drawn.
"This direction will draw the viewer in perfectly," he said. "You

can normally tell by the sketch if the painting will be good."

I tore my eyes away from his blind eye. "Thanks," I murmured, fighting a guilty blush.

"Where'd you get the idea from?" he asked, pulling a pencil from his shirt pocket. He twiddled it through his thin fingers.

"It was a dream," I managed, but he didn't reply. "The sketch isn't finished yet," I stated the obvious. "I don't know what's missing, but I'll figure it out."

In seconds, he pulled up a stool and sat down. He traced his finger along the swirl. "Feels like you're flying," he said.

I almost leapt up. "That's what I was going for."

His shoulders rose. "You said this was a dream?"

His questions were beginning to feel like an interrogation, full of judgment. I opened my mouth to defend the fantasy, but the bell rang.

"Nice work," he said as he stood. "Keep it up."

He walked away as quickly as he had appeared, and I was left to my thoughts. Strangely enough, I wanted the boy to stay. I liked my friends, but I only had two—Robb and Crystal—and I wanted others to talk to.

I pushed my feelings aside as I collected my things. Jonathon moved right past me as if we hadn't spoken moments before, and I turned to watch him return to my canvas. I was looking at him as I left the classroom, and I collided with someone.

"Sorry," I mumbled as I shot down, picking up the two books I had dropped.

"It's okay, Jess," he said, and I looked up at the person I stumbled into. Robb offered his hand, and I grabbed it. He lifted me up.

"I wasn't paying attention."

He looked over my shoulder. "What were you looking at?"

"Nothing," I dismissed the topic. "What are you doing here?" Robb didn't take art classes—unless girls were involved.

"Thought I'd walk you to homeroom," he answered, referring to the one class we shared until graduation.

"That's nice," I said, knowing he had other intentions. He'd been trying to talk to me about Zac all week, and I'd avoided the conversation successfully until now.

"Are you and Zac planning another date anytime soon?" he asked.

I rolled my eyes. "We haven't even been on one, Robb," I said. "We're just friends."

"Zac doesn't seem to think so."

"Why does that matter?" I bit back, surprised by my harsh tone. Apparently, my conversation with Jonathon was still bothering me.

"Zac's my friend," Robb continued, oblivious to my thoughts.

"And I'm your friend, too," I pointed out, and Robb paused. I turned on my heel, realizing I had glared at him, and I rubbed my eyes. "Sorry," I muttered. "I haven't been sleeping well."

"What's going on?" he asked, but I didn't answer. He leaned over and tapped my arm. "Come on, Jess."

I started walking, trying to prevent myself from speaking, but I couldn't stop myself for long. "I've been having nightmares."

A frown consumed his smile. "I knew we shouldn't have taken you to that forest."

"It wasn't the forest—"

"Wasn't it?" he asked, and I didn't respond because he was right. He exhaled, placing a hand on the nape of his neck. "Just ignore the dreams, Jess. It's not a big deal."

I wanted to argue, to tell him how surreal they were, how much they had been affecting me, but he didn't understand. Clearly.

When we entered homeroom, Robb took his seat next to Crystal. My assigned seat was across the room, which was probably a good thing considering I would spend the entire hour talking if I could.

I fell into my seat, and the period bell rang as my partner walked in. He kept his headphones on until he made it to his seat, hanging them loosely on his neck when he took them off. I had known Eric Welborn for eight months now, but we didn't talk. Instead, we stayed to our sides of the table, and I often fought the urge to look at him.

He wasn't a bad looking guy, but his attitude was awful, and I didn't want to push it if I didn't have to. Zac, however, was beyond handsome. His thick, black hair shadowed his dark eyes and tanned skin like the midnight sky. He was taller than Robb, but cockier, and he had been pursuing me more since the summer. On top of that, Robb was his wingman, and he was trying to convince me to accept his friend.

As my teacher, Ms. Hinkel, began talking, I pulled out my notebook and drew a line straight down the middle. I'd make a pros-and-cons list if I had to. I doodled Zac's name at the top and froze when Eric shifted in his seat.

His stare locked onto my paper until I met his eyes. They sliced through me like the cold wind from last night's dream.

"Thought you were taking notes," he grumbled as he yanked a pen out of his pocket and turned away, leaving me to stare at his shoulders.

The air left my lungs, but I was filled with the urge to scream at him. He didn't know me and had no right to read over my things, whether I was taking notes or not. But his glare wasn't just aggravating. It was confusing. He seemed upset, and I doubted it was over note taking. His emotional response was the only reason I could hold back. Between Jonathon and him, I'd turned into a softy overnight, and the nightmares didn't help. I couldn't even stand up for myself, and I had no idea why.

6

Eric

I WASN'T GOING TO VISIT JESSICA, BUT I COULDN'T STOP MYSELF AF-
ter everything that happened in class.

Robb talked her into going out with friends, including Zac, and I dwelled on her doodles. She'd written his name down, and the notion struck a maddening match in my heart.

Once the sun set, I walked most of the way to her house and carefully transported into her bedroom. Nothing had moved. Her bed was against the far wall, and her blinds were pulled up, allowing moonlight in. The silver coloring stretched across her torso, and her dark eyelashes moved when she dreamt. At a distance, I watched her flip over, and I held my breath as her curly hair moved across her pillow. I wanted to wake her up, but I knew I couldn't. Seconds were enough for me. I had to leave.

I melted into the shadows, but a hand grabbed my arm and pushed me against the wall. Jessica's desk shook, and I froze as a boy sprung up from the shadows, his hair as wild as his green eyes. It was Pierce.

Our eyes locked. "What are you doing here?" we hissed simultaneously.

I tilted my head toward Jessica. "Are you joking?"

As the words left my mouth, Jessica mumbled in her sleep and curled up in her blankets. We watched her, holding our breath, but she didn't wake up. We looked back at each other.

"Outside, Shoman." Pierce's breath seethed between his

24

teeth. "Now."

"Fine."

He disappeared, but I lingered, glancing at Jessica one last time. Her back rose, and a part of me hoped she would awaken. Another stronger part of me understood that would be the worst scenario.

I left.

My body reformed with mist and grace, and I shook my arms in front of myself. Black and blue droplets splattered across the front lawn, and I stared at the unusual scene, remembering how Jessica had showed it to me months ago. I still hadn't figured out how to control the power.

"I'm up here," Pierce said, snapping his fingers to gain my attention.

"I know why I was here." I waited for his excuse. He was my best friend, but I wasn't going to trust the fact that he was in my girlfriend's bedroom.

The veins on his arms pushed against his skin. "Let's walk," he said, jabbing his thumb over his shoulder. Without my consent, he walked away, and I was forced to follow.

He crossed the lawn, dipped past the sidewalk, and walked onto a trail that led to our school. His pupils radiated in blackness, and I had to look away from him to keep myself from searching his eyes for something I didn't want to see. Our silence was heavy, aside from the tapping of our shoes as we strode yards away from Jessica's house. The tapping was so deafening, it seemed to affect my heartbeat.

"I'm her guard," he said. Pierce had taken two steps before he realized I had frozen.

"What?" I asked, remembering how I'd already heard the information. I knew she was getting one, but I never suspected Pierce.

He pushed at his nose as if his glasses were still in place. "I was assigned to keep an eye on her since I can be in both worlds. We have class together—"

"Why does she need a guard?"

She was safe, wasn't she? That was the entire point of erasing her memory—so she couldn't activate her powers and figure out the situation. She would be entirely human, and Darthon would have no one to chase. It had been the perfect plan, but Pierce's responsibilities insinuated a flaw.

Pierce remained silent, and an owl's hoot echoed through the trail. I tore my eyes away from my friend and searched the branches for the bird. It was nowhere to be seen.

"You're supposed to stay away from her, Shoman," Pierce said.

"She was doodling Zac's name in her notebook today." Now that I was confessing it aloud, my actions felt selfishly ridiculous.

"Ouch."

"I know it's a stupid excuse—" I began, but Pierce waved his hands in the air.

"I'm not reporting you, Shoman," he said. "I'm just reminding you of your duties." He smirked. "I was kind of expecting you to show up one of these nights."

I chuckled. "That obvious?"

He nodded, but he didn't have to. "I need to show you something."

He pulled out his cell phone and the screen blinded my eyes. I blinked, and he turned the brightness down, tilting it my way. "Look familiar to you?" he asked.

Lightly drawn over a canvas was a sketch of Hayworth from the sky. I recognized it immediately as the night Jessica flew for the first time. I reached up to grab it, but Pierce pulled it away.

"Where'd you get that?" I asked.

"Class." He returned the phone to his pocket. "It's Jessica's work."

I sucked in a breath, and my ribs pushed against my lungs. "She remembers?"

"No," he corrected. "She's having dreams."

"She's dreaming about me?"

Pierce swayed from foot to foot. "I'm not sure," he admitted. "She didn't tell me much."

"You talked to her?"

"I'm her guard," he said with a hardened voice. "And we have class together."

I tried to picture Jonathon Stone approaching Jessica Taylor in art class, but I couldn't. The timing was too perfect.

"Luthicer tweaked my schedule," Pierce added.

I folded my arms. "Maybe if Luthicer's memory swipe worked, he wouldn't have to do that."

"It technically worked, Shoman," he said. "She's not aware it's a memory or she'd be right in front of us."

I kicked the crumbling pavement. "Why didn't you tell me earlier?"

"Why do you think?" He tapped his forehead. "You blocked me, remember?"

Now that you brought it up. I rubbed my temples, ridding myself of the heavy barrier I'd put up days before. "Sorry about that," I muttered.

Pierce whistled low. "You forgot, didn't you?"

I refused to respond because the truth wasn't worth hearing. "Do the elders know about this?" I asked, studying Pierce's reaction. He didn't flinch, and I knew the elders were aware. "Of course they know."

"They thought it would be better if you didn't."

"And look at the success their decisions have had," I spat.

"Exactly why I'm telling you now," he said.

"You're telling me because I broke the rules."

"Which is something I enjoy advocating," he agreed, adjusting his stance. "But you can't see Jess again. You have to trust in her safety, especially with me around."

I craved an argument but held back. "You have her bedroom sealed?" I knew how he found me. I used the same spell to keep Noah out of my things.

He folded his arms across his chest in response. "Can we go now?" he asked, jumping up and down. "It's starting to get cold."

"Sure, princess," I joked, unable to feel the chill from the upcoming winter. It was only August, and nighttime still felt nice to me. But it didn't to Pierce, and that was enough to re-mind me of the battle ahead. I didn't have time to worry about Jessica's personal life. I had to concentrate on defeating Dar-thon—killing him. Even if I didn't want to, he had to die, and I was the only one who could do it.

7

Jessica

I COULDN'T GET THEIR WORDS OUT OF MY HEAD.

What are you doing here?

The two boys were in my bedroom, and then they were shadows, disappearing into a black vortex of misty ash. When I woke up, I could barely breathe, and I still couldn't, even though it'd been hours. I was in homeroom, and the dream owned my every thought. My mind was about to burst.

"You okay?"

The sudden whisper couldn't tear me from my thoughts, but I did freeze when I realized who was speaking to me. Eric Welborn.

"What?" I asked.

He gestured to the pen in my hands. Ink splattered over my notebook, and I realized I'd been tapping it. I tore the ruined page out. Pieces of paper sprawled across the desk, and I swiped them off. "I'm fine," I said, but my voice shook.

"You seem a little jumpy," he continued.

We were in study hall, and our teacher was gone. Everyone was talking, including the guy who'd hardly talked to me since the semester started.

"How was your summer?" Eric changed the topic. He looked different, more rested, and his stare was concentrated on me.

"It was good," I stuttered through my surprise. I wasn't ex-

29

pecting him to talk to me at all. "It went by too fast."

"It did," he agreed, pushing his long sleeves up. "Go out of town or anything?"

"No." I swallowed my nerves. I'd spent most of the summer looking for more information on my biological parents, but I couldn't even find where they were buried. "Did you?" I followed the script of back-to-school talk.

"We always stay in town."

Our conversation halted, and I turned back to my notebook. As much as I wanted more friends, I wasn't sure what else to say. He sat next to me, but he didn't seem to be the socializing type, and I doubted he would talk to me again.

"That's really annoying, you know," Eric said.

I glanced back at him. For the second time, he gestured to my hand, and I realized I had done it again. My pen was emptying out on my paper. I sighed, apologized, and flipped the page over. I didn't need to fill up our desk with ripped up pieces.

"What's going on with you, Jessica?" he asked.

A blush rose to my cheeks. No one used my full name, but he said it in a way that comforted me. It felt personal.

"Rough night, I guess." I pushed my seat back. I would not touch my pen again.

Eric's stare relaxed, and the space beneath his eyes smoothed over. "It couldn't have been that bad," he spoke quietly.

I half-laughed. "I feel like I haven't slept in weeks."

He hesitated. "Nightmares?"

I gripped the table, unable to look at him. Even my closest friends hadn't been able to guess. "Yeah." I fought my embarrassment from crawling over my skin. "I know it sounds childish—"

"What kind of nightmares?" he interrupted with more questions. "Just curious," he added.

I dug my nails into my hands. I wasn't sure I wanted to talk about something I didn't understand with a stranger.

"A lot of them," I finally admitted, feeling the heaviness on my chest lift. Eric was surprisingly easy to talk to.

"Do they repeat?" he asked.

"Are you an expert or something?"

His lip pulled up into a smirk, but he didn't say anything.

"They're all different," I clarified.

His smirk faded. I expected him to respond, but he collected his things, tediously placing each notebook in the order he had taken them out. He repeated these motions every day, and I knew what they meant—the bell was about to ring.

"Hope you sleep better," he said, and the classroom erupted with the shrill ring of our transition bell. He stood, put on his headphones, and was gone as soon as he finished talking to me.

I watched him leave, wondering about the strange conversation. Unlike Robb, I didn't feel as if Eric judged me. He listened, asked questions, and remained attentive, like we had been friends for years. I yearned for a connection with someone ever since school began. I didn't care that he was Eric Welborn, the social outcast. He seemed nice enough to me, and I made a mental note to talk to him again.

"Jess," Crystal called out from the doorway. "Are you coming or not?"

I grabbed my bag and threw my pen out as I passed the trashcan. "Can we ditch?"

Crystal popped her gum. "Is that even a question?"

She looped her arm through mine, and we left. I didn't care about breaking the rules for one day. I needed a distraction, and school obviously wasn't working. Crystal, however, would.

"We could meet up with Robb," she suggested, knowing he had taken the day off.

"What's he doing?"

Her lip ring flashed beneath the fluorescent lights. "He's at Zac's house," she said. "With Linda."

I rolled my eyes, but Crystal was adamant about it, and I gave in. Ever since the summer, Zac hadn't been as domineering. He was fun, and Linda was lightening up. They were starting to feel more like friends, and friendship was all I needed.

8

Eric

"WHAT'S AN ELEVEN-LETTER WORD FOR FATE?" JESSICA ASKED, twirling her pen as she stared at her crossword book.

I glanced around the classroom as if there were a chance she was speaking to someone else. She hadn't attempted conversation with me since last week, but she looked up, and I held my breath.

She pointed her pen at the white boxes. "I need an eleven-letter word for fate." I didn't respond, and she rolled her eyes. "I'm stuck."

"Preordained," I said.

She blinked her blue eyes. The color reminded me of the sunrise over the river.

Her pen bobbed up and down. "You're right," she said, scribbling it in. Even her handwriting was perfect. "Thanks." She filled in a few more before pausing.

I read over her shoulder. "Silver," I said.

"Which one?"

"Five down."

She leaned back. "Looks like I need your help more often."

I couldn't help my grin. The moment was like old times, and I would live in the lie if it were only for a second.

"Jess."

I scooted back as Robb pulled up a chair and sat down

next to her. Girls stared at him from across the room. I didn't understand what they saw in him.

"I need to talk to you," he said, but Jessica didn't speak until Crystal sat on the desk next to ours.

If it were the previous semester, we would've been lectured, but our teacher had lightened up for our senior year. Her change in behavior was dramatic, and I wasn't the only one to notice. Ms. Hinkel rarely lectured, and I wondered if she were involved with the Marking of Change, nervous for her children or, perhaps, herself. It was impossible to know.

"We can't talk at lunch?" Jessica eyed the room full of curious stares.

"Lunch starts in two minutes." Crystal pointed at her sparkling wristwatch. "We can start now."

Jessica sighed. "Fine."

"The date," Robb spoke so suddenly my insides twisted. "Zac and Linda are meeting at my house, and then we'll come pick you up."

Zac. How I hated Zac.

"What about you?" Jessica asked Crystal.

She lit up. "I'll be at your house, silly," she said, tapping Jessica's arm. "We have to get ready."

"Get ready?" Jessica squeaked. "It isn't that big of a deal."

"It's a date," Robb said, and the word aggravated me.

"No, it's not," Jessica clarified slowly.

"But Zac—"

"I don't like him like that."

I turned away so they wouldn't see my grin. I shouldn't have been listening, but it was hard not to when they were inches away. Jessica didn't like Zac, and I was positive my week was made.

Her friends started to argue, but the lunch bell rang, and they stopped. "Usual place?" Crystal asked. They always sat outside.

"Go ahead of me," she said.

I froze. I sensed Robb's eyes on me, but he didn't say anything. Crystal grabbed his arm, and the two filtered out with the class. Jessica and I hung behind, and she exhaled a shaky breath when she met my eyes.

"Ever feel like people are making decisions for you?" she asked, and the Dark flashed through my memory. Shades and lights from a hundred years ago dictated my entire life, and there was nothing I could do but obey if I wanted to live.

"All the time."

"I bet you do, Eric," she said, lingering on her words as if she didn't understand them herself. Her eyebrows pressed together, and she shook her head, grabbing her bag. "See you later," she finished, walking out of the room.

I wanted to talk to her, to listen to her, but I knew I couldn't. She didn't know what her words meant to me, and I wondered if her subconscious was aware of what she'd said. A part of her, no matter how small, recognized our fates, and I was forced to fight that as much as I was fighting myself.

I couldn't stay in school any longer. I had to go to the shelter and train.

Grabbing my things, I pulled my keys out of my pocket and rushed to the parking lot. I avoided the lunchroom and used the side door to escape. No one would notice, and if someone did, no one would stop me. The teachers had learned to leave me alone as much as the students did. I wasn't interested in lectures, and their words wouldn't stop me from getting around the rules. Especially with Luthicer's help. He was useful for some things, after all.

"Hold the door."

I recognized the loud voice before I saw his black hair, and I let the door shut, knowing it would lock.

"Sorry, man." I moved past Zac.

He raised his hand as if he would run it through his mane, but he stopped himself. Apparently, he didn't want to mess up his carefully constructed hairdo.

"It's cool," he said. He was the tallest teenager I had ever seen. "You think they'll notice if I just go around the school?"

"Teachers are hawks around here," I lied, continuing to walk.

"Thanks anyway."

I didn't bother speaking to him again. I needed to get away from him fast. If I didn't, I would confront him about Jessica, and I no longer had the right to. She had her own life, and I had to survive mine without her. We had agreed on it, and that was enough to push me forward. That and my car.

I jogged over the small slope leading down the left side of the school to where the black Charger waited for me. In seconds, I was inside and revving the engine, sighing at the beautiful sound. It was mine, the only solace I had left. I took off, my thoughts slipping away with the speed, tearing out of the parking lot as if I could drive away from it all.

9

Eric

BEING A CAPABLE SHADE WASN'T ENOUGH. I HAD TO BE ABLE TO fight as a human as well, and today was my day to train as one.

Luthicer watched as Camille held up my punching bag. I threw one last punch before I stopped to catch my breath. Kickboxing was more of a cardiac workout than I thought.

"You should probably stretch," Camille said.

I swung my arm over my chest, and she walked over to the wall. She grabbed a bottle of water and tossed it over. I stopped stretching to catch it, and water droplets trailed down my arm with my sweat.

"Thanks," I said.

She started to walk over, but Luthicer tapped her arm. "Can you get the timesheets?" he asked, referring to a workout sheet trainers used for young children after the Naming. "I left them in my office."

Camille opened her mouth to remind him that I didn't use them, but Luthicer lowered his brow, and she obeyed, heading to the door. Her dark eyes met mine, and she widened them. I prepared myself for the worst. Luthicer didn't want Camille around for a reason.

I opened up my water bottle and took a quick drink. "What was that about, Luthicer?" I asked, refusing to rollover for the half-breed elder.

He patted the wall. "You should work on your core," he said. "Sit ups."

Hesitating, I moved forward and sat down, making sure my feet didn't touch the wall. Then, I began. We continued this for a few minutes, but Luthicer didn't look at me.

"Do you hate the Light?" he asked, his voice rigid and quick.

I sat up to rest on my knees. "They're my enemy."

"That's not what I asked."

I cleared my throat and wiped the sweat from my brow. I needed a shower, not chit-chat. "Sure," I gave in to the conversation. I hated Darthon and Fudicia, but they weren't everyone in the Light. "Hate" seemed like a strong word for a group of people.

Luthicer's cheeks were sunken in as if they'd dried up with his thoughts. He looked as tired as I felt.

"You are aware of what will happen to the sect if you defeat Darthon, right?" he asked.

My stomach muscles twisted from more than my workout's intensity. "They'll lose their powers," I responded as if he had given me an oral exam. It was a vital piece of information. Whoever won would retain power. Whoever lost would lose their identity.

"But some will die."

I tried to ignore this fact, but it was true. To have half of your life ripped away would prove to be too dire for some. We had seen it happen to banished shades. It was only natural for it to happen to lights, too.

"I'm aware," I said.

Luthicer threw his white beard over his shoulder like it was a fashionable scarf. "And what do you think about that?" He asked a question that wasn't on the exam. The prophecy didn't say how we were supposed to feel about it. It was factual, and that was all we were expected to know.

I rubbed my temples as I tried to comprehend the direction of our conversation. "It doesn't really matter."

Luthicer pressed his back against the wall as he glided to

the floor. "It does," he argued, slowly turning his neck to meet my eyes. "If there is a battle involving others—not just Darthon and you—I need to know you believe in their malicious nature."

"I know they're evil, Luthicer." I remembered the determination in Darthon's eyes. His actions held no sympathy or hesitation, and I witnessed his brutality on my own family. Not to mention Fudicia. She had killed Abby when she was fourteen. To describe the Light as ruthless was an understatement.

"You didn't always know this," Luthicer continued as if he hadn't heard me.

I lay on my back, stretching my leg over my stomach. "At least I figured it out."

While Luthicer stared at the farthest wall, I studied him longer than I ever had before. The shadows that hung beneath his eyes were darker than usual, and his wrinkles seemed deeper. Still, he was calm and didn't move.

"Why are you here?" I asked.

His dark eyes lightened. "Did you know I was born to the Light?"

"No." I ignored my racing heart.

He ran his long fingernails over his long sleeves. He pulled them up and revealed white slashes of scarred flesh.

"They're evil," he said. "And they raise their children to be as well."

I tried to tear my eyes away, but I couldn't. The scars were old, patched up in places with healed skin, but the bumpy ridges remained. Some were burns while others were round, hinting of puncture wounds. He had obviously been tortured, and I suddenly understood why Luthicer wanted me to go through the pain of the torture machine.

I stretched my other leg before sitting up. As I gulped my water down, Luthicer waited patiently for my response. I didn't have one. There were no words to sympathize with something I couldn't understand, and I wasn't about to fake that I could.

"They've been evil since the beginning, Eric." Luthicer used my real name as if it would help reach my conscience.

"They attacked our people in a moment of peace. We were balanced. We were free—"

I knew the story. The Light and the Dark lived among humans, but the humans weren't completely oblivious either. They suspected some of those with power, generally the ones who couldn't remain silent. They had been labeled as witches or gods. Ultimately, there wasn't much of a difference in their eyes.

The Light took advantage of it. They depicted themselves as holy, and the people followed them, believing every word about the evil creatures that came out at night. Unbeknownst to the humans, we were the innocent ones. When we confronted their lies, the Light slaughtered us. They wanted power and did anything to achieve it. If it weren't for a select few—the oldest ones who stripped everyone's powers—the war would've continued, and the Light would've succeeded. But the power couldn't stay dormant forever, so it followed two bloodlines. I was one of them. Darthon was the other. The separation of balance created Jessica's bloodline.

"Were you exiled?" I interrupted his history lesson.

"I'm sure that's what they'd say," he said in a half-grunt. "But I left." His lips pulled into the largest grin I'd ever seen him display. His teeth were crooked. "After I did as much damage to them as I could."

My throat tightened as I pictured a much younger version of Luthicer, but my imagination was halted by a lack of information. "What did you do?"

"I killed fifteen of them. Maybe more." His voice dropped. "I was thirty-five."

I didn't know Luthicer's current age, but I wished I did. I wanted to do the math to figure out if it coincided with my birth.

"It had nothing to do with your birth or Darthon's," he said, hinting at my existence. "I had a daughter with a human."

This was news to me.

"She's human, of course," he said, raising a finger. "But the Light didn't care."

"They wanted her to fight?" I asked, thinking I had to have heard him wrong.

A human couldn't fight a shade. They would simply be a body to clean up, but he nodded.

"I could not allow that to happen." Luthicer pulled his sleeves down. "But my abandonment didn't come without a price."

I didn't ask what happened after. I didn't need to. The point was his sect physically and mentally tortured him, not the details of how it happened.

He continued to fiddle with his sleeves as if he wanted to retract his honesty. "I know you don't like me, Eric," he said, standing up. "But I am on your side, and I have been my entire life—even when I didn't know it."

I wanted to tell him he was wrong, that I liked him, but I couldn't. Although I'd heard his story, my emotions had yet to catch up, and I needed time to reflect on everything before I'd be more comfortable with his dedication.

"And I want you to believe me when I say they are evil— all of them," he continued. "They aren't evil as humans. In that form, they are people just like us. But, unlike shades, their conscience disappears with their transformation." He lingered on his words as if it were the first time he'd spoken them. "It's one of the reasons half-breeds struggle so much. When transformed, half of our conscience disappears."

"Do you struggle?" I asked, wanting to know how my enemy's mind worked.

Luthicer's face twisted, and he turned his torso away as he opened the door. He left, but his last words echoed behind him. "Not anymore."

10

Jessica

MINUTES TICKED BY, BUT THE SUNSET REMAINED ABOVE THE Midwestern plains. The sky was plastered with stormy clouds, and the wind pushed against the glass near our table. We drove to a nearby town to eat at *La Bella Luna*, but I barely gave the building a glance. The setting sun was enough.

"How's your dinner?" Zac's voice sounded too close.

"It's fine," I said and brushed him off.

Crystal bumped her ankle against mine. I didn't have to look at her to know what she meant. I was being rude.

"How's yours?" I asked him.

Zac waved his fork over his empty plate. "I love this place," he said.

I laid my hands on the oak table. The wood was cool beneath my wrists, but the restaurant seemed warm. The golden lighting spread across the red floors and blackened walls like a sunlit river.

The restaurant was beautiful, definitely romantic. I wasn't sure how to convince Robb or Crystal that Zac would never be more than a friend. They didn't take no for an answer, and it was the only answer I had.

From across the table, Robb bumped into his girlfriend's arm. "Want to order dessert?" he asked Linda.

Her lips thinned. She hadn't touched her salad. "I thought

we were seeing a movie," she said.

"We can later," Robb said, but he didn't check his watch. Both Crystal and Linda took a long time to get ready, and the food did, too. The movie had started an hour ago.

"We could watch one at my place," Zac suggested.

"Dad has to get up early," Linda excused her half-brother as if he were a child. "We'll go to a later show."

"Maybe you should ask everyone else how they feel," Zac said, and I flinched at his hardened voice. "What do you want to do, Jess?" he asked, but all I could concentrate on were his black eyes, consuming the light around us.

Crystal pushed her chair backwards. "I'm going to the restroom," she announced, standing on platform sandals too tall for her. "Come on, Jess." She wobbled away as I stood up.

We had swerved through two rooms before we reached the restroom. She leaned her body against the door and pushed past me. I followed her and locked the door behind us.

Habitually, Crystal pulled a pen from her purse and threaded it through her fingers. "What is going on with everyone tonight?" Her lip ring twinkled as she ranted. "Linda and Zac keep fighting, Robb isn't paying attention, and you're barely talking. Not to mention that I'm the fifth wheel—the fifth—not the third."

"You're not the fifth wheel," I said, but Crystal cocked her hip.

"Zac's into you," she said. "Like really into you."

"Wasn't that your plan?"

Her eyes darted to the ground. "I don't know."

I couldn't believe what I was seeing. Crystal Hutchins was insecure.

"You like him," I accused.

Her face lifted up, her mouth open. "Who?"

"Zac."

Her cheeks burned, but she didn't deny it.

I sighed and fiddled with the tips of my curls. "It's fine, Crystal. Really," I said, finally understanding why she was pushy. She liked Zac, and she wanted him around. If he came around me, she would get to see him, but it was starting to bother her. It was written all over her ink-covered palm.

I took her pen away and placed it in her purse. "I don't like him, Crystal."

"Not at all?" she squeaked.

I held back the truth. I wasn't sure what I thought about him, but I didn't want to say I hated him. Zac seemed nice, but he wasn't my type.

"Go for it," I encouraged, trying to block my thoughts out.

"I can't," she said. "It'd be too awkward after prom."

My dinner churned against my stomach. "What about prom?"

Crystal's glitter mascara caught the light. Purple spots blocked my vision.

"You guys danced," she said. "And he kissed you—"

"What?" My voice was high-pitched as it echoed off the mirrored walls. I couldn't remember.

Crystal's shoulders rose. "Are you feeling okay, Jess?" she asked, gesturing to a fainting couch in the middle of the room. Someone knocked on the door, and Crystal shouted back, "Someone's sick in here."

I sat on the couch before I fell. My brain felt like it was pushing through my forehead. Gripping the rough fabric beneath me, I released a deep breath.

Crystal scurried to my side. "What's wrong?"

"I don't feel well," I admitted, rubbing my temples and searching for any memory of prom, but nothing surfaced. "I must be coming down with something."

"I'll have Robb drive you home." She stood up, but I pulled her down.

"In a minute," I said.

Crystal scooted an inch away. "You're kind of freaking me out, Jess."

"I'm sorry," I muttered.

Her elbows rested on her knees, her head in her hands. "This is because of Zac, isn't it?"

"No," I promised.

Crystal's eyes turned red. "I would've said something earlier, but I don't exactly have many girlfriends," she admitted, curling her fingertips through her black roots. "Linda doesn't count."

I wanted to respond, but I couldn't. My mind remained clouded, and Crystal's confession was adding to it. I liked Robb and Crystal, but I still felt like I barely knew them. I didn't know how to fix it.

"Something is wrong with me," I spoke the words without considering the aftermath.

Crystal straightened up, and I immediately wanted to ask her to forget what I said.

"What are you talking about, Jess?" she asked, gesturing more to my dress than anything else. "There's nothing wrong with you."

I stopped her. "I'm having dreams."

"So what?"

"So, I can't sleep," I added. "I can't think. I can't do anything but feel like I'm going insane, and I don't know what to do about them because they won't stop, and they seem so real, and—"

Crystal laid her hands on my shoulders. "Breathe, Jess."

I did what she said, but I didn't feel any better.

Another knock rapped against my eardrums, and Crystal walked over to answer it. I listened, but I didn't turn around. Robb was there, along with a manager, and Crystal apologized.

"I think we should take her home," she whispered, but the sound was louder than anything else I'd heard in my life. In that singular moment, it was the only thing I could hear. If I hadn't known what a panic attack was before, I knew now.

"Jess?" Robb walked around the couch.

I stood up before he could touch me. "I'm okay," I said.

His expression didn't budge. "How about I take you home?" he asked, gesturing to the exit. "You can get some rest."

"Rest is the last thing I need," I mumbled, marching forward.

Even I had to admit that it was time for me to leave. Otherwise, I would probably ruin everyone's night, and that was the last thing I wanted. Instead, I wanted Crystal and Zac to work out, but it didn't seem probable. Zac stood by the exit doors with his jacket draped over his arm. Crystal was gone.

Robb stopped in the doorway. "Where are the girls?"

"Still at the dinner table," Zac said, looking past Robb to stare at me. "I thought I could take Jess home with you."

"No," Robb said, and Zac suddenly seemed taller. Robb adjusted his shirt. "I'll be fifteen minutes, and they don't need to be here alone."

"So, I can take Jess home," Zac offered.

"Not in my car," Robb said, pushing past his friend. He opened the door, and cold air rushed in. It was late. "Let's go, Jess."

"Thanks anyways, Zac," I said, but he didn't respond. I rushed outside, feeling cold, nauseous, and everything in-between.

Robb took my arm as if I couldn't walk on my own. I wanted to pull back, but he did before I had the chance. He unlocked his blue Suburban, and I climbed onto the passenger seat as he got in the driver's side. The engine shook the car, and Robb blew into his hands before grabbing the steering wheel. It was colder in the car than it was outside.

"This is going to be a harsh winter," he said, turning the wheel as he pulled out of the parking lot. I agreed, but I was unfamiliar with Hayworth's average winter. Since arriving in January, it had only snowed once.

"It doesn't normally get this cold until October," he continued.

I fought the urge to argue with a local. October was only a month away.

My stomach twisted again, for no reason in particular, and I closed my eyes to fight the feeling away. My body was reacting to nothing.

"It's those nightmares, isn't it?" Robb's brown eyes left the road and pierced me through the darkness. "You told me, remember?"

"That was weeks ago."

"But you haven't been the same since." His grip loosened on the steering wheel. "You always look tired."

"Thanks."

"I didn't mean it as a bad thing," he clarified. "I'm saying it because it's true."

I turned to the window and felt him glance over a number of times before he accepted my silence. I didn't want to talk about it with Robb. He had blown me off the first time, and I didn't want it to happen again.

The Suburban came to a squeaking halt. My bedroom light spread onto the front lawn, and I exhaled, calmed by the familiar sight.

"Want me to walk you up?" Robb asked.

I shook my head, but he got out anyway, leaving his car running. I jumped out and walked next to him.

We didn't talk, and I reached into my purse for my keys. I curled my fingers around them and pulled them out. They jingled as I lowered my hand to my hip. "Thanks for driving me, Robb."

His eyes darted around the lawn, and I looked over my shoulder. "What are you looking at?" I asked.

His neck snapped as he turned it back. "Nothing," he said. "I thought I saw something. Probably an animal."

"I hope so," I said, fighting the urge to search the neighbor's trees for whatever he saw. A part of me hoped it was an animal, but a bigger part of me wished to see one of the boys from my dream.

I barely turned to the door before Robb spoke up again, "What are you dreaming about?"

My neck tightened like I was being choked. "Nothing important." I cleared my throat, but Robb didn't budge, and I dropped my eyes to the ground. "A boy."

The words, spoken aloud, sounded weirder than I expected. It sounded dangerous, not comforting, and I could sense Robb's discomfort. He'd shifted away, and his back was pressed to the wall. He crossed his arms before uncrossing them and shoving his hands in his pockets.

"Have you thought about calling the police?" he asked.

"Why would I do that?" I squeaked. "It isn't real."

Robb's lip pulled into a smirk, but it dissipated quickly, leaving me to wonder if I had seen what I did. "You seem upset enough that I figured you thought it might be." His eyes searched my yard again.

"Do you think I should?"

He pushed his back off the wall. "I think the more attention you give your dreams, the more dreams you'll have," he said. "The dreams will stop if you want them to."

"I'll try that," I said, but I wasn't sure I wanted them to stop. "I should get back to Zac and the others."

"Thanks again," I said.

He threw his arm over my shoulders and hugged me from the side before striding down the sidewalk and disappearing into his car. I went inside before he drove away and tried to ignore my gut.

Someone—or something—was in my yard, and it didn't feel protective like the boys from my dreams. It felt malicious, and it was focused on me.

11

Jessica

H E STOOD BENEATH THE SHADOWS OF THE TREES, BUT HE WAS immune to the darkness. His blond hair illuminated without light, and his face didn't cast a single shadow. The man didn't move, but he seemed to be vibrating, causing the leaves to shiver above him. On a windless night, he was the eye of a storm—still, but awaiting something.

I, immediately, feared I was that something.

His abnormally widened eyes were black pits, but I somehow knew he was staring at my bedroom. And I wasn't awake.

The image flashed on and off in my mind as I clutched my blankets, desperately searching for reality, but I was stuck. I couldn't wake myself up, and my skin was burning. Even my pajamas felt like they were ignited by electricity.

He was in the yard, but I could feel a hand on my chin, a blade to my neck. The air was warm, but my mind was frozen. I wanted to move, fight, and run, but I couldn't. I could only scream.

———◆———

My scream shattered the nightmare, and I sprung up, blinking the image away furiously. I leapt from my bed, sprinted across my bedroom, and slammed against the window as I searched my front yard for him. He was gone, nothing more than a nightmare, but I didn't believe it. I could feel him. His presence remained.

"Jessie?" My father burst in my bedroom with my mother following. His puffy eyes were red when they met mine.

My mother's face was pale. "Are you okay?"

My chest knotted, pushing against my breath, and I rubbed my forehead. I couldn't speak. I didn't like lying. I never had.

"We heard you scream," my mother continued as my father walked over to the window.

He looked out the window, and his eyes scanned the yard. I wanted him to see what I couldn't, but he grabbed the blinds.

"I wish you'd shut these," he said, pulling the cord. The blinds slammed into the windowsill.

I fought the urge to argue. If the blond man was there, I wanted to see him coming.

"I must have been sleepwalking," I suggested, grabbing my jacket off my desk chair. I draped it around my shoulders. The clothing felt like the embrace I needed.

"Let's get back to bed," my dad said, moving past me as if he were the one sleepwalking.

My mother hung behind. She teetered on the edge of speaking, but her lips pushed to one side. She grabbed my door as she walked out of my room. "Goodnight, Jessie," she said, shutting it softly behind her.

Alone again, I stood with shaking knees. I grabbed the cord and pulled my blinds up, half-expecting the blond man to reappear. But he didn't. Even his presence was gone now.

I sighed, and my breath fogged the window. When I touched the glass, it was cold, and goose bumps trailed over my arm. I wanted to let go, but I couldn't. I wanted to feel the cold until it meant something—like it was supposed to mean something—and I curled my fingers against the condensation. I had to dream again.

I was ready for the insanity to consume me if it meant I could understand what was happening.

12

Light was at her house, and it was a powerful one.
I slammed on the brakes, and my car's engine vibrated
through my sudden panic. My hand slapped against the
door as I shoved it open, and the electric air sizzled against my
lips.

"What are you doing here?"

I whipped around with my fist in the air, but Pierce
grabbed my wrist. I sucked in a breath as he tossed my hand to
the side. He was glaring, and I was too.

"Do you feel that?" I asked, spreading my fingertips out,
but everything that had been there dissipated.

"No," Pierce said.

"You were here for a reason," I argued, gesturing toward
Jessica's house. It was only a few yards away.

"I bet you were, too."

"I was driving by," I said, attempting to keep my voice
down. He was keeping something from me, just like the elders.
"A light was at her house."

"Near her house," he corrected. "Not at it."

"Is that relevant?" I spat.

Pierce eyed my car. "Are you going to turn that off?"

"No."

His sigh came out rigid as he swiftly shut the driver's door.
"We shouldn't be talking out here," he said, remaining in his

shade form.

"Why aren't you a human?" I asked, knowing he was prepared for something. The light was powerful, and it was near Jessica. That wasn't something to ignore, yet Pierce wanted me to. "What's going on?"

"We're handling it."

I surveyed the road. "Who else is out here?"

"Eu and Bracke."

My hands shook. "My father?" *This was a big deal.*

"It's not a big deal," Pierce spoke as if he could hear my thoughts.

"Where is he?" I asked, searching my radar for my father.

The neighbors were up, and a few kids were smoking cigarettes in the park. A dog walked around by itself, and Pierce touched my shoulder.

"He's busy—"

As I prepared myself to disappear, a circle of smoke curled through the air, and my father appeared. His shoulders rose, and his eyes were slits. I knew the look. He was preparing to yell at me.

"You're looking for me?" he asked.

I ignored the accusation. "I want to know what happened," I said, surprised by my hardened voice.

My father didn't react to the tone as I had hoped. He remained calm and pointed to my car. "Go home, Eric."

"I know more than any of you," I growled, but my father walked toward me as if he could shepherd me to my Charger. "She's frequently dreaming."

He stopped. "What are you talking about?"

I repeated myself. "She told me," I said, "in class."

My father turned to Pierce, but his hands went into the air. "They're in homeroom together," he defended. "I can't stop her from talking to him."

"You shouldn't have talked back, Eric," my father said.

My eyes shot to the ground. "It doesn't matter," I said. "She told me, and it means something, especially if lights are coming near her."

My father's jaw locked as mine did, and Pierce put a hand on my father's shoulder as if he needed to be held back. My father shrugged him off.

"Why would she talk so openly?" he asked.

I had to defend her. "She only told me."

"How do you know that?"

"She didn't say a word to her friends. She was too busy griping over—" I cringed. "Zac."

My father blinked. "Who's Zac?"

"Don't ask," Pierce interrupted.

My father turned back to me. "Did Jess say anything else?"

"She has dreamt every night since school started." My words didn't seem real, but they were. She'd opened up to me more as a human this time around, and I wondered how strong her subconscious was.

"You're telling me Luthicer's spell only worked for one month?" My father continued his interrogation, but I couldn't answer. Only Jessica could. "Someone had to trigger something."

Pierce and my dad focused on me, and my anger sizzled like the Light. "I didn't do anything."

"Eric." My father didn't believe me.

I grabbed my hair with fists. "I'm trying to help, and you're accusing me of being the problem."

"Because I don't believe you."

"I'm leaving," I muttered, yanking my car door open before getting inside.

My dad grabbed the door. "Calm down before you drive."

I pulled hard, and he moved his hand before the door squished his fingers. My foot laid on the clutch and gas, and I was gone, speeding away until the trees became blurs of midnight blue. I had to get away, far away.

"Eric." Pierce's voice broke through the sound of my engine, and I shifted again. I wanted to see how far I had to go before the Dark couldn't penetrate my thoughts.

"Don't speed," he continued.

"Get out of my head," I said, blocking him.

My father's voice echoed behind. "*You're going to crash.*"

"*I never crash,*" I replied, downshifting to take a corner. I was getting on that highway whether they liked it or not.

His voice paused, but his presence floated around, and I knew he was sensing my actions. I saw the highway, sped up, and aimed for the on-ramp. My fingers drummed against the steering wheel as the car flew across the blackened pavement, curling up to aid my escape.

"*You're going to crash,*" my dad repeated quickly.

I tightened my grip. "*I don't crash.*"

"*Slow down,*" he screamed, and my concentration shattered at the exact time my tires hit the on-ramp.

My wheels skidded, and the back of the car leapt. Air froze in my lungs, and a rush of sounds pounded against my ears. Pierce's voice returned, accompanied by my father's yelling and the brief squeal of the tires.

Then, I was flying—floating upward toward the windshield, and I squeezed my eyes shut when the horizon began tilting dangerously. I felt myself transition away from my human form, and even with the car spinning I could feel the seatbelt against my chest. A sound ripped the air just before I lost consciousness.

The smell of smoke broke through the blood dripping from my nose. I thought about moving, but nothing happened. After a moment, a moan finally escaped me and I blinked through the dusty debris.

I coughed, but my chest resisted the effort, squeezing my lungs. I coughed again, and tears sprang to my eyes. My fingers curled around the seatbelt latch, and I pushed. I fell, and my left shoulder collided with the crushed door. Glass scraped my skin.

"Hey." A man was in front of me. He hadn't been there before, and he was already fading into the darkness.

"Stay with me," he said. He reached in and grabbed my jacket. When he yanked my body out, my shoulder wiggled unnaturally.

I lifted my hand to help him, but then I saw my skin. I had

turned back into a human.

A sharp pain shot through me, and I sucked in a breath.

Before I could comprehend it, I was opening my eyes to a flashlight. The man had been replaced by someone else, and this one wore a uniform. Purple lights flickered behind him. Jessica's purple rain drifted through my vision until he shook the flashlight at me.

"What's your name?" he asked.

I tried to look past him, but the purple lights were gone. They were never purple at all. They were red and blue—police lights.

"Er—Er—Ar—Aec—Eri—c." Every sound I made hurt.

"Eric?" he guessed, and I sensed another person. I was being tied down. "Is your name Eric?"

I opened my mouth to speak but spit blood out instead. He wiped it away, but I tasted it. "We—Well—Welborn."

"Eric?" he repeated, and the gurney was lifted. My stomach felt as if it had been left on the ground. "Eric Welborn?"

I couldn't nod. My head was restrained. But it didn't matter anymore.

The man's eyes widened, and he looked at the men carrying me up the hill. With every step they took, the lights became brighter, and consciousness became harder to stand. "Be careful," he said. "That's James Welborn's kid."

13

THE LIGHTS WERE AS DIM AS MY THOUGHTS, AND I HAD TO CON-
centrate every time I opened my eyes, only for them
to shut again. I drifted in and out so many times that I
wasn't sure whether I was awake or asleep.

"Keep resting, honey."

The words were soft-spoken and unfamiliar. My own family didn't talk to me that way, but I felt like my mother would
have if she were alive.

I shifted, wanting to see the woman, but she was gone—
replaced with a man I had seen every day of my life.

"How are you feeling?" my dad asked, leaning on his elbows.

I made a feeble attempt to speak, but all that came out was
a cough. Pain wrung my chest, and my brow crumbled as he
handed me a sippy cup.

"Take it easy," he said. "You broke a few ribs." He stared at
the wall behind me. "You almost punctured a lung, Eric."

My human name explained my location. I was in a hospital—a human hospital. I swallowed the water to drown my
panic. "How long have I been here?"

"A day."

The only time I had left was melting away, and I wasn't
even allowed to live it. I scanned my body, but it didn't look
as bad as I felt. My arms weren't broken, but one had a large

gash running down the side. I couldn't see my legs, but I didn't think I wanted to.

"What happened?" I asked.

My father straightened. I turned my neck without any pain and stared at him. He didn't respond until I repeated myself.

"You don't remember?" he managed.

I searched for any recollection. I had a feeling of spinning. That was it.

"Nothing," I said, lowering my voice. "Why am I here?" I couldn't fathom why they would bring me to a human hospital when the shelter could heal me in minutes.

My father cleared his throat and rolled his shoulders back. "You were angry," he spoke slowly. "And you crashed your car."

"What?"

"You got in a car accident," he continued, ignoring my reaction. "It was just you. No one else was involved, but another driver found you and pulled you out."

I expected my memory to return, but nothing came. I was teetering on the edge of nothingness. "I—" I couldn't complete the sentence.

"What's the last thing you remember?" he asked.

I opened my mouth as if it was the easiest question in the world, but it wasn't.

I knew the Marking of Change was close. Jessica didn't have her memory, but her subconscious was aware of the Dark, and I could barely stand it. Pierce was her guard, and Camille was too busy training to be around me. I went to training. Afterwards, I drove by Jessica's house.

"I sensed a light," I said before the memory even came and stopped myself before continuing. I didn't know what to say. I had argued with Pierce, and my father appeared. I didn't agree and drove away.

I lifted my hand to rub my head, but my dry skin was cracked. I half-expected to see blood, but I was clean. I dropped it in my lap, and every muscle in my body tingled.

"They gave you morphine a while ago," my dad said, standing up from his chair. "It should wear off, but I imagine they'll give you more." He cupped his chin and whispered, "I've been monitoring what you say."

"I said something?"

"Almost," he admitted. "You were telling the nurses you weren't allowed to be on drugs, because of the fight."

I was going to be sick.

"You have to get me out of here," I said.

"I'm trying, but—"

"But what?"

My father crossed his arms and lowered his face. His complexion was paler beneath the fluorescent lights. "The doctors are determined to heal you."

I got it then. I was Eric Welborn, James' kid, and he had money. The politics of Hayworth were astounding.

"You're lucky you lived, Eric," he muttered, looking over his shoulder before continuing. "If you were human, you'd be dead."

"That bad?"

He nodded.

I groaned and stared at the ceiling. The lights didn't burn my human vision as much as they did when I was a shade, but it reminded me of my inhibitions. I couldn't transform, and I knew what my father had done. He had taken my powers away.

"How long will this take?" I asked.

He sat down before standing up again. He was pacing. "Until you heal naturally," he said. "We can't give them another reason to be suspicious. We don't know who these nurses are."

"So, get one from the Dark."

"It's not that simple," he retorted.

I drank more water because I had nothing else to say. We were quiet for a number of minutes before he sat down on the edge of my bed and reached for my hand. He pulled back at the last second. "I'm glad you're okay, son."

"Thanks."

His breathing was heavy, and he turned toward the hallway. Mindy and Noah were probably at home, but they had to know. Strangely enough, I wanted to know what they thought.

"Mindy took Noah home," my father said, practically reading my mind. "Camille and Pierce were here earlier, but they had to train. I'm sure they'll return tomorrow."

I cringed at the reminder. "What about my training?" I asked, knowing I couldn't fight as a human, let alone an injured one.

My father patted the bed instead of my leg. "Don't worry about that now."

"But—"

"Concentrate on getting better, Eric," he said, locking his brown eyes on mine. Despite his harsh tone, he seemed much warmer than the man I knew as a child. "Just don't crash again."

I couldn't help the smirk from spreading onto my face. "Sounds like I have nothing to crash."

He chuckled. "That is a fortunate fact."

"I wouldn't call it fortunate." I tried to suppress even a light laugh. My chest hurt, but my actions disappointed me. If I'd listened to Urte, I would've handled my anger better and not destroyed my only possession—my pre-murder gift.

"I am sorry."

"I wonder—" he began quietly, "if you crashed because you lost control or because you were trying to leave Hayworth."

His words clouded the hospital air worse than the smell of sanitizers. The thought of fate controlling my life was always present, but the destruction it would use in order to succeed was unfathomable. No one knew whether events in our everyday lives were preordained. We had either little control or none. The idea of bringing on my early death just by defying fate was terrifying. But the worst part wasn't even about me.

Jessica's parents died trying to escape, but she didn't. She could leave whenever she wanted. She could be free.

14

Jessica

"**M**Y UNCLE IS THE ONE WHO FOUND HIM," SARAH SHRILL bragged, leaning to the right of her palette. I couldn't help but hear their conversation in art class. She was talking to Mitchell from across the room. "He couldn't believe he was alive. His car was in pieces."

Mitchell blew air out of his nose. "Too bad the car is gone."

"He's spoiled if you ask me," Sarah said, pointing her brush toward him. "I guarantee he gets a new one before he's even out of the hospital."

"He's still in the hospital?"

"He should be," she said. "My uncle said he wasn't in good shape. He didn't even recognize him."

Mitchell cringed. "That bad, huh?"

"I can't believe he survived another wreck. You'd think karma would catch up with him."

My stomach dropped, and my eyes froze on the twist of my painting. I couldn't continue. My fingers were shaking.

"Hannah didn't even have a chance in the last one," Mitchell said. "I wonder who was with him this time."

"No one that my uncle saw," Sarah responded. "He was there until the ambulance team took over. They said Welborn was lucky to be breathing."

"I bet. How'd he crash this time?"

My homeroom partner doing crosswords flashed through

59

my memory, and I stared at my backpack. My crossword book was still in the front pocket, even the puzzles with his handwriting.

"My uncle said he was speeding," Sarah continued. Her tone disgusted me. "He guessed Eric was going over a hundred. Big surprise, right?"

"I've seen him speeding before," Mitchell added.

"I think most people have," she pointed out. "He's hard to miss."

"Got that right," Mitchell said. "The guy asks for it. He's going to die young."

"Probably deserves it, too."

I didn't want to listen to my classmates. They were heartless. I wanted to stand up and leave, but I couldn't. The teacher was at his desk, and he would see me if I made my way to the door.

"You okay?"

I followed the squeaky voice to Jonathon Stone and hesitated to answer his question. "Yeah. Are you?"

His thick eyebrows furrowed together. "Why wouldn't I be?"

"You don't normally talk to anybody," I remarked, pointing to his little chair in the corner of the room. "You kind of keep to yourself."

"I've talked to you before."

"About a painting," I retorted.

He pushed his glasses further up his nose. "You looked so worried," he said as his eyes—or his eye—traced across my face. "I had to ask if you were okay."

"Thanks, but I'm fine," I snapped.

Jonathon ignored my bitterness. "You sure you don't want to talk about it?" he asked.

I stared at him, wondering again how he could ask me personal questions so easily. "I'm sure."

"Who wants to guess how long Welborn is out of school?" Mitchell's question gained my attention.

"I say one month."

"He bounced back in a week last time," Mitchell argued.

Sarah twirled her brush through her fingers. "But he wasn't hurt."

"Welborn enjoys sulking around too much," Mitchell said. "He'll be back."

"Good call," Sarah agreed but shook her head. "I don't see how someone so awesome can change so much."

"He used to be pretty cool," Mitchell agreed.

Sarah tapped her forehead. "Hit his head in too many wrecks."

They continued to talk, and I gripped my seat to keep myself from walking across the room and slapping them. I didn't understand how they could be so cold.

"Don't worry about Welborn," Jonathon said.

My neck cracked when I turned to him. "What?"

He gestured toward the gossip. "You were listening," he said. "I figured you were worried. Are you friends with him?"

I hesitated. Jonathon wasn't going to give up.

"Kind of," I sighed. "He's my partner in homeroom class. He wasn't there yesterday, and I guess I wondered where he was."

"He's fine," Jonathon said, dragging his fingers over his palm as if he were drawing.

I ignored his habit. I wanted to know about Eric. "How do you know?"

"Our fathers are best friends," he said. "I know Eric really well."

"I didn't know."

"Not many people do," Jonathon chuckled. "But we're friends."

"I didn't know he had friends," I said, hoping my honesty wouldn't come across as harsh as it felt.

"He has lots of friends, Jess," Jonathon said, standing this time. He walked over to his palette, and I followed him without hesitation. If he could come to me, I could do the same thing to him.

"I didn't mean that as a joke," I clarified, sitting next to him.

He picked up his paints. "Eric and I tend not to talk during school."

"Why?"

"That's just how we are," he said. "He does his sulking thing, and I do my artist thing." His foggy eye seemed to focus on me. "I thought you met my father."

"I did?"

Jonathon's thick glasses slid down the bridge of his nose. "George Stone? He was at Eric's house when you two were working on your science project last year."

It came to me like a distant whisper—the bickering, chasing Eric down, his wit, and everything else I despised about the project. But the other memories happened like a burst of lightning—the willow tree, his house, his room. Everything was a dream I had to fight to remember, but it had only been six months.

Remembering George Stone was a migraine. When he had opened the door, his voice had frightened me. He had longer hair, but his lack of facial hair made him look younger than I had originally thought. I didn't think he had kids. He didn't seem to be that kind of man.

"I did meet him," I managed through the headache. "Weird."

Jonathon turned his entire body toward me. "My dad likes to give me his autobiography every night," he joked, explaining how he knew.

I laughed. "Fun."

"Very."

"My uncle said the ambulance crew thought Welborn broke some ribs," Sarah continued, louder every minute. I might as well have been sitting next to her. "He might even have permanent eye damage. It was swollen shut."

I focused on Jonathon. "Are you positive he's okay?" I whispered.

He scooted closer. "Positive as can be," he said. "I talked to him once, but I don't think he'll remember. He kept drifting in and out."

Jonathon was not making me feel better.

"He blacked out?" I asked.

He snapped his mouth shut as his gaze drifted over my expression. "He'll be okay, but he isn't in good shape. Her uncle was right about that much."

"What exactly happened?"

"He was speeding in that Charger of his, and he lost control," he confirmed Sarah's story. "He's not too happy about totaling his car. He loved that thing."

"I think I'd be more worried about my health than my car," I said.

Jonathon laughed under his breath. "That's Eric for you," he said. "He only fractured three ribs, and he has a pretty nasty black eye, but he'll be walking around in a few days. No worries."

"Fractured ribs?" I cringed, but I was glad to hear his eye wasn't permanently damaged. "Doesn't that hurt?"

"Sure, but he can manage a few bumps and bruises. He's a tough kid."

A part of me already knew that. Just by the look in his eyes, I knew he was tough. He was complicated, too, and I was convinced Eric was simply misunderstood. He was always nice to me, and I couldn't help but feel the desire to be nice back to him. I wanted to make sure he was okay.

"Will you see him tonight?" I asked.

Jonathon's focus returned to his palette. "I'm planning to," he said, suddenly refusing to look at me. "Want me to say hi for you?"

"Can you take me?" I asked, and Jonathon went rigid. My stomach twisted. "I'd like to say hi myself."

"I don't know if that's the best idea, Jess," he said, each word as deliberate as the first.

"Please," I begged, touching his arm. "I just want to make sure he's okay myself."

"But—"

"Please, Jonathon." I was desperate for his help. "Please?"

Jonathon glanced over before staring at his painting, sighing. "I guess I can't stop you."

"Thank you." I hugged Jonathon without a second thought. He felt like a friend now, and Eric, in a way, had always been one. It would be nice to see them both outside of school, even under the circumstances.

"You're welcome," Jonathon said, tense beneath my arms.

I let go. "Meet up after school?"

"I'll have Teresa take us," he said.

"Teresa?"

"Eric's—" Jonathon took a moment to breathe. "She's a family friend, too."

The name was like my other memories—familiar, but a migraine. I repeated the name until I got a mental picture of her up on the hill, underneath the willow tree as she talked to Eric. She used to pick him up every day after lunch. "Short, black hair?"

"You've seen her?"

"I think so," I said. "Last year sometime."

"She has an old, silver BMW." Jonathon eyed the clock. Class was almost over. "Meet me out front."

"Sounds perfect," I said, standing as the bell rang.

15

Jessica

THE CAR DOOR SQUEAKED WHEN JONATHON OPENED IT, AND TE-resa was already turned around, focused on him. Jona-thon's face turned red.

"Teresa, this is Jess," he said, climbing into the passenger seat as I got in the back.

She was pretty, but she was even prettier close up. Her pale skin was flawless, and her cerulean nails were as bright as her eyes. Behind the black bob, she gawked, and her mouth opened. I expected her to say something, but she only put on her dark sunglasses.

"She's coming to the hospital with us," Jonathon explained.

"Jonathon—"

"Not now," he grumbled.

I straightened up to peer into the rearview mirror. Teresa was tightlipped until she turned to me. "Hey, Jess."

"Hi."

"Are you strapped in?" she asked, and I nodded. "Good."

She drove away from the cracked curb, and no one spoke. Jonathon turned up the radio to mask the awkward silence.

It was fifteen agonizing minutes before we reached the hospital. I got out of her car as quickly as I could and followed them into the giant building. Like most people, I didn't like hospitals, but I was willing to deal with it if it meant seeing Eric. The rumors made it sound like he would never function again.

"He's this way," Teresa said, seemingly calmer, and we were buzzed into a section and I didn't even see an attendant. I walked behind them, only stopping when they did.

A middle-aged man stood outside of a room, and I recognized him as Eric's father. His demeanor was so like his son's that I couldn't forget him.

"Mr. Welborn." Jonathon gained the man's attention.

He looked up, and his expression dropped when he saw me. "Jess?"

"Hi, Mr. Welborn," I squeaked, waving. "I'm surprised you remembered my name."

"Well," he cleared his throat. "Eric doesn't have many girls over."

Eric's name twisted my gut. "Is he okay?"

"Other than his ribs, he's perfectly fine." His father sounded more confident than anyone else had. "They have him on a lot of painkillers, so he's been sleeping a lot."

Jonathon leaned to look past Mr. Welborn. "Is he awake right now?"

Mr. Welborn stepped aside. "Just woke up, Jonathon," he said the boy's name like it was a curse.

Jonathon hung his head, and Teresa moved toward him. Their rigid movements amplified my nerves, but I fought the urge to step back. I was here to see Eric, not to worry about whatever family drama was happening.

"You can go in and see him, Jess," his father spoke to me like an old friend. "He's in there."

I hesitated, staring at the white curtains used for doors. Eric and I were classmates, but I still didn't know what he would think about my visit. I looked at Jonathon and Teresa. "Don't you guys want to see him?"

"Believe me, Jess," Teresa began, opening the curtain. "He'll be more ecstatic to see you than us." With her free hand, she pushed me toward his room. "I have to talk to his dad anyways."

"Are you sure?" I wanted them to come with me. "I mean,

if you want to see him—"

"I'm positive," she insisted. "Have fun."

She pushed me again, causing me to stumble, and I grabbed the doorframe as if I could still hold myself back, but I couldn't. I was in his room, and there he was, lying in bed. His brown hair matted to the pillow like it hadn't been washed in days, and his arm was wrapped. One of his eyes was swollen shut, a giant, black ring surrounding it, and his cheek was puffy and red. The rest of his face was blotchy and pale, but I had never been happier to see him before.

"Jessica?" he croaked, sitting up. His eyes were glazed over. "What are you doing here?"

"I—I—" I hovered in the doorway. "I'm not sure, really," I admitted. "I heard you were in a wreck, and I wanted to make sure you were okay."

Eric's brow rose, but it crumbled in seconds. I wondered if the expression caused him pain. He patted the bed.

I walked across the room and sat inches away from him, and a rush of memories twisted through my mind. Last semester, we had sat on his bed when we worked on our project. He leaned against me that night, and I was nervous. This time, I was nervous for him. I didn't want to hurt him.

"I'm okay," he said, managing a promising smile. "Except for the eye, that's not so good."

"And the ribs," I reminded him.

He chuckled, wincing as his chest moved. "Those aren't so great either," he agreed, but his smile remained as if he couldn't let it go.

I wanted to smile back, but couldn't. It felt uncomfortably sick to see him in such a state, and I felt selfish for being unable to control my emotions.

His fingers tapped the space between my hands. "How'd you get here?"

"Jonathon. We have art class together," I said. "I didn't know you were friends with him."

"And I didn't know you knew him."

"Small world."

"Small school," he retorted.

"It is," I admitted, hesitating to say anything else. It was too strange to look at Eric. I was used to seeing him in class, listening to music through his headphones. Now, I doubted he could even tilt his chair back without some part of him hurting.

"I'll be okay," he whispered, and chills ran up my neck. He could read my body language better than anyone else I knew. "It could've been worse."

"It should've been worse." I relied on the information I had heard. He was lucky to be alive. My biological parents had done the same thing, and they were dead. A part of me wanted to lecture him on his recklessness, but a bigger part of me knew the most important thing was that he was alive.

I stared at my hands as I dug my nails into my palms. I heard the bed shift before I realized he'd grabbed my hand. He threaded his fingers beneath mine and pulled my nails out of my hand. When I looked up, he let go.

"I hope Jonathon is the one who told you," he said, but I barely heard him. My heart was pounding in my ears.

"Kids were talking at school," I said, hoping he hadn't noticed how hot my hands were. "Everyone knows."

He glanced at the wall. "Fantastic."

"It's Hayworth. What did you expect?"

"Some etiquette would be a little nice." He lifted his chin to stare at the ceiling. His neck was red from the seatbelt scraping him. "I suppose I couldn't hide it forever."

"Why would you want to hide it?" I asked.

He didn't respond the way I expected him to. "Does Zac mind that you're visiting me?" he asked.

I tensed. Eric barely knew me, but he wasn't holding back, and I wondered how much medication they had him on. Without knowing, I took a deep breath. "Zac isn't my boyfriend."

"So I've heard."

My face burned. "From who?"

He glanced down from his fixation on the ceiling. "Robb McLain is kind of hard to ignore when he talks to you at our table."

I cringed. I had always known Eric didn't like it when Robb and Crystal moved over to our table because he turned his music up. It was one of the reasons I thought he never heard a thing.

"Robb doesn't know what he's talking about half of the time." Even though I didn't have to defend myself, I wanted to.

Eric smirked. "Robb likes you."

"What?" My breath escaped me. "There's no way. He's my friend."

"A close friend."

"Girls and guys can be close friends," I said.

"But Robb doesn't want to be just friends."

"That's gross."

"It's the truth," he said, winking his good eye at me as he snuggled into his bed like a child. His cheeks turned a light pink, and his eyelashes batted. His medication was affecting him more than I thought.

"Thanks for checking on me, Jessica," he said.

My irritation dissipated. "You're welcome," I whispered, and the white curtain was yanked open.

Mr. Welborn walked in, and his eyes fell on his son. "I think Eric needs rest now," he said.

I stood up.

"I'm fine, Dad," Eric argued, but he yawned and shut his eyes. "I—I'm wide awake."

He fell asleep as the words left his mouth. I stared, unable to tear my eyes away. Eric Welborn looked peaceful, even with a black eye and broken ribs. I wanted to stay, but I knew I couldn't. He was exhausted.

I tiptoed out of the room, and his father followed me. I spoke when we were safely in the hallway. "Thanks for letting me see him, Mr. Welborn."

"Thanks for coming."

Teresa stepped away from the wall she was leaning on. "I'll drive you home, Jess."

"Thanks."

Mr. Welborn stopped me, and I waited. He ran a hand

over his chest, and his watch flashed beneath the lights. "Eric should be out of here soon, but he probably won't be back at school immediately," he said. "You could come over if you'd like."

"Sir?" Teresa spoke up, but Mr. Welborn raised his hand as if he could control her speech.

He was still looking at me. "Eric could use someone to talk to."

"I'd like someone to talk to myself." I accepted the invitation, feeling my chest lighten. Whatever burden I'd been holding was suddenly gone. "I'll visit soon."

16

Eric

I DIDN'T OPEN MY EYES WHEN I HEARD SOMEONE SPEAK, AND I KEPT them closed when I recognized my father's voice.

"She's gone, Jonathon." Footsteps echoed off the linoleum floor.

I almost thought Jessica was a dream, a hallucination brought on by drugs, but she wasn't. She had come to see me. I couldn't believe I had fallen asleep while she was with me.

"When?" Jonathon asked.

"Teresa took her an hour ago," my dad said. "Eric fell asleep."

"Eric, sleeping?" Jonathon's voice lightened. "What a shocker."

My father chuckled beneath his breath. "The drugs will keep him like this until tomorrow."

"I bet," Jonathon agreed. "Eric can't relax unless you force him to."

"Can you blame him?" My father's question lingered as he whistled a low tune. "Do you think this happened because he tried to leave?"

"Want my honest answer?"

"Yes."

"I do," he said.

My father's sigh bordered on a groan. "Me, too."

"But it doesn't mean anything," Jonathon rambled. "It

71

doesn't change anything."

"It means he can't run," my father said, and someone began pacing.

"He doesn't need to run," Jonathon said, but his voice was quiet. "Does he?"

My father hesitated. "No."

"Eric's right," Jonathon said. "You're a horrible liar."

My father laughed again. "I'm not lying. I'm just worried."

"You're allowed to be." Apparently, my best friend was my father's counselor. "This isn't working as we thought it would."

"I don't know what to do about Jess," my father confessed. "She loves him, even if she doesn't know it." My father paused and so did the pacing. "It's still strange to see them together," he muttered. "It's the only time I see Eric act like my son. I'm afraid he won't be able to hold back, that he'll remind her—"

"I won't tell her," I said, finally opening my eyes. My father seemed much taller standing when I was lying down.

"Eric," he scorned. "You're supposed to be sleeping."

"I'm almost asleep," I said. "Does that count?"

He folded his arms across his chest. "You shouldn't be listening to our conversations."

"Maybe you shouldn't have them in my room," I suggested.

My father rubbed his chin, trying to conceal his grin. "You and your eavesdropping."

"Me and my eavesdropping," I repeated. "When will I ever stop?"

My father masked his laughter as he sat down next to Jonathon. "I don't know where you got that attitude, but if you got it from your mother, I'll be sure to say something when I see her again."

It was the first time he had mentioned my mother since she died, and I turned away from him. I didn't like to think about how she died, how she committed suicide and left us here to deal with the prophecy. I barely remembered her. It was almost like she hadn't existed, but I thought about her more and more the closer the Marking of Change got.

Rustling interrupted the tension. "Mindy dropped these

off earlier," Jonathon said, lifting a plate covered in tinfoil. "Lemon cakes."

My mouth watered. "I love those things," I said, reaching for one.

My father placed them on the counter. "You'll only get sick on this sugar right now," he said. "You need to rest."

"Can I have one after?"

"You can eat them when you get home."

"That's in two days," I whined.

"Two days it is then."

My only hope was crushed by protective wrap. "This is cruel," I mumbled.

Jonathon snatched one and stuffed it into his mouth. "Sorry," he spoke, showing off the dessert I was supposed to eat.

I groaned. "I cannot wait to get out of here."

"That makes two of us," my father agreed.

Jonathon pumped his fist into the air. "Three."

We laughed, and my ribs stung.

Before I knew it, I would be home, but it wouldn't be the home I was used to. I would no longer be able to participate in the Dark. I would have to heal my human body until the doctors cleared me before I could transform. If I didn't, my identity would be risked. I needed to heal fast enough to train before the battle. If not, I would be stuck with what I already knew, and I was sure Darthon would know more than me. I wouldn't win.

17

Jessica

WHEN I WALKED INTO ART CLASS THE NEXT DAY, THE PAINTING was finished. Purple streaks dripped from the sky, and swirls of blue melted through the twists like liquid sapphires. Every aspect of my painting was how I'd left it except for one thing—the sky reflected off a river, and not just any river. It was the river from the forest.

The piece represented every emotion of my flying dream. Every inch of the painting meant something, and the canvas was practically a photograph from my vision. The river created the perfection I'd been striving for, but there was one problem. I hadn't painted it, and there was only one person I knew who could've done it.

Jonathon Stone.

He was sitting in his usual corner, his back facing the class, and I had to tap him on the shoulder to get his attention. I recognized the artist stare plastered on his face when he turned around. His painting engrossed him. It was of a woman I'd never seen before.

"Who's that?" I asked.

He took off his glasses to rub his eye. "No one important," he said, replacing his glasses.

"She must be if you're painting her."

He gestured to the empty spot next to him. I retrieved a chair and sat down, but he didn't talk. The painting was vivid enough that I looked for a photograph in his lap, but there wasn't one. He was painting from memory.

He laid his paintbrush down. "It's my mom." He straightened his spine, but his shoulders, somehow, remained slumped. "She walked out."

"Oh." I didn't want to intrude any more than I already had. "Thanks for finishing my painting."

"I'm sorry I did that." His fingertips shook. "But I couldn't stop myself."

"I'm glad you did," I clarified, but his guilt was apparent.

"It wasn't mine to finish."

"I couldn't finish it myself," I pointed out.

"I know."

I wondered how he recognized what was missing. His eye for color and the shape of a piece was beyond masterful. I had only started painting in our class, but I already felt a connection to it, and I envied how much passion he had for something I was unable to complete.

"You'll get there one day," he said. "You're very good."

"Maybe you can teach me," I said, hoping he would tutor me, but he didn't respond to the invite. My cheeks burned. "How'd you know what to do?"

"I followed your style," he began, pausing as if he were contemplating an explanation. "Sometimes an outside perspective is the clearer perspective."

"That's unbelievable," I breathed, staring at him as if I were staring at one of the greats. "You're really something, you know that?"

"Thanks," he squeaked. He was uncomfortable, and I hated to be the one who caused that.

"How's Eric?" I changed the subject.

"He'll be home tomorrow."

Tomorrow was earlier than I was expecting.

"That's great," I said, wondering how soon I should visit him. I wanted to, but I didn't want to seem pushy. "Is he excited?"

Jonathon chuckled. "More than he was when he got his

car."

The reminder silenced us. Eric's car was gone, but at least he was alive. I looked around the classroom and studied the students who treated Eric like simple gossip. It was bad enough that Eric's car wreck happened, but kids constantly compared it with his last car wreck—when Hannah died—like it was nothing. I wanted the gossip to stop.

"Well, I'm glad I could help you with your painting," Jonathon said, splitting through my thoughts.

I stood up. "I'll let you get back to yours."

He gestured to his. "Any thoughts?"

It was his mother. I couldn't possibly help him with it.

"Be honest," he said.

I breathed, looking over the curve of her cheekbones, the lightness of her eyes, the watery skin of her face.

"Her complexion could use some color," I suggested.

He turned back. "I'll consider that," he said. "Thank you, Jess."

"You're welcome."

I felt strange helping someone who helped me, but that's what friends did, and Jonathon felt more like a friend now than when he first talked to me. He practically saw my dreams. I thought about what he said.

Maybe all I needed was an outside perspective to understand my dreams, and I already knew the perfect person to talk to. I only had to figure out when I would see him next.

18

I WAS FINALLY HOME, BUT I WOULDN'T BE ABLE TO GO BACK TO school until tomorrow at the earliest, and that wasn't even guaranteed. My father wanted me to rest as much as possible. The injuries weren't life-threatening, but I had to heal quickly, and I couldn't cheat by turning into a shade. The doctors might be in the Light, and then I would be a discovered shade. I was more useless than before.

I fought the urge to throw my stress ball at the ceiling. My ribs were already burning from the first throw. I couldn't strain myself, even if I wanted to. If my car wreck had taught me anything, it was the fact that I didn't own my body. My life held the future for hundreds, and I couldn't be selfish anymore. Not even as a human.

A small knock echoed through my bedroom. I slowly sat up to see Mindy in my doorway. Her hand grasped the door. "How are you feeling?"

I kicked my feet off the bed and stood up. "Better."

She'd been checking on me every hour since my return, and I couldn't help but feel more empathy for her. As far as I knew, she was human, and humans healed dreadfully slow. I hated to think how slowly her emotions healed.

"Your father wants to talk to you," she said.

I tensed. "About what?"

"Not sure," she admitted, tying her bright, red hair into

a ponytail. I knew the look. She was getting ready to prepare dinner.

"Need help cooking?" I asked.

Her head moved back like my words shocked her. I had to remind myself that they probably had.

"I'd love that, but your father—"

I had already forgotten. "I'll go talk to him." I moved past her, and she went to the kitchen. Those few words were the only ones we had exchanged all week.

I managed to get down the hallway without much trouble. I was used to pain, but I wasn't used to human pain. It was different—more constricting and lingering. I ignored it as I entered his office and hoped he wouldn't notice.

"Shut the door behind you." He didn't glance up from his paperwork.

I shut the door and locked it, wondering if his paperwork involved more news from the Dark. They usually avoided writing anything down, but had gotten desperate with the upcoming fight.

I waited for him to finish reading. He continuously flipped papers over, only moving his hand up to gesture to the chair in front of his desk. I sat down, grateful to be off my feet, and he stared. His glasses made his eyes look too large for his face.

"Mindy said you wanted to talk to me," I said, trying to look over his paperwork, but he laid his palm on top of them.

"I do."

I cleared my throat. "What about?"

"How are you feeling?" he asked, but I didn't respond. He knew I had three weeks before anything would change.

"What do you want to talk about?"

"Teresa was over earlier." Apparently, she had been the one to drop off the papers. "She said you've been refusing to talk to her."

"She's already lectured me once," I said, thinking of Camille.

She had been different ever since she began training. She planned on fighting, and I didn't understand why. It was between Darthon and me, but everyone was acting like Hayworth would be at war.

"I don't need to hear it again," I said.

"She's protective of you, Eric," he said. "That's her job."

"And my job is to prepare," I repeated the very words she had told me in the hospital.

"She's worried about you." His words lingered, and the meaning changed in the silence.

"She thinks I'm going to do something stupid again," I guessed.

My father laid his fingertips on his forehead. "Not exactly."

My heartbeat thumped against my injuries. "What is she worried about then?"

He stared past me. His pupils glanced over the decorations littering the office, and the light flickered over his hesitant expression. "As your father, I should talk to you about your depression," he said. "If you're considering suicide—"

The words were worse than the torture machine. "Camille thinks I tried to kill myself?"

His wrinkles deepened when he closed his eyes.

I leapt up, unable to remain still. "I did not crash my car on purpose," I said.

My father spread his hands out like he could force me to sit down again. "You have to understand—"

"I'm not my mother." My words escaped with a hiss. "It was an accident. I'd never consider that."

My father didn't speak, but he didn't have to for my anger to rise. My mother's suicide had affected my life more than any other event I could consider. I'd dealt with the aftermath my entire life. I couldn't contemplate inflicting that pain on others. I'd seen what it could do. That was enough for me.

"Then, we can drop it," my father said. He didn't want to talk about it any more than I did.

I gripped the back of the chair. "Now."

"Okay." He bent over to open a drawer. "I have something for you."

He shut the drawer and laid a black box on his desk in

front of me. I waited for it to do something—to open up in a magical way like an object from the Dark would—but it didn't. It was a simple box.

"Take it."

I picked it up. "What is it?"

He pointed at it, and I opened the box. I stared at the object inside and had to sit down when I realized what it was. "Dad—"

"Don't argue against it, Eric," he said. "Your mother would've wanted you to have it. Believe me. She talked about it all the time when she was—" *Alive*. Even he couldn't say certain things aloud.

I wanted to run my finger over the object, but I couldn't. "What am I supposed to do with this?"

"It'll help you through this, Eric." His chair squeaked as he reclined. "I promise."

I opened my mouth but snapped it shut as I closed the box. Without being able to look my father in the eye, I stood up and walked out of the room. There was nothing left to say. There were only things left to do, and I had to begin now. I had to finish what I was born to do, and I had to do it as a human— as my mother had seen, even before her death.

19

I WAS HELPING MINDY WITH THE DISHES WHEN THE DOORBELL RANG. It didn't interrupt our conversation because I hadn't been able to speak yet. My father's words still rattled through me. I was surprised I had even heard the doorbell.

"I got it," Noah chirped, running downstairs. He slammed into the door before he opened it. "Hey, Jess."

The name stopped me.

"Jess is here?" My dad stood from the table and left his coffee there. He went to the stairs before I could.

"Hello, Mr. Welborn." I heard her voice before I saw her. "Is Eric home?" She quieted when I appeared at the balcony, and her bottom lip hung open for a millisecond. Her presence twisted my insides.

"Hey, Jessica," I said, trying to ignore her blue sweater. "How are you?"

"I was about to ask you the same question," she said. She was curling her fingers against her side. She was as nervous as I was.

"Come on in, dear," Mindy shouted, rattling the dishes at the sink. "I'll make you guys some apple cider. How does that sound?"

Jessica's face lit up. "That'd be nice," she said as Noah ran back upstairs. Jessica watched him but didn't join us until I waved her up.

"Do you like cinnamon in yours?" Mindy asked, and Jessica nodded. "I'll get right on that. You two should sit." She tapped the table.

Jessica followed her suggestion before I did. She sat with her back to the railing, and I sat next to her. Her stare lingered on my hands, and I moved my scratched fingers around.

"I'm healing," I said, and she bit her lip. It drove me crazy. "Thanks for visiting."

"Jonathon told me you were back." She was barely breathing. "I thought I'd visit again."

"It's good to see you," I said, wanting her to relax, but even I was struggling. My father was lingering behind us, and I didn't want to say anything he'd find inappropriate. He would lecture me about getting too close to her.

"Here you go, Jess," Mindy said, placing two cups of apple cider in front of us. The drink reminded me of the cooling autumn outside my house. Winter would be here in a few weeks.

"Thank you," she said.

Mindy beamed, grabbing my father's arm. "We'll let you kids talk," she said, and my father didn't protest as she dragged him down the hallway.

The kitchen was silent, aside from Jessica sipping her drink, but I couldn't pull my eyes away. Her presence was too surreal, like this past summer before her memory was erased.

"I didn't know you had a brother," Jessica said.

I grasped my cup. Jonathon's theory was correct. More than her shade memories were gone. She had met Noah before and knew he was my stepbrother. I didn't know what to say other than what I said the first time.

"Noah's my stepbrother," I said. "He's always snooping around my bedroom."

"He looks up to you," she said. She hadn't responded the same way last time.

"What?"

"He's a younger sibling," she said, steam moving past her nose as she breathed into her hot drink. "He's snooping because he looks up to you." She winked. "I bet he's been nicer

82

since you've gotten back from the hospital."

She was right. Noah had helped as much as Mindy had. They'd checked on me periodically, leaving me alone when I was resting. Noah even stayed out of my bedroom. But it took hearing Jessica's words for me to realize it. She had that effect on me, and I missed that about her more than anything.

"I'm coming back to school soon," I volunteered, unable to hold back the information.

"When?"

"I'm not sure," I admitted. "But I'm trying to get as much rest as I can."

She ran her finger over the rim of her cup. "I don't think I've been so excited for homeroom class," she said.

"I doubt Ms. Hinkel feels the same way," I joked, and her giggle lightened my dark mood.

"I like talking to you, Eric." She was blushing again, but she wasn't trying to hide it. "Why else would I visit you?"

"Because you can't stay away?" I wasn't joking, but she thought I was.

"Don't let your ego show," she said, trying not to laugh. She took another sip of her drink and placed it on the table. We fell into a silence, but it wasn't an awkward kind. It reflected an understanding that'd grown between us over the past few months. It was familiar.

Too bad the silence was interrupted with the front door opening. George Stone bounded up the stairs and halted at the sight.

"Jess," he lingered on her name, his stare darting between the two of us. "How are you?"

"Mr. Stone," she said, but her voice teetered. I wondered how she remembered him but not Noah. "I'm good. How are you?"

"Good," he said.

My father appeared as if he had been waiting in the shadows. "Jess came to visit Eric," he clarified what he couldn't say aloud—Jessica didn't have her memory back. She was simply here.

"That's good," George said, turning his back to us. They muttered words under their breath as the door opened again, and Jonathon appeared within moments.

Jessica waved. "Hey, Jonathon."

"H—Hey," he stuttered.

Something was wrong.

"How are you?" Jonathon repeated the same polite script everyone did, but Jessica didn't answer.

"I should go," she said, standing up slowly. I wanted to stop her, but I knew I had to talk to my father. "I came at the wrong time."

"No, you didn't," I said.

"We didn't plan on coming over, either." Jonathon took my side.

Jessica tapped my arm. "I'll come back another night," she said, moving past me.

I followed her. "Let me walk you out."

"Okay," she said, and we walked downstairs. She slipped her shoes back on, and I opened the front door, feeling my friend's eyes on my back as I left with her.

Jessica walked to her mother's car, keys in hand, and turned around at the last second. Her hair was much longer than I remembered it, and I fought the urge to move her curls out of her face.

"I didn't realize Jonathon's family was so close to yours until he told me," she said, attempting a short conversation, but I hesitated to continue. Our secret wasn't something I wanted to expose to everyone.

"I'm really glad you stopped by," I said.

Her cheeks rose with her smile. "Me, too."

I opened her car door. "I'll see you again."

She stared at the gesture as if she couldn't comprehend it, and I let my hand drop off the vehicle. I didn't know what she wanted from me. She seemed interested, but then she acted as confused as I already felt.

"Get some rest, Eric," she said, climbing into her car.

"I will," I promised, shutting her door. She met eyes with

me through the tinted windows, and the shade seemed to change her blue eyes into the purple ones I had seen when I first met her. I wanted to kiss her, but the car jumped as it shifted into reverse.

I stepped back, shoving my hands into my pockets as she backed out of my driveway. Her headlights blinded me as they cut through the dark and disappeared through the trees. That's when I sensed him.

"She doesn't remember Noah," I said, knowing Jonathon had appeared next to me. He had already melted back into his human form.

"So, I was right," he said.

My jaw locked. I didn't want to say it aloud because there was a chance she would never remember those things. It was a risk we knew of when she agreed to it, but it didn't make it any easier to accept.

"Do you think she'll figure it out?" I asked.

"She could."

"This could be a problem," I said.

Jonathon sat down on the sidewalk. "It already is." He was more willing to speak the truth than I was.

"What should I do?" Jessica was coming around me, and there was nothing I could do, even if I wanted to. "I don't know how she feels something for me when she doesn't even know who she was."

"Who she is," Jonathon corrected, laying his arms on his knees. "And I think both of you always knew."

"What do you mean?"

He sighed. "Last semester," he began. "You like to pretend you didn't know who she was until you saw her human face, but you did."

"I didn't."

"I've never seen you open up to another student, even when they begged you to," he pointed out. "She never gave up on you, and you eventually gave into her." Jonathon leaned backwards as if he couldn't stay still. "You both knew it. You just denied the truth."

I wanted to argue again, but I couldn't. I thought about the time she woke me up in my car, the time I asked her about adoption. I suspected her then, but she dismissed me, and I accepted her answer without another thought. Maybe Jonathon was right. We always knew.

"Everyone should've realized you were the first descendant from the beginning," Jonathon continued. "You were always more powerful than the rest of us."

I thought back to our childhood—all the times I succeeded in training before anyone else. I figured it was talent, nothing more, and I was wrong. "The elders must have had suspicions," I said.

"I know I did," he said, and he flashed a grin. "Don't look so shocked."

"I don't understand why you're telling me this now."

He dropped his face. His glasses slid down his nose, and he pushed them back up. "I'm tired of seeing you this way," he said. "You used to be excited to be the descendant—"

"Then, I grew up and realized what responsibility was."

He shook his head. "You don't really believe that, do you?"

I wanted to punch him, but his words were too quiet to start a fight over my maturity. "I like to think I understand it." Especially after seeing Darthon.

"I don't think we can," Jonathon said. "Not now."

"Not when I'm a human," I joked, but Jonathon's expression didn't budge.

"Being human isn't that bad," he said.

"What makes you say that?"

"I can't paint when I'm a shade." He glared at the darkness as if it were a cracked mirror. "Have I ever told you that?"

I swallowed my nerves. "No."

His eyes crinkled, and he shoulders rose. He seemed more like Pierce despite his human appearance. "There are things only humans are capable of," he said, standing up to leave me to my thoughts. "Just remember that."

20

Jessica

WE WERE BENEATH THE WILLOW TREE, AND THE HEAT OF THE day lingered on my bare skin. I stood between the dangling leaves, breathing in the cooling night air like it could soothe my sunburn, but nothing stopped the humid heat. A pound of hairspray couldn't keep my curls down.

His fingertips skimmed the nape of my neck. His lips lingered on my shoulder, and chills ran down my arm.

"What are you doing?"

He wrapped his arm around my waist. I knew who it was without seeing his face. The boy from my dreams.

"Enjoying this," he whispered.

It wasn't the voice I was expecting.

I spun around, nearly smacking him with my sudden movements. His sleepy face was tanned with sunlight and red with happiness, but I was still in denial. I had to look up to meet his eyes, and his height made me as dizzy as his identity.

Eric Welborn.

———— ◆ ————

I woke from the dream in a way I never had before. I wasn't scared, but I wasn't dreaming of the boy I had previously seen so many times. I was dreaming of the one I was visiting.

I jumped out of bed and rushed to my bathroom. Turning on the faucet, I splashed water on my cheeks. The images remained, and I opened my eyes, blinking away water droplets to stare at my reflection.

My hair was black.

I fell over, smacking my head on the wall, and scrambled back to my feet. In the mirror was the reflection I'd been used to my entire life, but my round face was blotchy and dripping. My curly hair was frizzing from the water.

I sucked in a breath and slumped on the countertop. Crystal and Robb were right. My dreams were affecting more than my sleep. My vision was warped, my imagination was out of control, and my heart was obsessed with a man I had only seen in my sleep.

Eric Welborn was a different story. Why I dreamt of him was unknown to me. I had spent a lot of time worrying about him, but I didn't think I let him consume my thoughts as much as I obviously had.

The fantasized kiss was stolen time from the dreams I wanted to figure out. Even with a shake of my head, I couldn't get the images out of my mind. Eric Welborn was overwhelming. If I wanted to have my other dreams again, I would have to avoid him.

21

Jessica

EVERYTHING WAS REMINDING ME OF ERIC—THE TEACHER'S green shirt, the heat blasting from the ceiling, the smooth desk in front of me, the empty seat next to me. I couldn't get my mind off him, and it didn't help that everyone seemed to be talking about his arrival.

"He should've taken the opportunity to drop out." The girl spoke behind me without any clue that Eric was now one of my friends.

"I know," her friend agreed. "I really don't understand why he keeps coming back."

"No one does."

I ignored their words and watched the clock, tapping my fingernails against the desk. It seemed like everyone had already seen him and his injuries. I didn't think he looked that bad, considering the accident. His black eye looked the worst, but his internal injuries were the most detrimental. I hated to think about the pain he was in. I also hated to think of how I dreamt of him any more than I already had.

"You weren't kidding when you said you were excited for this class."

The voice controlled me.

I stopped tapping my fingernails, and I straightened up, looking into the eyes of the boy who had kissed me in dreamland.

"You're back." I blurted it out.

Eric was right in front of me, and the entire classroom had dropped their voices to whispers. He didn't seem to notice. Instead, he slipped into his chair with an ease that suggested he had never been injured at all. I wanted to know how he remained calm all the time.

"They never stop talking, do they?" he joked, gesturing his head at the girls behind us. Apparently, I was wrong. He had heard everything.

"I guess not."

"How much did I miss?" he asked.

I tried to ignore his lips as he talked. The dream was distracting me more than I hoped.

He pulled out a notebook from his backpack, and his shoulders shifted beneath his black shirt. He stared at me. His black eye looked darker against the color of his clothes. "Jessica?"

"What?"

He cocked a grin, and I was suddenly relieved that he hadn't lost any teeth in the accident. "I asked how much I missed."

A blush crept up my neck, and I turned to the front of the classroom. "Not that much," I said, but I didn't know. I couldn't collect my thoughts. "I'm sure Ms. Hinkel will want to see you."

"Speaking of which—" His voice faded as our teacher entered the classroom. Her focus immediately landed on him, and she waved him up to her desk.

I studied his walk, half-expecting a limp, but he was fine. How someone could survive crashing at speeds over a hundred miles per hour was beyond me. He was a walking miracle.

"We'll start class in a few minutes," Ms. Hinkel announced, and everyone erupted into chatter. This time, no one spoke of Eric, and I wondered if they knew how good he was at eavesdropping.

"Jess." Crystal swung into Eric's chair at the opportunity to talk. Her lip piercing matched her fluorescent clothes. "Robb's parents are going out tomorrow night. He wants us to come over."

I glanced at his empty seat. He was missing more school than usual. "Where is he?"

"I don't know," she said, waving her hand around. "But he's really excited to have the house to himself. It never happens."

"Okay," I said. "I'll have to check with my mom, but I think I can come over."

"Great." She was glowing.

"What's going on?" I asked, suspicious of her lightened appearance. She always had an attitude in school.

"Zac called me last night."

"And?"

"He wants to go out sometime," she said.

I patted her knee. "That's awesome."

"I'm excited," she said, kicking her feet like a child. I had never seen her as happy as she was now. "We haven't made the plans yet, but I hope it's soon. He says he has good news."

My stomach twisted at the words. I didn't know Zac, but it was hard to imagine any news coming from him was good.

"Maybe he'll come over to Robb's," she continued.

My eye twitched. I rubbed it, and I opened my eyes to Crystal's mouth hanging open. She was facing Eric, and he didn't look as happy as he had before.

"Can I have my seat back?" he asked in a low tone.

Crystal leapt up, leaving without another word. By the way she reacted, it was hard to remember they used to be friends.

He sat down so suddenly that his chair moved backwards. I wondered if he remembered what he had said in the hospital about Zac and Robb, but I didn't want to ask.

"You okay, Jessica?" His whisper was barely audible.

"Of course."

His gaze landed on the blank notebook in front of us. "You really are a terrible liar," he said as the teacher took over the class' attention.

Eric was right. I wasn't okay. I was more worried about Crystal dating Zac than I wanted to admit.

22

THE SUN WAS SETTING ON HAYWORTH, AND THE USUALLY GOLD-
en glow was gray and cold. It hovered over the still trees,
and I breathed in the dense air. I knew the feeling. Rain
was coming, and it wouldn't surprise me if it would be the last
time before the transition to snow. Winter was coming earlier
than usual.

The realization hit me as soon as her energy did. It was
electric, but dull, and I knew Camille was in my father's office.
Darkness followed, and the hair on my arms stood up. Whatever was happening in my house was big, and I didn't know
about it.

I rushed inside. Mindy and Noah were nowhere in sight.
They were gone, confirming my thoughts, and I ignored the
overwhelming sensation to transform. If the elders were in my
house, they could handle my identity.

"What's going on?" I began talking before I even had the
door open.

They, however, hadn't stopped talking.

"We've already decided this is the best plan," Luthicer said.

Eu stood by his side in agreement. He was practically the
other man's shadow.

"But Camille is hesitating," Bracke—my father's shade
identity—said, but Camille didn't speak. Her white hair was
longer than ever before.

"My student has accepted full responsibility," Luthicer continued. "She wants to go."

"There's a better way," Urte said.

Luthicer folded his arms. Even with his sleeves down, I couldn't forget his scars.

"What's going on?" I repeated.

Everyone turned toward me with meek interest, but Luthicer's face budged.

My mind went to the worst place possible. "Is Jessica okay?" I asked.

"She's fine," Camille grumbled. She was rigid with nerves.

"Then, what happened?"

"It doesn't concern you," Eu said.

I shut the door behind me as a response. I was staying whether they liked it or not.

"This meeting is for the Dark," he continued, stabbing at my inability to change.

"If you haven't forgotten, I'm in charge of its survival."

"Not anymore, kid," Eu retorted.

I glowered at the people of my community. "What does that mean?"

"We're declaring war," Luthicer said, taking a seat for what seemed to be the first time in my life. He was quiet and so were the others.

"War?" The word held too much definition for three letters.

"The Light wants to meet," my father informed me. "We already know why."

I couldn't breathe. "How long has this been going on?"

"A few days," Urte said. "We didn't want to worry anyone."

"You could've worried me."

"You don't have time to be bothered," he said.

"This is about my injuries," I guessed. "Isn't it?"

"If they're offering a war, they don't believe Darthon can beat you on his own," Camille said. "It's a good sign."

"It's a trap," I said.

Her black eyes slid into thin lines. I hated how the lights

didn't have irises.

"We have to consider it," she said.

"So, what do you have to do with it?" I interrogated her.

"I'm making the deal with them."

My ribs felt as if they were breaking again. "No, you're not," I said, pointing at her as I shouted at my father. "They could kill her."

"She's more than capable—"

"I'm guessing they want to have this meeting in their realm," I said, knowing they would only send a half-breed for one reason. "They could kill her in there—in a second. She wouldn't even stand a chance."

"They won't do that."

I didn't bother looking at her. "They will declare war with your death, and you know it."

She twitched in my peripheral vision, but Luthicer remained calm. "I'd go myself," he said. "But they requested your guard, Eric."

"Even more reason to ignore their request," I said, throwing my arms into the air. "Aren't you the one who told me about their ways? You can't believe they'll keep their word."

"If it's death they want—" Camille began, but I shouted over her.

"They'll get it in war," I said. "They don't need one beforehand, and neither do we." I was shaking. "Have you even considered how easy it would be to figure out my identity if you get killed as Camille and Teresa disappears? Everyone knows you're close to this family. Don't be an idiot."

Luthicer stood up. "We have considered that, Eric, but we can't ignore this. A war would improve our chances."

"Our destined chances?" I argued. "We're going to win."

"We can lose."

"Then, let me lose," I said, refusing to move.

Among my stillness was a pounding heart.

"If they truly want a war," I chose my words carefully, "they'll be willing to meet on equal territory."

"There's no such thing, Eric," Luthicer said. "We're more

powerful here, just as they are in their realm. Either way, one side will have to forfeit safety."

"We're talking about war," I pointed out. "What is safe about that?"

"That's why I'm going," Camille interjected.

I resorted to my last tactic. "Then I'm disowning you as my guard."

"You can't do that," she said, her voice squeaking to octaves I've never heard before.

"Actually, I can," I said, searching my memories of the training I had as a child. "If a guard is chosen for you, you can disown them and choose another." I turned to my father. "Can't I?"

He blinked his ice-blue eyes as if he were clearing his vision. "You can," he said. "But the Light wouldn't know."

"I'll make sure they do," I threatened.

"If you transform, you would heal, Eric," Luthicer said, knowing I could break my father's binding spell. "You'll expose yourself."

"Wouldn't be any different from Camille getting killed," I pointed out.

Camille threw her arms down. "Why do you have to be so difficult?"

I didn't budge. I wouldn't let it happen. Even though we hadn't been talking, she was still like my sister.

"I won't see you die for the situation I caused," I said. "Not if I can prevent it."

"You can't prevent this war, Eric," my father said, stepping away from his desk. "We've already decided to agree to it."

I knew they were right. I didn't know how long I had between healing and the fight. I'd be weaker, and Darthon was already stronger than I was. Fighting on my own would be riskier, especially if the Light showed up with every warrior they had. Despite our refusal for a war, they could do it anyway, and I would have to fight an army.

"Then wait for them to come to us," I said. "They'll show up on their own."

Urte sat on the desk, running his hand over his beard. "Let's give them a week," he suggested. "If they don't communicate, we'll consider other methods."

Camille wouldn't have to go.

I grinned. "Deal."

"Then, this meeting is done," my father said, moving toward the door.

Eu disappeared in a cloud of smoke, but everyone else remained. My father stopped near me like he was about to speak, but only laid a hand on my shoulder. I stared at the wrinkles beneath his eyes. He was too tired to say anything. He dropped his hand and left the room. Urte followed him.

"You shouldn't have done that," Camille said, but she wasn't as rigid as she had been. Her movements confirmed her reluctance of what I stopped. She knew what would happen to her, and she had accepted it.

"You shouldn't have agreed to it," I said.

She moved across the room in a flash. I half-expected her to slap me, but she did the opposite. Her arms were around my shoulders, and she squeezed me into a hug.

"Thank you," she whispered, sizzling into light as she left the room. She was gone, and Luthicer was the only one who remained.

"I'm waiting for the lecture," I said.

"Eric." His hardened tone was quick. "You impressed me tonight, even if you are just a human." He pulled on his sleeves, and then he was gone, electricity running down my spine. Even he had to admit what I hadn't considered before.

I was more powerful as Eric than I had ever been as Shoman.

23

Jessica

"HE WAS JUST STARING AT ME," I WHISPERED, LETTING MY brown hair fall over the side of Robb's bed as Crystal painted my toenails. She had already redone my makeup and threatened to put some on Robb when he complained. She didn't, but I kind of wished she would.

"We've heard it before, Jess," Robb said.

Crystal shushed him as rain pinged against the window. "I didn't hear all the details," she said, waiting for more. She winked. "Sounds romantic, even if it isn't real."

I fought a blush. I didn't want to think of my dreams as romantic, but they felt nice aside from the last one. I wouldn't tell them about the one with Eric. "Another man showed up."

"Another one?" Crystal was about to fall off the bed, but I couldn't laugh.

"He was frightening," I admitted, thinking of the man standing in my front yard. I wanted to talk about my dreams with Eric, but it was too awkward once the Stones showed up. I only had my friends to confide in now.

I turned to Robb, but he hadn't looked at me all night. "That dream happened the night you dropped me off."

"From the date?" Crystal asked, but I stared at Robb. He was transfixed on the rain.

"You said you saw something," I said.

He finally glanced up. Thunder smacked against the house,

and the lights flickered. "I don't remember," he grumbled.

I sat straight up, almost kicking the bed with my freshly painted toenails. "You have to," I said.

Crystal interrupted, "You're going to ruin your pedicure," she said, grabbing my feet as Robb stared at them.

"Don't ruin it," he said, his face locked into the same dull expression he held all night. His parents were gone, and he practically begged us to hang out at his house for once, but he didn't seem as excited now that we were here.

"I was hoping you remembered what you saw," I said.

Crystal glanced between the two of us. "Do you think someone was actually there?" she asked.

I shrugged, staring at Robb. He wasn't saying anything.

Crystal tapped his shoulder. "Why are you so quiet?" she asked.

"Just stressed out," he sighed. "Family stuff."

"Is everything okay?" she asked, and he said something, but the thunder drowned him out. When Crystal asked him again, he remained silent. He never talked about his family. Everything I knew about them was from Crystal or Zac. I had only seen them in the photos lining the walls, and a photo of a dog sat on Robb's desk. I recalled his pet had died when Eric and him were still friends.

"We don't have to talk about it," I said.

Robb's face relaxed. "I must have seen a raccoon or something." He finally gave an answer, but it wasn't what I wanted from him.

"You seemed a lot more concerned when you dropped me off," I argued.

Picking up the controller, he turned on the television that hung on the far wall. He had left the conversation.

I sighed, and Crystal rolled her eyes. "So—"

She stopped as the garage opening rattled Robb's bedroom. He leapt up, and Crystal gaped at him. He shushed her before she could talk. "I'll be right back," he said, moving toward the door, but it opened before he could get to it.

"We need to talk," Zac said, bursting in as Robb leapt

98

up. Zac's eyes widened as he looked around the room. Rain dripped off his clothes. "I didn't know you guys were hanging out."

"Did you run up those stairs?" Crystal joked. "You got up here really fast."

He chuckled, pulling a stack of papers out from under his shirt. He was still in his school uniform, and he was soaked, but his papers weren't. "I'm in a hurry," he said. "I thought I could talk to Robb since our parents are out together." As usual, I learned more from Zac than Robb.

"What's the paperwork for?" Crystal asked, leaning onto Zac's leg.

"Transfer paperwork," he said, his cheeks reddening beneath his tan. "I'm going to Hayworth," he said, and he met my eyes. "Good to see you're feeling better, Jess."

Crystal spoke up first. "You're transferring?"

Robb went back to his chair. "Linda is, too," he said.

Zac sat down next to Crystal. She lit up, but Zac kept looking over at me.

"We don't have to talk about that," he said, pressing his back against the wall. His entire torso was facing me, and I suddenly hated being against the corner of Robb's room. "What were you guys talking about?"

"Nothing," I said, but Crystal spoke at the same time.

"Jess is having freaky dreams."

Zac lowered his face, and shadows melted across his wet forehead. "What kind of dreams?"

"Just a bunch of boys," Crystal answered.

I tapped her, hoping she would get a hint, but she didn't. Only Zac noticed my gesture.

"Why don't you want to tell me about it?" he asked, showing off his overly white teeth.

"It wasn't that," I lied. "We already finished the conversation."

"Jess thinks someone was outside her house the other night," Robb said, turning around to stare at Zac.

Zac's eyes didn't leave mine. "Why would you think that?"

"I thought Robb saw him," I admitted.

Zac looked back at his friend. "Who'd you see?"

"Not sure," he said, contradicting his raccoon answer.

"You said you didn't see someone," I said, but the boys stared at one another, refusing to move. I didn't understand. I had to wave my hands to get them to look at me again. "What did you see?"

Robb sighed. "I thought—"

"He didn't see anything," Zac said, leaning over to punch his friend in the shoulder. "He's just kidding."

"I was just freaking you out, Jess," Robb said.

Crystal threw her hands into the air. "Not funny," she said. "You two are so immature." She tapped the top of my foot. "Do you like them?"

I tore my eyes away to look at my toes. Yellow stars settled on sparkling purple polish, and I felt the first burst of relief I had all night. "They're beautiful."

"I thought you'd like them."

"They're just toes," Robb grumbled.

Crystal groaned. "Do you have to ruin everything?"

"Trust me," he said. "I didn't ruin anything."

Zac stood up from the bed and grabbed his papers. "I'll come back later," he said, only turning to wave to me. "See you later, Jess," he said, and no one stopped him. He dipped out of the room before anyone could speak, and we waited until the sound of the garage door stopped.

"Well, that was weird," Crystal said, laying down on her stomach. Robb watched her as she kicked her legs back and forth.

"I don't think either of you should date him," he said.

Crystal gasped. "I don't like him. Jess—"

"I've known you long enough to tell, Crystal," he said. "Just trust me on this one."

Crystal's face was beyond red. It was an entirely new color. "What's your problem?" she asked, rolling over to pick up her things.

Robb stopped her. "I'm not trying to start anything," he

said, speaking quickly. "I just wanted to say what I thought."

"Maybe you shouldn't have."

"Crystal—"

She grabbed the door, but I was the one to stop her this time. "Come on, Crystal," I started. "At least he didn't say anything in front of Zac."

"Are you seriously taking Robb's side?"

"I'm not taking sides," I clarified. "I don't want anyone to fight."

She seethed for a moment, but Robb sighed and reached for her hand. She didn't shake him away. "I'm stressed out," he said. "I didn't mean it."

"You didn't?"

"I'm in a bad mood," he admitted.

"So, don't take it out on me," Crystal said, stomping across the room. She yanked a mirror out of her purse and pushed her bleached hair to the side. Her face wasn't red anymore, but I doubted she felt any better. Her hands were still shaking.

I cleared my throat to avoid the silence and watched as Robb put his head in his hands. He was a complete wreck, and he wasn't trying to hide it anymore.

"Is there anything we can do to help?" I asked.

Robb lifted his head, peering between his fingers. "To help what?" His voice cracked.

"You," I said.

His chestnut eyes looked over my face. He didn't say anything, but his eyes glazed over as his thoughts consumed him. He was far away, but I didn't know how far away he actually was.

"We should go out soon," Crystal suggested, answering for him.

Robb straightened up. "Where?" he asked, his voice rushed with desperation.

"The bars."

"I don't know about that," I started, but Crystal waved my worries away.

"We're going, and it'll be a fun way to relax," she said. "I'm sure you could use a break from your dreams."

"They aren't that bad."

"You freaked out when Robb said he saw something. Not to mention the freak out in the restaurant." Crystal argued.

Robb agreed. "You need to relax just as much as the rest of us."

My stomach twisted, but they were right. "I could try it."

Crystal cheered. "Let's go this weekend."

"I need two weeks." Robb made a money gesture with his fingers. "It'll be more fun if we wait."

"Then, it's decided," she said. "We'll go then—just the three of us."

"No Zac," Robb clarified.

"Or Linda," Crystal added.

He laid his hand out for a handshake. "Deal," he said, and it was done. We were going, and we were going to forget.

24

I STRETCHED MY LEGS AS FAR AS I COULD WITHOUT STRAINING MY ribs. I breathed, released, and did it again before looking back at Teresa. She was sitting on the railing overlooking the river, eating a Popsicle despite the cooling weather.

"Aren't those for the summer?" I asked.

Her blue lips spread into a sugary grin. "I like them more in the cold," she said. "They don't melt as fast."

"You're strange."

"And you're missing out," she retorted, kicking her legs against the metal. It tinged, vibrating beneath her, and I wondered how the metal hadn't moved when Jessica had jumped onto it the first time we met.

I looked away, trying to distract myself with the park, but I couldn't. She was always on my mind, and I hated the fact that she hadn't come back over since the time she left early. Our talks at school had stopped, and I didn't understand why.

"How is she?" Teresa asked.

I winced. I was hoping she'd avoid the topic since we just rekindled our friendship.

"She seems good," I answered, attempting to sound enthusiastic, but Teresa knew me better than I wanted her to at the moment.

She plopped down on the grass in front of me and pressed her feet against mine. "I'll help you," she said, and her black hair bobbed to the right as she swished it out of her eyes.

I grabbed her hands, and she pulled me forward into a stretch that was hard to do on my own. The human healing process was beyond me.

"I am sorry," she said, pulling me a little bit further.

"About what?"

"What I said to your father."

I sighed, and she let me go so I could straighten out. Her face was paler than I remembered, and I wondered if it was from training. Most of her free time was spent in the underground shelter.

"Did my father tell you what he gave me?" I asked, thinking of the black box. I had put it in my desk and couldn't bring myself to take it out again.

"No." Teresa's lips thinned. "What did he give you?"

I stretched my arm across my chest. It stung, but it was easier than the other stretch. "I need you to drive me to school tomorrow."

"You're changing the subject."

"I'll have a lot of catching up to do," I continued.

She rolled her eyes. "There's the Eric I know."

Her words brought me back to a time she spent chasing Jonathon and me around, struggling to stop us from getting into trouble. Half of the time, she didn't stop us—she joined.

"Do you ever miss it?" I asked.

She closed her eyes. I hadn't realized how long her eyelashes were until they were all I had to stare at.

"Sure, but we can't go back to it." She knew what I was referring to. She never needed an explanation. "We can only go forward."

"Who says it'll be resolved once we win?"

"No one," she said. "But it's a start, and I think we could all use a new one."

I agreed. "You'd be relieved of your guard duties, Ms. Young."

She lifted her finger, shaking it back and forth. "I'll always be your guard, Eric," she said. "Don't think you're getting out of this friendship that easily."

I chuckled, and she reached out for my hands again.

"I thought we were done stretching," I said.

She leaned further to grab them. "We won't be done until you're better."

"That might take a while."

"Stop talking," she ordered.

I followed her instructions and stared at the grass between my legs, wishing it wasn't drying up despite the previous rain. If I could choose my powers, I would've wanted the ability to freeze time. I didn't want winter to happen.

I tried to let go of Teresa, but she strained herself to grab my hands, locking me in a position. "Don't move," she said, knowing what I had just realized.

The Light was near, and the last thing we needed to do was react to the energy humans couldn't feel. I continued my stretch with beads of sweat forming on my neck. If they appeared, I didn't know what we'd do. For once, I wished I had my telepathic capabilities. Shoman could talk to Camille without any hesitation, but we were restrained to human silence.

I moved my leg to the side, and Teresa let my hands go. I stretched once more, and she stood up. "We should go home," she said, acting better than I could.

I nodded and rushed to the street, knowing Teresa's BMW was only feet away. We climbed in, and Teresa sped off, cranking her radio to drown out our thoughts. I gripped the door handle and waited every agonizing second before we reached my house. She slammed her car into park, and I rushed inside before she could even get out of her car. The front door smacked into the wall, and Mindy jumped from the couch downstairs.

"Eric?" Her voice could've split glass. "What's wrong?"

I caught my breath as Teresa whisked past me. "Just trying to get back into shape," she dismissed my stepmother's worries. "Is Mr. Welborn here?"

"No," she said, sinking back into her chair. "He left with George an hour ago."

"Thank you," Teresa said, climbing the stairs without an invite. I followed her, and she silenced my bedroom when we got inside. The Dark energy teased my insides to transform, and I gritted my teeth against the churning sensation.

Teresa, on the other hand, stood still as her body transformed into the half-breed she had always been. I knew she was communicating with someone. When she flickered back into a human, I grabbed her arm.

"What's happening?" I asked.

Teresa stared past me. "The Light," she said. "They agreed to a war."

25

Jessica

"WE AGREED TO COME HERE, DIDN'T WE?"
The fair-haired adults radiated past the pallid couple sitting across from the room. The two couples stared at one another, ignoring their dimly lit surroundings.

"How do I know you are Darthon's parents?" The pale woman was the furthest from my viewpoint. I didn't recognize any of them, but she seemed most out of place.

"How do we know you're Shoman's?"

A flurry of words resulted in a deafening static until the oldest man slammed his hand on the table. "There isn't a purpose for us to agree to this," he said. "We are destined to win."

"But win what, Bracke?" The illuminated woman revealed his name. "A battle? One death? Who says we'll give up at that?"

"You won't have powers," Bracke argued.

"We still have weapons."

"We are immune to human devices."

"Not if you're a human when we use them," the woman's counterpart—an equally glowing man—threatened.

Bracke grabbed his counterpart's hand. "Aren't you confident in Darthon's capabilities?"

The woman smiled. "But we're also confident in our own," she said. "Darthon is not the only one who wants to see the Dark fall."

Bracke's grip tightened. "You want bloodshed, even if it

means your own people."

The yearning in their sharpened expressions confirmed it. "It would be a proud death if we died together." They spoke in unison. "We may not know Shoman's birthday, but we can feel it coming. Knowing the date is your only advantage," they continued. "We know much more."

———————•———————

When I woke up, I was standing in my front yard, and the daylight was smothering my sleepy eyes. I rubbed them with shaky hands, and images of my dream flashed behind my eyelids. My eyes sprang open, but the images didn't disappear. The women. The men. The sound of their voices was unforgettable.

"Jessie?"

I turned around and saw my father, returning from work in his pressed clothes. "What are you doing out here?" he asked. "Your mother said you were napping."

I remembered lying down to rest, but I didn't know how I ended up outside. Swallowing my nerves, I said, "I'm going for a walk."

"But we should have dinner on the table soon—"

"I'll be back," I blurted out, rushing down the sidewalk before he could stop me. I didn't care if he lectured me later. I had to get away.

The images of the glistening people fluttered through my mind as I forced my tears back. My brain was splitting. The people didn't even look real. Their colors were washed out, and their words were muddled with death, discussing it like a minuscule thing. It didn't make sense. And my gut knew it involved the boys I'd seen.

My strides widened as I broke into a run. My hair whipped into my eyes. It was the only part of my body I could feel. Everything else was numb as if I weren't truly alive. I felt like I only existed in my dream—a ghost, a deniable existence—and the town passed by in rushed blurs of nothingness. I didn't stop until it was my only choice.

My knees buckled, and I grabbed the nearest object. The wood prevented me from falling over as I inhaled oxygen with the desperation I had felt all year. The tears I had held back were gone, yet I regretted it. I wanted to feel. I wanted to sob. I was praying for tears, hoping that something—anything—would make me remember the reason I had left the safety of my own bed. But not even a single tear would create itself in my depression. Not one. No matter how hard I tried to concoct one.

"Jess—"

I spun around as if I'd been trained to fight. My hands were up, and my body froze into a stilled stance. It wasn't until I saw his face that I relaxed.

"Zac?"

In the midst of my panic attack, he had driven up to the side of the curb and parked Robb's car. I hadn't even noticed, but I did see what he was looking at—my hands. I dropped them to my sides, but he followed my fingertips.

"What are you doing here?" I asked, hoping to distract his attention away from whatever stance had overcome me. I had never even punched someone. "Why do you have Robb's car?"

Without speaking, he opened the car door and stepped out. He towered over me as he closed in. "Are you running from someone?" he asked, laying his palm on my shoulder.

I leapt away from his touch. "No."

"You're jumpy," he accused.

"I'm not."

His face flinched, but he didn't attempt to get closer. "You're kind of far from home, aren't you?"

I glanced over my shoulder, surveying the road. He was right. "I'm a long-distance runner," I lied. I couldn't remember the last time I'd jogged outside of gym class.

He cocked an eyebrow as if to argue my statement. "You aren't wearing shoes, Jess."

I had to look down to confirm it. He was right. Again.

"Feels more natural to me," I stuttered, grateful I'd at least worn sweatpants.

"I didn't know you worked out," he continued, and I shoved my hands into my pockets only to take them out again. I wanted my hands to be in front of me, and the gesture didn't go unnoticed. Zac watched me.

"Why don't you tell me what you're running from?"

"Because I'm not running from anything," I said. "I'm just tired."

"How about I give you a ride home?"

"I can walk."

He grabbed my hand, and I froze. Even his loose grip was frightening. "Let me take you," he said, pointing a finger at my wrist. "You look like you scraped yourself on that fence."

I jerked away, more startled by his touch than by the blood I'd seen forming on my skin. It stung.

"If you walk, I'll only drive next to you until you make it home," he spoke as he walked back to Robb's Suburban. "Wouldn't want something to happen to you between here and there." His words sounded more like a threat than a comfort.

"I doubt that would happen—"

"This town isn't as nice as it seems," he said and didn't look at me as he opened the passenger door.

I hesitated. "Are you seriously going to follow me?"

His chuckle shook me. "Try walking."

He meant it. I groaned and stomped over to the passenger side. Without the adrenaline, I was starting to feel the ground beneath my bare feet, and I had to admit it felt nice to sit down. I shut the door, and he drove away.

"Thank you," he said, even though it should've been the other way around. "I wish you would've agreed to it sooner."

I glared out the window. "I told you, I was—"

"Exercising," he finished, and I saw his momentary stare in the window's reflection. "I don't know why you feel the need to lie to me."

"I'm not lying." This time, I was facing him.

"Your feet," he said, pointing to the floor. "They're not calloused enough for your alleged technique."

I squeaked and slapped a hand over my mouth. He didn't

even jump at my sudden noise. He was as calm as the people in my dream that caused it all.

"It's personal," I said, hoping he'd stop prying.

"Isn't everything with you?" he asked.

I curled my fingers into fists. "Did you offer me a ride to mock me?"

He didn't respond as he turned the car down the street I lived on. "I remember where you live from prom," he murmured, explaining something I'd never asked him to. "I've never apologized for what I did that night."

My head throbbed. I had no idea what he was talking about.

"I shouldn't have kissed you without asking," he continued.

I stopped him. "What are you talking about?" I panicked as Crystal's words from the restaurant resonated through me. She had said the same thing.

Zac blinked. "You don't remember?"

"No."

His face twisted like all his features were trying to meld together.

"I'm sorry," I started, but he stopped me.

"I suppose that's a good thing," he said, but his voice was strained. "It means we can start over." We—like he had grouped us together.

The tires crunched as he pulled into the driveway, taking one inch at a time. It felt like we'd never get to the front door, and I straightened my legs to prevent them from shaking. When he parked, I rushed for the exit, but the lock clicked.

My heart squeezed.

"Do you dislike me, Jess?" The whisper didn't help.

I gripped the door handle. "Why would you ask that?"

"Why would you avoid answering it?" he retorted. His cheekbones looked higher beneath the overhead light.

"I think you're a nice guy," I said, but his expression didn't budge.

"You're still avoiding it." His intensity was suffocating with the few inches between us.

I couldn't breathe. My chances of successfully lying had diminished.

"I thought it was from prom," he admitted. "But it can't be that if you don't—" He didn't finish his sentence.

"Thanks for the ride," I excused, yanking the lock up without permission. I pushed the door open and sprang out, slamming it behind me before I mustered the energy to run inside. I didn't want to be alone with Zac. Not even for a second.

26

"ARE YOU SURE YOU DON'T WANT TO COME, ERIC?" MINDY asked, twirling her nimble fingers through her red curls. Her wedding ring shined in the setting sun.

"I'm fine," I said, dismissing myself as Noah hobbled by, tripping over his suitcase. I laid my hand on his head and lifted it from his hands. He froze, and I avoided looking at the surprise on his face. "Don't strain yourself," I muttered, walking over to the packed car. I found a place for his belongings and shut the door.

When I turned around, Mindy perked up. "That was nice of you."

"He'll be able to get it himself soon," I said.

Noah straightened his shoulders. "I could've gotten it myself," he argued, but his voice was light. He was happy.

"You can get it at your aunt's house," I said.

He jittered. "I will."

I fought a smile from spreading over my lips. My stepbrother was getting taller, and I hadn't noticed.

"You'll be in middle school next year, won't you?" I asked, and he strode over to the car.

"Yeah." He didn't seem as excited as a preteen should've been. I wondered if he looked like his father—a man that skipped out when Noah was born.

"Are you going to be okay by yourself?" Mindy asked.

I rubbed the back of my neck. "Shouldn't be too difficult," I said, but my father didn't speak. He was the one to convince them to leave for the week, but it wasn't out of sincerity. His absence would help disguise his identity since he talked to the Light. I had already told my teachers he had been gone all week.

"We'll be right down the street," Mindy continued, but I knew that was an understatement. They'd be on the opposite side of the town—far enough away that I was surprised it was considered part of Hayworth. Apparently, the town stretched further across the wheat fields than I thought.

"George should be back at any minute." I tried to soothe their concern. I didn't have a car to get around, but Camille and Urte would be good enough chauffeurs for the week. It wasn't like I had plans to go anywhere—aside from a meeting with the elders. I still didn't know what the Light meeting had entailed, but I'd find out. For once, I would miss my father's presence.

He laid a hand on my shoulder, but he didn't look at me. "Don't forget your doctor's appointment," he said. "We'll be back for Thanksgiving."

The approaching holiday was a reminder that it was already November. I had one month left.

"I know," I said, wondering if I referred to their trip or my predicament.

"Have a good time." Mindy winked. "And no girls over."

Jessica. The idea of having her over was merely a fantasy, but it felt like a possibility despite the fact that she hadn't come over in weeks.

"I won't," I promised, searching for my father's gaze. He had already turned his back.

My stomach twisted with nerves. Whatever had happened during the meeting was clearly bothering him, and I had less than an hour before I would find out for myself.

"Bye," Noah said, rushing toward me. Before I knew it, his arms wrapped around my torso in a hug, and then he was running to the car. They got in, and I lifted my hand to wave. Mindy waved back, and they left. They were gone, safe for now.

I stood there until George pulled into the driveway in a car I'd never seen before. I gawked at the rusted can that was his vehicle. When he got out, it rocked from side to side.

"What," I began, "is that?"

He shoved the keys into my palm before answering. "Yours," he said. "It was Mindy's sister's."

I couldn't speak.

George shrugged. "It's why they wanted you to go," he explained. "But we both know that couldn't happen." Not with the meeting taking place. "I picked it up, so you'd have it while they were gone."

I stared at the old metal key in my palm. It was as weathered as the vehicle, yet it felt better than the Charger I'd been given. It wasn't a death gift. It was freedom.

"I don't understand," I said.

The car looked European by the size, but it was impossible to tell given the condition it was in. The antenna had been stolen, and the mirrors were cracked down the middle. I wasn't even sure what the color of the car was supposed to be. One door was blue while the others were stained brown with dirt. A pearl paint peeked through.

"They didn't even stay to tell me," I said.

"Because it doesn't matter," George said, opening the door. It clanked like it would fall off. "Family doesn't help one another to be praised."

Family. The word was something I had never expected.

"I'll have to thank them when they get back," I said.

George pointed at the driver's seat. "Are you going to drive or not?" he asked. "It doesn't go over forty, so you don't have to worry about crashing at high speeds again."

It was supposed to be a joke, but my thoughts prevented my laughter.

"Something wrong, Eric?" George asked.

I got into the car before he could read the expression on my face. I couldn't tell him what I was thinking.

"Let's go to that meeting." I turned over the engine as he sat down in the passenger seat. The car vibrated beneath us.

"Is the meeting bothering you?" he asked as I drove the automatic down the driveway.

"No." That was my last concern. The war was my first. More people would die, and I didn't know what Mindy and Noah would do if my father died.

I no longer wanted to win solely for Jessica. I wanted to protect my family, too.

————◆————

The meeting wasn't in the usual spot. On top of that, it was in a house I'd never stepped foot in before. Smaller than mine, it was in Jessica's neighborhood. Being close to her wasn't the hardest part. The identity I faced was.

"Make yourselves at home," Eu said, but he wasn't Eu. He was Quin Stephens, Eu's human form and the owner of a restaurant in town. His wife, Ida, worked at the hospital. She was Chinese, but I couldn't recall seeing an Asian woman in the shelter. Even races changed in their supernatural forms. I wondered what else could.

"Please, take a seat," Ida said, handing me a glass of water.

I followed her instructions and sat down on the nearest chair I could find. A coffee table was placed in the middle of a circle of seats, but imprints on the carpet told me they had moved their furniture around just for the meeting.

"Why didn't we meet in the shelter?" I blurted out.

Ida placed her tea on the table between us. "The shelter was too risky," she said in a quiet voice.

"And this isn't?" I asked, glancing over the photos on the table. They had three daughters, all under the age of thirteen. They hadn't been Named yet.

"It's our anniversary," Eu—Quin—explained as he laid his hands on his wife's petite shoulders. "It doesn't look very suspicious this way."

"Will it just be us?" Urte asked, remaining as George. His son, Jonathon, stood behind him.

The couple nodded. "Luthicer cannot reveal his identity."

My stomach lurched. "And you can?"

"We offered," Ida said.

"You see, Eric," Eu continued. "Ida stepped in as your mother during the meeting."

I couldn't move.

"We couldn't allow Darthon's parents to realize you only had a father."

"It was a risk," George said, aware of the information. He sat next to me, but Jonathon remained standing.

I gazed past them and met Ida's brown eyes. "Thank you," I said.

Her expression softened. "I don't need any praise, Shoman."

When Ida used my Dark name, George's words of family resonated. To her, I was saving her family's lives. Risking hers was nothing if it guaranteed her daughters' survival.

My fingers tightened, but I forced them to relax. I didn't want to seem unappreciative, but the gesture stung. If my mother hadn't killed herself, it wouldn't have been necessary. The small, black box she'd left behind suddenly seemed selfish.

"What were his parents like?" I asked.

"As intense as we expected them to be," Ida said. "But they didn't say anything about the third descendant."

The report unnerved me. "They should've."

"We expected them to," Ida agreed. "But it seems we've over-thought their actions. They want bloodshed—not a strategy to win but a strategy to take out as many people as possible before they lose."

"I don't believe that."

"It doesn't change the decision either way," Eu spoke up. "We agreed to a battle."

"How are we supposed to cover up all the deaths?" I asked. "It's not the Middle Ages. We can't blame something like the black plague."

"You worry about your training, and we will worry about the funerals," he said.

"Your birthday is the concern," Ida added.

I tightened my grip on my glass. Condensation dripped between my fingers. "I'll be healed soon," I started to argue, but Ida held her palm up.

"The Light can feel it approaching," she clarified. "Your identity is in more jeopardy than ever before."

My heart slammed against my ribs. "Is it possible they already know?"

They didn't respond, but instinctually, I felt as if they did.

"December 13th." George's words lingered. "It falls on a Friday this year."

"Great." I muttered. "Friday the 13th. Just what we need."

"That's just an old superstition," he said.

"Some of us call those omens."

"Enough," Eu interrupted. "We don't have time to worry about that. People are already booking hotels near the area."

I tensed. "Why would they do that?"

"The holidays," he suggested, but everyone knew it was a lie.

"It's too early for that." George was the first to say it aloud.

My hand shook as I placed my cup down. It rattled against the glass, and everyone stared at the swishing water. "They know," I said. I didn't know what to do.

George grabbed my arm. "It's entirely possible that shades and lights who have left are being drawn in by the increasing energies."

"That means the war is part of the destiny," Ida agreed. "The prophecy never clarified you two would be the only ones involved—just that Darthon and you would fight." *To the death.*

I ignored their comfort. "If they know my identity, they surely know Jessica's."

"Then, why not attack her?" Eu pointed out.

"It could be a part of their survival plan," I said, wondering if I believed in my argument or not. The Light could've been tempting us with the belief that they knew, so we would reveal our identities out of desperation.

"It could be a trick," Ida spoke my thoughts out loud. "We

must be careful with our decision."

I turned to face Jonathon. "Where is Jessica right now?"

He was the only one who remained calm. "At home," he answered. "The Light hasn't approached her street since Eric's car wreck."

The information was the only comfort I'd had all night.

"We aren't bringing her memory back," I decided.

"But your birthday—"

"Let them come to me," I said, leaping to my feet. I was pacing like my father. "We'll have to narrow down Darthon's identity."

"How?"

I thought of my car wreck. "If he's like me, he can't leave this town."

"We don't know if that's why your car wreck occurred," Eu argued. "It's a simple theory."

"We're left with theories, and they have facts," George grumbled.

I placed my hand over my mouth to prevent myself from speaking. I had a car. I could test the theory out, but it could result in more injuries that I didn't have time for. I was about to be healed, and I could fight, even if Darthon showed up at my house. Risking anything was more of a threat than Darthon's potential knowledge, yet I was contemplating it.

"I'm going home," I announced.

I had to test my boundaries if I were going to get any- where at all. No one stopped me, and I left the room, walked down the hallway, and hesitated at the sound of children. Eu's daughters were playing a board game.

"Eric."

I turned around to face their father. Quin got within inch- es of me so he could shut the door. It didn't prevent me from hearing their loud giggles.

"I didn't know you had children," I managed.

"I do." Quin held the doorknob with whitened fingers. "And it'd be best if you forgot such information."

I knew what he was really saying—don't lose focus.

It was the main reason the Dark insisted on keeping fellow shades' identities a secret. If we knew, especially from a young age, we'd treat one another differently. We might even reveal ourselves. It was the only rule I was positive we shared with the Light. It was risky, even for them. Identity was a delicate process to create, but simple to destroy.

"Thank your wife again for her help," I said, knowing it'd be the last time I mentioned Ida to him. I walked away, but he grabbed my jacket.

"Don't make any rash decisions, Eric," he said.

I pulled back. "Who said I was going to?"

His upper lip twitched. "You forget that I grew up with your father," he said. "I can recognize that expression, even under the darkest circumstances."

I looked over Eu's face as Quin Stephens. He was thinner and taller. His nose protruded over his mouth, and he was much younger than I had always suspected. He was another man I didn't know, but he knew me, and that was enough for me to agree.

"I'll think it over," I promised, ending our conversation in a way I hadn't anticipated—rationally.

27

Jessica

"WE'RE GOING TOMORROW," CRYSTAL ANNOUNCED, FLOP-ping down on her bed. Her face was practically in my lap.

"Going where?" Robb mumbled, flipping through his math homework. A calculator dangled off his leg.

Crystal swiped the technology away from him. "The bar," she said, demanding his attention. "You guys should've saved enough money up by now."

"I have," Robb said, glancing at me.

"I could borrow some from my parents—"

"Too risky," Crystal said. "Why would you borrow money for a sleepover at my house?"

"I'm—I'm sorry," I stuttered. "I didn't think it through."

"No worries." She waved me away. "I'll cover you."

Robb shut his textbook with a loud thump. "You're really set on this outing, aren't you?"

She stuck her bottom lip out. For once, she didn't have her piercing in or makeup on. She looked three years younger. "I thought you guys wanted to."

"Sure," Robb said, but his words didn't match his tone. Crystal looked like she was about to hit him, but she stopped when his phone rang.

He jumped, yanking it from his pocket, and stared at the screen. He didn't move, and Crystal leaned over to see the name.

"What does Zac want?" she asked.

Robb pulled it away from her eyes. "I'll be back," he said, answering his phone as he left Crystal's bedroom. His voice drifted down the hallway.

Crystal slouched against the wall. "Why wouldn't he answer it in front of us?" she complained.

"I don't know," I said, snatching my coat off Crystal's chair.

She sat up. "What are you doing?"

"Going outside," I responded. I had to ask Robb why Zac had his car two days ago, and the opportunity to do it in private was diminishing.

"Jess." Crystal sounded hurt. I knew she was worried about Zac. "He's on the phone."

"I know." I finished buttoning my coat. "But I have to ask him something."

I dashed after Robb and prayed Crystal wouldn't follow. I made it to the front door without her calling after me and sighed as I laid my hand on the door handle. For reasons unbeknownst to me, I didn't want Robb to hear me.

I cracked the door open and slipped through. The cold air smacked me, and I inhaled with careful precision. I didn't want to make any more noises than I needed to.

Tiptoeing across the driveway, I heard Robb's voice from behind the garage. "I can't tomorrow," he spoke into his phone. "I'm going out with Crystal." He paused. "No one else is going."

I clutched my jacket, wondering why he lied about me.

"We'll talk when I get home," he continued, and I used his talking to my advantage. I stepped closer. "About ten," he said.

I could hear Zac's deep voice on the other end. "Okay. See you then," he said.

Robb's phone beeped. He hung up just as I smelled it.

I leapt out, unable to stop myself, and Robb spun around with his mouth hanging open. A cigarette dangled from his bottom lip.

"You smoke?" I asked.

His shoulders dropped. "It's disgusting, I know," he sighed, his back against the garage. "And, no. I just—" He stopped speaking when I stepped closer. He looked awkward with a cigarette in his mouth, like he wasn't even breathing it in.

"How'd you even get those?"

"I'm eighteen, Jess," he said, pulling the tobacco stick from his mouth. He held it between his fingers as the cold wind blew by, lighting up the end. "Can I ask you something?"

"Um—sure," I managed, unsure of how the situation had changed. I was supposed to be the one asking questions, not him.

"Why have you stopped arguing with Crystal?"

A squeaking noise escaped my lungs, and his lips twisted as he put the cigarette back in his mouth. It bounced as he talked, "Don't get me wrong, Jess, but last semester, you made it pretty clear you don't drink. Ever."

"I've had a drink before," I argued.

Robb took a drag, and he squinted. "Taking a sip from your mother's wine glass doesn't count."

Heat rushed over my cheeks, and he leaned forward, skimming my face with his knuckle. His hand smelled like smoke. "That's what I thought," he whispered.

I dropped my face to avoid his touch, but his hand lingered in the air. He flicked his cigarette onto the ground. It bounced past our feet in a trail of smoke, sizzling out quicker than I expected it to.

"I don't think you should come tomorrow," Robb said.

My neck popped when I looked up. "Why?"

His sigh was a visible fog in the chilly weather. "Mixing alcohol and emotions is never a good combination."

I crossed my arms, contradicting my words. "I'm not emotional."

"Who said I was talking about you?" His brown eyes were torn as he closed the distance between us.

"What are—" Crystal's voice broke through us as she leapt around the corner. I jumped away from Robb, but he didn't budge. Her eyes darted around, but they slid into a glare.

"We weren't doing anything," I blurted out.

Crystal pointed to the ground. "Lola will freak if she finds cigarette butts in her yard."

"Yeah. Yeah," Robb grumbled, bending down to pick it up. He walked right past us, but Crystal's focus was on me.

"Did something happen?" she asked, shivering in the wind. She hadn't even bothered to put on a coat.

"Just complaining about my dreams again."

Crystal folded her arms. "I don't get why you complain about them," she said, and I expected her to pry, but she winked. "Those boys sound cute."

I thought of the people I had seen in my recent dream. They hadn't been the two in my bedroom, yet I had recognized Bracke's name. It sounded bizarre, but so was the conversation. I couldn't make sense of it, but I couldn't admit to them that I was even more conflicted than before. Crystal was worried enough.

"Are you girls coming in?" Robb shouted from the door.

"Yes," Crystal responded, but I grabbed her arm and pulled her around the corner.

"Is something wrong with Robb?" I mouthed. I didn't want him to hear.

"Why don't you ask him?" She was loud enough for him to eavesdrop.

I tightened my grip on her arms. "He seems bummed."

She rolled her eyes. "Linda and him keep breaking up," she dismissed his peculiar behavior. "It's normal."

But Robb's gestures weren't, especially if he was focused on his on-and-off-again girlfriend.

"She isn't coming tomorrow," Crystal clarified, looping her arm through mine. "You won't have to worry about drama."

But, apparently, I had to worry about Robb's emotional state.

I leaned into Crystal for support as we walked toward the doorway into her house. "Do you think you'll be able to sleep over tomorrow?"

"Yeah."

She leapt a few inches into the air, practically pulling me

with her. "I can't wait." She ran up the three steps to the door and put her hands on my shoulders. Without warning, she shook me.

My head rattled, and I blinked at her when she stopped. "That's the Jess I know," she said, seeing something in my face I couldn't feel for myself. "It isn't healthy to dwell on everything around you all the time." She pushed the door open, and the heat washed over my skin. "You'll get wrinkles before your twenties."

I wanted to say I didn't care about that, but I couldn't bring myself to do it. Robb was right about one thing—I had stopped standing up for myself, even though I didn't know why. It was as if I'd lost part of myself that brought me fulfillment, and I was trying to fill it with empty distractions.

28

Eric

I T HAD BEEN THREE DAYS SINCE MY FATHER LEFT, THREE DAYS SINCE speaking to Eu, and three days since I contemplated leaving. I stood next to my car, considering my options. I doubted I could leave Hayworth without getting hurt, but I needed to know if it were factual. It would help narrow down Darthon's identity. If I couldn't leave, he couldn't either, which meant he probably went to my school. It would mean he could only be one of the boys in Hayworth. I didn't know where to go from there, but it was a place to start.

I got in and turned over the engine.

It rumbled down the street as I drove through Hayworth, unsure of my decision. It had been made, and I could still change it, but I didn't want to. I passed Jonathon's house first. His little brother was outside, but Brenthan didn't recognize my new car. He didn't even look up. I hoped George wasn't looking out of a window.

Jessica's house was next, but I couldn't bring myself to look. Her bedroom window was in the front, and the reminder was too tempting. I passed Eu's shortly afterwards, and a part of me wished he had seen me, so he knew I was making the decision after I had carefully thought it over.

Even if I were rebelling against the Dark, I had to try to leave Hayworth again.

I erased all thoughts from my mind as I neared the highway ramp where I'd crashed. I wasn't thinking, but my stomach was twisting, and my palms were sweating. The unwanted reaction was uncontrollable, but I concentrated as Urte had taught me in training, and it disappeared as the car sped up, tilting to the left as I readied to merge.

The moment had the potential to hurt me again, to ruin my success, but I kept my eyes open. I wanted to see what my future truly entailed. I wanted to see if I could figure out Darthon's identity before he knew mine.

I held my breath as I made it to the top and merged over. My grip loosened when nothing happened. I exhaled as the car continued forward on the highway, but disappointment seeped into me.

Darthon could be from any town, and I'd lost control of my car by myself. The only theory we had was gone, and Hayworth melted behind me as undeniable proof. The people who were booking hotel rooms had to have been shades and lights moving in for the fight, and the war seemed more destined than ever before.

I had to prepare myself, but I couldn't return in that moment. I wanted to see the next town over—something I had never seen before. Even if it only lasted one night, I could pretend I was running away and belonged somewhere else. I could forget the ramifications of my tested actions.

Tonight, I wouldn't find Darthon in Hayworth, but he wouldn't find me either.

29

Jessica

THE BAR WAS LOUD. I ALWAYS EXPECTED THEM TO BE CHAOTIC, and this one was too loud to think. I hadn't even had a drink yet. I was nervous enough about getting in, but they hadn't even carded me. My burst of nerves seemed as useless as the fake ID Zac had created. It sat in my purse, unused, and I couldn't believe I had it. A year ago, I wouldn't have risked it, and my past-self lectured me through the cranked music and smoke.

"I didn't know it was legal to smoke inside," I said, thinking of the Kansas laws, but no one heard me.

A crowd of young adults—slightly older than us—screamed at a basketball game on the television, and I wondered if they hadn't been carded as well. One of the boys even looked like he was wearing the same uniform Zac sometimes wore.

"On the house," Crystal said, setting down three beers. They sloshed over the rim as she sat down and pointed her thumb over her shoulder. "Jeff won't stop hitting on me."

I glanced at the puppy-eyed bartender behind the wooden countertop. He was talking to another customer, but he was watching Crystal. He was probably why we got in so easily.

"He gave me a free shot, too." She had to speak abnormally loud for us to hear.

Robb grabbed his glass, indifferent to her small talk. He

downed a few gulps, but he didn't flinch. All I could recall was how my face twisted with disgust the only time I had accidentally sipped my dad's beer.

"Go ahead, Jess," Crystal encouraged, drinking hers with the same nonchalant attitude as Robb.

I touched the glass, pulled away, and grabbed it again. I didn't want to look out of place with all the bartenders around. I was paranoid about getting caught, but I was more worried about the effects of drinking. I'd seen my parents drunk enough to know how secrets slipped. It was how I learned my biological parents had died.

"It isn't that bad," Robb added, speaking with his glass to his lips.

I glanced down at the brown liquid one last time and sipped it. I tried to fight my expression, but I cringed. It tasted how I remembered.

Crystal giggled, tapping my arm. "It gets better after the first one."

"I don't see how that's possible," I admitted through a small cough.

"You'll see," Crystal said, chugging more. She was already halfway through the first one.

I followed her example but closed my eyes to prevent myself from spitting it back into the glass. It was disgusting. The taste, the smell, everything. I forced myself to continue until it was halfway gone. I met Robb's widened eyes when I put it back on the table.

"See?" Crystal exclaimed, bouncing up from her seat. "I'll get a second round."

"Already?" I squeaked.

Robb rolled his eyes. "She just wants to talk to Jeff."

Crystal ignored him as she strode away. She was acting as if Zac didn't exist anymore.

"Jess?" Robb spoke up, and I drank again. I didn't know what he would say to me after the night before. "Why did you follow me outside?"

"I need to ask you something." The confession slipped out

effortlessly, and my sips turned into a heated flush across my body.

He raised his brow. "Why didn't you?"

I gestured to Crystal. "I wanted to ask you alone."

He placed his empty glass on the table. I hadn't even noticed he finished it. "You can ask me now."

I bit my lip. It felt strange to talk so loudly about private matters, but I knew he wouldn't hear me if I didn't. "Why did Zac have your car the other day?"

Robb's calm expression faltered. "What are you talking about?"

He had to have known. "I was jogging, and Zac drove by in your car," I explained. I didn't want to tell him what his friend had said to me.

"You jog?" Robb asked.

"Why does everyone seem to have a problem with that?" I whined.

He chuckled. "You're a little too fragile to be running around by yourself."

My muscles in my arm tightened. "How'd you know I was by myself?" I asked, too focused to be irritated by his fragile comment. He knew about Zac's run-in with me. "Robb—"

"I needed new brakes, and I was too busy studying to take it in myself," he said. "That's it."

I didn't have a reason to distrust him, but it didn't seem like enough. "What classes were you studying for?"

He rubbed the back of his neck, glancing over his shoulder to survey Crystal. She was coming toward us. "What's with the interrogation, Jess?" He leaned across the table. "Just tell me what's bothering you."

Zac was, but I couldn't say it without it getting back to him, and that was the last thing I needed.

"Round two," Crystal announced, slamming more drinks on the table. This time, there were shots with the beer.

Robb gladly picked his liquor up. "You chase with the beer," he said, but his tone made it sound less like an explanation and more like he was talking down to me.

I grabbed mine, refusing to drop my eye contact. "I got

that part," I mumbled.

Crystal clinked hers against mine before Robb's. "To the night," she toasted, tipping hers back at the same time Robb did. I followed and gripped the table when my throat burned. I wouldn't cough this time.

"What was that?" I managed, but my voice sounded rough.

"Vodka," Crystal said, sipping her beer. I mimicked her. The mixing of the two was as unpleasant as the beer by itself.

After a few more sips and a couple of minutes, I could feel my fingers tingling. I stretched them out and stared at them like I'd see sparkles, but they were my usual nails.

"Feels good, doesn't it?"

Robb's voice startled me as much as his closeness did. He moved to sit next to me, and he placed his elbow on the back of my chair. I tried to scoot away, but my feet slid across the ground and didn't gain traction.

"It feels weird," I admitted, standing up. "I should go—" My legs wobbled, and Crystal shot up, wrapping her arm around my waist. She forced a little dance like we had planned it and put me back in my seat.

"Don't stand out too much," she hissed. Other drinkers had seen the entire thing. "We'll get caught."

I couldn't believe two beers and a shot had affected me so much. I had to remind myself that I was a teenager with less experience than I wanted to confess.

"I'm not handling this too well," I said, surprised by the giggle that escaped me.

"It doesn't matter if we stumble out after a few," she said, sliding a new drink over I hadn't even seen her get. "Two, however, is a problem."

I didn't reach for the glass, but Robb did. He took a sip from it, setting it down in front of me with a stillness that made my insides twist. He wasn't even buzzed. "It's always better after the second glass." His words came out like a dare, and I snatched it from him like I had to prove myself.

I sipped it and steadied my hand as I put it down. The liquid didn't slosh around, and I grinned back at my friends. "You're right," I said, surprised my words weren't a lie. "It is."

30

THE TOWN WAS BIGGER THAN HAYWORTH, BUT THAT WASN'T A surprise.

I drove through the gridded streets with ease, wishing Hayworth had been planned as properly. I had the place memorized in a few minutes, and I watched as my clock ticked by.

It looked different in the dark. Older, but busier. People were everywhere, walking around in their own worlds, some of them clearly enhanced with alcohol. I stopped at a red light and watched as a group of boys passed by the front of my car. They didn't even bother looking over, but I half-expected to see Zac among the group. It was the weekend, and their clothes were pressed. The amount of money floating through the somber town was astounding. Hayworth was only fifteen minutes away, but the atmosphere changed as if I had passed a state line.

I wondered if the town's hotels were also booked, but it was too late to ask. Bars were closing, and the lights were going out. I should be heading home myself, but I couldn't bring myself to turn the car around. I wanted to see everything, even though it was repetitive——a store after an eatery after a coffee shop. If I had left Hayworth earlier, I could've gone inside.

I turned a corner only to face a mansion. Outside lights streamed down the sides, and I slowed down to peek at the carved words at the top. *St. Lucy High School.*

I recognized the name for one reason—Zac and Linda went there—and I tore my eyes away from it. I didn't want to think about the guy whose name Jessica had been doodling in her notebook. She warned me that she might date, and she would scorn me for getting distracted when she got her memory back. When, not if. I knew we would be together again, but the thought shattered like the lightning that smacked against the sky.

I tried to ignore the omen, but rain splattered across my windshield, and my heart sank. I turned the car around.

31

Jessica

"A CAB WON'T BE HERE FOR ANOTHER HOUR," CRYSTAL COM-plained, jumping in place as she tightened her coat. The bar was closed, and a misty rain fell from the sky. "I have to go home now." Her mother had called, and Lola was furious.

Robb hung up his phone. "Zac isn't answering, but his house isn't far from here," he said. "We could walk."

Crystal groaned, but she wobbled forward. "Fine."

I didn't have much of a choice. I followed her, concentrating on my feet. They felt like they secretly consumed alcohol on their own.

Everything looked different. The sidewalks were wider—until a car drove by, then the sidewalks thinned into balance beams. Some lights were dim while others were as bright as the lightning above us. The storm blinded me, and the mist didn't help. It was making my skin crawl, and I kept grabbing my arm like I was fighting off mosquitos.

"I hate getting my hair wet," Crystal said as she stomped in front of Robb and me. Her bleached hair had sprung out in tiny waves. I didn't even know she straightened it.

"Why did you have to wear that?" Robb's voice glided over my shoulder as his hand landed on my hip.

"Wha—" I looked down, staring at his touch, but I didn't move away. He was warm in the cold rain.

"You should wear dresses more often," he continued, and my blush increased the liquor's heat I was already feeling.

"I told her that a long time ago," Crystal joined the conversation, but she didn't seem to notice Robb's touch. She was too busy tying her hair into a bun. We continued to walk behind her, and she whined about Zac's house the entire time. Her feelings for him had magically returned now that bartender Jeff wasn't around.

A screeching noise made her stop talking. A two-door Mercedes parked at the curb, and the window sprang down to reveal a blonde woman. "What the hell are you doing?" she asked, and I recognized her as soon as I saw her glare land on Robb.

Linda.

Robb stepped away from me. "We were walking to Zac's, but—"

"He's busy," Linda cut him off.

His chest sank. "Great."

"Now what?" Crystal groaned.

Robb sauntered up to Linda's vehicle. "Linda—" He didn't have to ask.

"I can only fit one person at a time," she sighed, dragging her manicured nails through her hair. They looked like claws.

"Me first," Crystal volunteered, running to the other side. She was sitting in the passenger seat before I realized it. Time was moving too fast.

Linda's glower was the first thing I saw clearly. "I'll be back for you in fifteen," she said, but it didn't sound nice. It sounded like she was coming back to fight me.

Her Mercedes shrilled as she skidded into a U-turn and disappeared.

Robb sighed. "Ignore her."

"What is with you two anyway?" I asked, surprised by the harshness of my tone. I was no longer able to hold back what I was thinking.

Robb's brown eyes were wide, but they squinted when he looked away. "We're not together right now."

Right now. Like they would be together again.

"Are you upset with me?" he asked.

I didn't answer because I didn't know. My head was spinning too fast to collect my thoughts, let alone my feelings, so I buried myself with silence. My body tingled, and the feeling, somehow, seemed familiar in the darkness. The overwhelming vision of flying flowed through my veins, and I shifted from side to side as if I would take off at any moment.

"I really think we should talk, Jess. We have to talk about it sooner or later—Linda and I—Jess, I think you should consider—" Robb's rambling was breaking my concentration. "Zac told me, and Crystal said you're—dreaming."

It was beautiful. The sky, I mean. It was clearer than anything else around me, and the midnight color mixed with the stormy clouds like an obscure painting. I wanted to paint it right now—right now, like how Robb and Linda weren't together right now.

Robb grabbed my arm. "Are you even listening to me?" His face swayed from side to side, and I could smell the bar on him.

My shoulder blades were digging into the brick wall. "No," I said, but it came out sounding like, "Err—mo."

"Jess?" Robb was infuriated. "What do I need to do to get your attention?"

"Monthin." I meant to say nothing, but Robb wasn't deterred.

"I know one way," he said, and then he kissed me.

He wasn't suave, and he wasn't delicate about it. He was desperate, and the taste of beer glided over my tongue. I wanted to puke.

"Let me go," I mumbled, pushing his chest with my hand, but he shoved his leg against my thigh and missed my lips the second time. "Robb," I screeched, scratching him across the face.

He jerked back. "Stop shouting," he screamed back, latching onto the same wrist I just freed. His grip stung the insides of my hand.

"You're hurting me."

"You're overreacting—"

I screamed as loud as I could and yelped when his hand wrapped around my throat. I froze, eyes locked with Robb—my friend—as he glared down at me. His threatening gaze was as tenacious as his hold. I wasn't sure if he was going to kiss me or yell at me again, but he was interrupted.

A vehicle squealed onto the curb, and the door opened before it came to a complete stop. "Hey!" A man's shout caused Robb to drop his hand. "What are you doing?"

"Stay out of it," Robb growled back, but he didn't bother looking over. Instead, he grabbed my arm and pulled me forward. "This isn't your problem."

I stumbled, looking behind me as the other man followed. He was a silhouette in the headlights. "Let her go."

Robb released me but spun around like he was going to fight. The other guy punched him across the face first. I fell to the ground in shock, landing in a puddle of freezing water as the rain escalated. Robb reared back, and the other guy grabbed his wrist, twisting it around his back before kicking him forward. Robb stumbled, splashing water across my face, but he didn't look at me. He refocused on his opponent.

"I'd think twice before you turn this into a real fight," the other guy warned.

Robb stared at him. "Whatever," he growled, turning his shoulder as he stomped away. "She's your responsibility now." I watched him turn a corner before I realized the other guy was kneeling next to me.

"Are you okay?" he asked and froze when I met his eyes.

He had the most beautiful eyes I had ever seen—as green as the blooming world in the summer. They sparkled in the rain, and they misted over as they searched mine.

"Jessica?" His voice had dropped into a whisper.

I studied his face, trying to put the facial features together. When I did, I could hardly breathe. Eric Welborn.

"I'm fine." I was too embarrassed to say anything else. I couldn't even look at him. Instead, I stared at the cuts on my shins and pushed myself up. My knees shook, and I grabbed the nearest wall to support myself. I stumbled against the brick wall, the world spinning as fast as my stomach was churning. I lost my balance, tumbling to the ground, but he caught me.

"Whoa." His breath brushed against my neck. "You've been drinking."

"Just a little," I said, hoping it didn't sound as slurred to him as it did to me.

"A little?" Eric didn't have to say he didn't believe me. "I think you've had too much, Ms. Taylor."

My name reminded me of the fact that I was with a fellow student. He would tell, and everyone would know what Robb had done. What had Robb done? The memories already slipped away with my raging emotions.

"I didn't—" I sniffled and gasped for breath through my tears.

Eric tensed as I dug my nails into his shirt. His warm clothes comforted me. I just wanted to crawl into bed—bed, and be warm—warm and comfortable—comfortable and wait—wait for my dream boy to come back to me. I didn't want to be here.

"What did Robb do to you, Jessica?" Eric's voice hardened.

I wiped the tears from my face, telling myself it was only rain that drenched my body. "What are you talking about?" I tried to lie despite the fact that he had seen, but Eric wasn't playing along.

"Robb." His eyes were no longer sparkling. They were cold and blank. "Robb McLain."

My drunken mind wasn't agreeing with my thoughts. Nothing in my body wanted to work, but my hand met my neck, and the soreness traveled through me. "He—he choked me."

Eric's jaw locked as he looked away, but he didn't stop holding me up. When he cursed, his voice shook his torso. It was only then that I realized my hand had gone from my neck to his shirt. "I'm going to kick his ass tomorrow—"

"No," I begged. "Please. No."

"I don't want you to get treated that way," he said, shifting his tone with disappointment. "And you shouldn't either."

I wanted to shout at him, but I pulled away instead, and my knees hit the ground again. I didn't care that I was sitting in a puddle. The cold water had already seeped into my clothes.

A wave of water moved over my feet, and I glanced up to see Eric kneeling in front of me. He wasn't leaving. "You're really shaken up, aren't you?" The thunder made it almost impossible to hear him.

He was still for a moment, but then he moved, and the lightning blinded me. His arms were wrapped around my torso, and he had pulled me into his lap. His embrace startled me, but I couldn't move. I didn't want to move.

I relaxed against him, drawn into the moment. I needed this more than anything. It wasn't until I pressed my ear against his chest that I heard it.

Thud-thump. Thud-thump. Thud-thump. The heartbeat was unmistakable. It was his heartbeat—the dream boy's—and he was here, with me, holding me, being with me. He wasn't gone.

"I was afraid you'd never come back," I whispered against his shirt, unable to move away from the familiar sound I yearned to hear.

"What?" Eric leaned back instead. "What did you just say?"

"Nothing, Shoman," I muttered, wishing he would move back, but he was moving further away.

He stood up, and his hands shook when they grabbed mine. He pulled me to my feet. "I should probably get you home—" he started to speak, but I intervened.

I kissed him.

He pulled away. "Jessica." His expression was contorted with intensity. I could still taste him on my lips, but he was rambling until he stuttered, "Don't."

I didn't listen.

I kissed him again. This time, he didn't fight it. His hands fell to my hips, and his fingers dug through my rain-drenched clothes. He pulled me closer and kissed me in a way I had never been kissed before. It was careful, light and loving, and my heart synced with the sound of his. He was everything until thunder shattered between us.

I leapt back, and the rain poured as cold as snow. I hugged myself with shaky hands as Eric exhaled. His breath fogged out in front of him, mixing with mine.

He didn't meet my eyes before he turned to his car. "I'll drive you home," he said.

I took a step forward, but my knees were shaking, and the clarity I had while kissing him dissipated. The drunkenness of my night returned with a vengeance, and Eric grabbed my arm to steady me.

"Thanks for the help," I heard myself whisper. I hadn't even thought of the words.

He glanced over his shoulder with pained eyes. "You're welcome."

32

Eric

"Jessica." I raised my voice as I reached behind my seat and tapped her leg. With the rain pouring down, I didn't want to take my eyes off the road, but she had stopped responding. "Jessica. Wake up."

A murmuring broke through the screeching of my windshield wipers. She was hardly conscious, and I was in trouble.

"Jessica, I need to take you home." I hoped the threatening tone would help her concentrate.

"No," she begged. "Please. Anything but home." She gurgled like she was going to throw up.

A curse escaped me.

My presence would be impossible to explain. No one would believe it was a coincidence, but I didn't have a choice. I couldn't take her home, and I wouldn't leave her on the street. I had to take her to my house, but that meant I had to tell Urte. I dialed him before I stopped myself.

"Are you okay?" His tone startled me.

"Uh—hey. I'm fine," I said. "But I need your help."

"Eric," Urte sounded like my father. "What happened?"

"It's a long story," I said. "My father can't know—"

His lecture began before he even knew the situation. He was programmed to expect the worst. Unfortunately, he was right this time.

"I didn't do anything. I swear," I rambled. "I just happened to be out and she—"

"She?" Now, he was really panicking. "You better not be talking about Jess."

I sighed, and that was enough of an answer. He scorned me, and I tried to get a few words in whenever he paused. "Yes, Urte. I know," I repeated. "Yes. Yes. She's fine. Just listen to me."

Urte was silent as I explained.

"She's passed out in the backseat of my car," I said. "I know I'm not supposed to leave Hayworth. It was a coincidence. She was with another guy from school. I helped her out, okay? She was in trouble."

My head was splitting as I squinted through the darkness. I had never realized how dark the night actually was until I was stuck as a human. But my emotions were the same. My blood was rushing with adrenaline, and it was taking everything in me not to drive to Robb's house and wait for him to return. I wanted to kill him for touching Jessica.

"I didn't do anything," I repeated, knowing I hadn't been listening. "I can't take her home."

"Yes, you can."

"And how am I supposed to explain to her parents why I was with her while she was drunk? They don't even know who I am," I pointed out. "She's coming to my house. We'll deal with everything else later."

He was shouting, and I put my phone on my lap until he stopped.

"You aren't changing my mind," I said.

"Then, I'm sending help." He hung up.

"Hey."

A girl appeared in my backseat, and her white hair flashed in my rearview mirror. I nearly lost control of my vehicle. "Camille."

She gripped the back of my seat, shifting herself beneath Jessica. "At least I didn't transport on top of her," she said.

I gripped my wheel as I hit the highway. The car rumbled as it picked up speed.

Camille looked like Teresa as soon as she spoke again,

"What the hell, Eric?"

"I already heard it from Urte."

"What happened?" she asked, and I looked at her in the rearview mirror as she scrunched up her nose. "And what is that smell?"

"She's drunk."

Camille lifted Jessica's feet into her lap. "Jess drinks?"

"She doesn't," I said. As far as I knew, Jessica avoided things like that, but I knew her friends didn't. "She was with Robb McLain. Crystal wasn't around, surprisingly." I couldn't bring myself to tell her what happened. "Jonathon wasn't either."

"He's busy tonight."

"Too busy to protect Jessica?"

"He's not her babysitter," Camille argued. "Drinking doesn't justify protection."

"It should." I waited for the Hayworth exit to appear in the misty rain.

"This isn't your responsibility," Camille said.

"She'll always be my responsibility."

"You're being stubborn." She glowered. "You should take her home and let her get in trouble like a typical teenager."

"So her parents can figure something out?" The words formed on their own. "I think Jessica remembers me."

"That's ridiculous—"

"She kissed me, Camille."

My guard didn't speak again, even after I took the exit and drove through Hayworth. I recognized Camille's silence as something from our childhood. Whenever we got into a debate, she accepted defeat with silence. The argument was over, but I wished I hadn't been able to win this one.

I kept my mind as mute as our conversation until I pulled into my driveway. The old car lunged as it crept up the hill. I shifted it into park. The rain was no longer pounding on the roof of the car, but the trees were swaying dangerously low.

"Let's get her inside," Camille said.

I unbuckled my seatbelt and stepped outside, joining Camille. I opened the door Jessica was leaned against and held her up, so she didn't fall onto the pavement. My fingers tingled. Jessica had control over me, even when she was unconscious. I had to concentrate.

"I can get her," Camille offered.

I shook my head and slipped my arm beneath her knees to pick her up. She curled against my chest, and her hand landed on my sternum. She grumbled as the hair fell out of her face, and I followed Camille to my house.

My guard opened the door, and we walked up the stairs. "Where are you putting her?" Camille asked.

I motioned my head toward my room. "I'll stay on the couch downstairs," I explained before she could argue.

"I'm sure you could use your father's bed," Camille said, pushing open my bedroom door.

"And risk him wondering why things were moved around? No, thank you."

"Good point," Camille laughed, but I couldn't bring myself to smile.

I laid Jessica on my bed and stepped back as quickly as I could. I didn't want to touch her any longer than I had to. I expected Camille to say something—anything, really—but she walked toward Jessica instead. She grabbed the straps of Jessica's dress and pulled them over her shoulders.

I spun around, putting my back to them. "What—what are you doing?" I shut my eyes as the sound of Camille's fingers grazing Jessica's wet skin filled my ears. A thud landed near my feet, and I peeked. A black bra was on my foot.

"Please, tell me you weren't planning on leaving this girl in drenched clothes all night," Camille said. "She'll freeze."

I stepped away from the undergarment. "But—"

"Honestly, Eric," Camille teased. "She's practically your wife."

"Stop it."

"Fine," she sung. "Give me a shirt."

I opened my dresser and pulled a clean shirt out. I tossed it over my shoulder, hoping Camille would catch it, and then grabbed a pair of boxer shorts. "You'll probably need these, too."

"Thanks."

I locked my knees, glaring at my wall. I wouldn't look. Not for a second. It would be too disrespectful to Jessica. Whether we were meant to be together or not, we weren't now, and I wasn't going to act like we were.

"Give me one more minute," Camille said, and the sounds of clothing moving ricocheted through me.

I had to distract myself.

I opened my drawer and picked up the black box my father gave me. I knew that my mother had given it to me for a reason, and the reasoning was starting to become clear, but I needed to do something before I actually used it.

"All done," Camille announced, and I shoved the box in my pocket before my guard saw.

I turned around and shuddered at the sight of Jessica in my clothes, asleep on my bed. "Won't she wonder how she was changed?"

Camille beamed. "Tell her you did it."

"What?" My chest was tight.

"I'm sure she'll understand." My guard collected the wet heap of clothes on the floor. "I'll wash these and have them back before morning."

"Thank you, Camille."

She walked toward the exit, only lingering to put a hand on my shoulder. "And, Eric?" she started. "Don't let this get to you too much." Her words remained minutes after she left, and I sat next to Jessica, unable to move.

"Don't let this get to me too much?" I repeated, laying my head in my hands only to peek through my fingers.

Even with my T-shirt on, I could see her bruises, and I wondered why Camille hadn't said anything. Then again, it was probably the reason she hadn't said anything at all. My guard trusted me despite my flaws, and it was Camille's trust that I valued the most in the Dark. The elders always assumed I did the worst. Camille knew I only did the worst when I was forced into it.

I sprang to my feet before I dwelled in my emotions. I walked to my door and then returned to Jessica's side, leaned down, and kissed her on the forehead. "Goodnight, Jessica," I said, staying by her side before I disappeared like everyone else had that night.

33

Jessica

THE AFTERNOON LIGHT WOKE ME UP. IT SPEWED THROUGH THE slit of the black curtains and landed across my eyes. I squinted, groaned, and turned over. My eyes were stinging, and my head was consumed by a migraine stronger than any headache I ever had before. The taste in my mouth was worse, but my blankets smelled wonderful—they smelled like a boy.

My heart lunged into my throat as I sprang up, glancing around the bedroom. It wasn't mine. It wasn't even in my house. But I recognized it—the stark cleanliness mixed with the strange light coming from beneath the desk. I knew it was a nightlight. I had figured that out last semester.

I was in Eric Welborn's room.

I leapt from the bed, and the cold carpet tickled my toes. I shivered, remembering the freezing rain. The entire night flashed through me like one of my detailed nightmares. I remembered Robb, and my neck burned.

I covered my mouth. I didn't need to deal with my emotions now. All I needed to do was get out of Eric's house, and get out fast.

I rushed to his door, grabbed the doorknob, and turned it. I listened for movements, but heard nothing. The house seemed to be empty as I crept into the hallway.

"Don't worry." Eric's voice broke my confidence. "No one

is home."

I froze, staring at the only part of the kitchen I could see—the table.

"I promise," he called out, and I tiptoed toward the table, half-expecting the entire family to be waiting for me, but he was telling the truth. He was the only one there, and he was boiling water on the stovetop with his back facing me.

I wrapped my arm around his T-shirt, wondering where my clothes had gone. My face was hot, and I was dizzy. It was the only reason I surrendered and sat down.

"How are you feeling?" he asked.

I laid my forehead on the table and reminded myself to breathe. I couldn't believe where I was or what had happened. My last memory was twisting any sanity I had left. I remembered a girl magically appearing in the backseat of his car. It didn't make sense.

The table rocked, and I looked up to stare at a cup of steaming liquid. Eric was sitting across from me. "Is this for me?" I squeaked.

He tilted his head. "Who else would it be for?"

I didn't respond as I grabbed the mug and sipped the hot tea. It soothed my throat and calmed my nerves. It was possibly the best drink I ever had.

Eric was staring into his mug. "Are—" he paused, and I noticed the shadows beneath his eyes. He hadn't slept. "Are you okay, Jessica?"

He was sincere, but his tone frightened me. He used the same one at the hospital.

"I'm fine," I lied, wondering how he had even driven me the night before. He didn't have a car, and I wanted to ask him about it, but he gripped his mug like heat couldn't burn him.

"And your neck?"

I nearly choked on my tea. "I'm okay," I repeated, but Eric wasn't moving.

"I'm going to confront Robb tomorrow," he said.

I straightened up. "I can handle it."

"Can you?" His tone was as rigid as his stare. It was the

148

first time he looked at me all morning.

"I'm capable," I argued, desperately wanting to stop the aftermath of my actions, but Eric wasn't giving up.

"You weren't last night." He scooted his chair back only to move it forward again. He took a drink and practically slammed his glass down. "I know you're capable, Jessica," he said. "But that's why I don't understand why you're acting this way."

I couldn't fathom what he was saying. "You're mad at me."

His shoulders dropped. "I'm frustrated."

"Why?"

"Because you're not acting like yourself," he said, meeting my eyes again. The emerald color of his eyes made me shudder, and heat crept over the bruises that had formed overnight.

"You don't know me that well."

He waved his hand over me. "Don't I?"

His words froze me, and I remembered kissing him. As much as I wanted to hate the drunken actions, I could still feel the clarity and comfort that had washed over me. For a moment, he was the dream boy I was looking for, and I had never been happier leaning against him. This morning, his words were cold.

I lowered my face. "You're being really mean."

"I'm being honest," he whispered, waving his fingers where I was focused on the table. He wanted me to look up, but I couldn't.

"I'm sorry," I said, rubbing my temples. "I'm just really confused right now."

"You don't have to tell me that, Jessica," he said, and I glanced up to see a small smile spread across his face.

He sighed, and it disappeared as if it had never existed. We sipped our tea to avoid conversing. I couldn't blame him for the silence because I didn't want to talk either. I wasn't sure what to ask first—how a girl had appeared in the car I didn't know he had, or why I was in his clothes. But I knew I had to ask one of them.

"I—I saw something strange," I stuttered.

Eric's eyes were slits. "You were drunk." Somehow, his words didn't seem sincere anymore.

"I didn't know you got a new car," I retaliated, but he didn't tense.

"I guess you've been in both of mine now," he said, and my stomach twisted. He really had a knack for controlling the conversation. "Anything else you'd like to know?"

"Your clothes," I said.

It was the first time I saw him squirm.

He spit his drink into his cup, coughing up the liquid he choked on. I tensed at his reaction and waited for his answer, but he couldn't speak through his constricted throat. He scooted away from the table and retrieved a glass of water. The few minutes passed like hours.

"You were soaked," he said, pressing his palms against the countertop. "I didn't want you to get pneumonia. Nothing happened between us."

Except the kiss. I doubted I imagined it like the woman appearing in his car.

"I helped you change," he continued. "That's it. I promise."

The words caused my head to spin, and I gripped the table, but it didn't help. I fell over, stopping in mid-air. Even though he had been across the room, Eric had caught me. My vision blurred but refocused on his burning eyes. They looked blue, and I had to blink to see his emerald gaze again. His stare was ablaze.

"Are you okay, Jessica?" His voice was rushed as he helped me up. "Can you hear me?"

My cheeks were as hot as the rest of my body. "Must be the hangover," I said, but his misty gaze shifted. "Why do you look at me like that?"

He let me go and turned his face away. "Look at you like what?"

Before he could step away, I grabbed the end of his shirt. "Your eyes," I said. "You look sad." I didn't know how else to word it. He was acting like our kiss had broken him, and his reaction was breaking me.

His hand snaked around his back, and he grabbed mine. His fingers shook when he pulled my grip off him, but he didn't let me go. "I'm fine, Jessica," he said.

"I'm sorry that I kissed you," I blurted out.

He dropped my hand then. "Wouldn't be the first time."

My heart lurched. "What?"

"That I've been kissed," he said, but his voice was tight. "It's okay." He collapsed in his seat in a way that suggested it wasn't all right. "I think I'll live."

"So, you'll forgive me?" My voice was squeaking, and Eric's cracked.

"If you stay out of trouble."

"I will," I promised.

He smirked his usual "I'm-one-step-ahead-of-you" grin and placed his hands behind his head. "Then, you're forgiven," he said, "by me, at least."

I didn't understand. "Who else did I upset?"

He cocked an eyebrow. "Don't parents get upset when their daughter doesn't show up?"

"I was supposed to stay at Crystal's," I said.

He chuckled. "You'll still get in trouble."

I cringed. I had lost everything I had taken to the bar, including my phone. "You're probably right."

He tapped his temple. "I have a lot of insight."

"Or a lot of experience," I retorted, and he opened his mouth to continue the banter, but the front door opened.

I jumped, but Eric stood up and laid his hand on my shoulder. "It's fine," he said. "It's just George."

"What is he doing here?" I hissed, but it was too late. George had already scaled the stairs to the kitchen.

"Hello, Ms. Taylor," he said, waving his cracked palm in my direction. I felt naked in Eric's T-shirt and boxers, but George didn't flinch. "I suspect you slept well last night."

I couldn't say a word to the man. He wasn't Eric's father, but he seemed to be more present than Eric's actual one. George was talking to Eric when I finally noticed the stack of clothes in his hands.

"Are those mine?" I asked.

The older man handed them to me. "Teresa dropped them off at my house this morning," he explained, and I wondered if I hadn't imagined the woman after all. "They just came out of the dryer."

I beamed when I grabbed them. "Thank you," I said, clutching the cleaned dress with desperation.

Eric pointed over his shoulder. "There's a bathroom across from my bedroom."

I ran faster than I thought my dizzy legs could take me. Slamming the door, I practically ripped Eric's clothes off to put mine on. With my attire returned, I felt like my usual self. Not my drunken, dangerous, and delusional counterpart. That wasn't me. It never had been.

I folded Eric's clothes and put them on the counter before I left the bathroom. I lingered in the hallway, wondering why George was accepting me when I heard them talking.

"Of course I didn't tell your father," George said, and his words slammed against my head. "You need to get this place cleaned up, or he's going to realize someone slept on the couch."

"I wasn't exactly sleeping, Urte," Eric mumbled. The nickname made me hold my breath. "It was torture having her here."

"You're going to have to forget about it," George said. "You are close enough to your birthday that you can't risk this. The prophecy will only tolerate so much."

"I had to do it," Eric said, and I heard his footsteps cross the room. He would see me any minute.

"You have to take care of yourself first, kid," George said.

"But—" Eric stopped speaking when he rounded the corner and saw me. His mouth hung open, and George started talking, but Eric lifted his hand. "You're already dressed," he said, and I stepped closer.

Unlike Eric, George's reaction was neutral. "I didn't hear you come down the hallway." George's words felt like a lecture.

"I guess I'm quiet," I muttered, trying to catch Eric's startled expression again, but it was gone. He was looking out of the kitchen window.

"Well, then." George whistled, clapping his hands together. "Are you ready to go?"

"Go?" I asked.

"Go home," Eric explained. "I have a doctor's appointment, so George has to take you."

"Oh." I turned to Jonathon's father, hoping this wouldn't become part of his daily update to his son. "Yeah. I'd love to go home."

34

Jessica

I LOCKED THE DOOR THE INSTANT I STEPPED INTO MY HOUSE. I WAS thankful George hadn't attempted a conversation, and I was hoping I wouldn't need to have one with my parents. But I doubted it.

I only got halfway upstairs before my mother shouted from the kitchen. "Is that you, Jessie?" She appeared soon after, but I kept walking toward my bedroom. She followed me. "Where were you? Are you okay? You look sick. What happened?"

"Nothing," I grumbled, grabbing a towel from my shelf as I went toward my bathroom.

She cut me off at the doorway. Her hair was a bigger mess than I was. She didn't look mad at all.

"Can I get a shower first?" I asked.

Her bottom lip quivered as she stepped to the side.

I walked past her with guilt leading the way. I had to get cleaned up before I explained myself, but I knew it wasn't fair. I pushed the thoughts away as I stepped out of my dress and into the shower. The hot water stung my neck, and I ran a rag across my back and stomach. The dirt in my hair felt like it would never come out, and I washed it twice before I was satisfied. If only the soap could wash away the memories of Robb.

Maybe Eric was right. I couldn't handle it.

The memories were as painful as the actual moment. My

friend had choked me, not to mention forced a kiss on me, and I was more broken than when I had given up on finding my biological parents. Strangely enough, I couldn't recall why I gave up during the summer. Eric saw it before I did—I wasn't acting like myself. Somewhere, I lost myself and didn't know how to get myself back. The only time I felt complete was in my dreams. Until I kissed Eric. I closed my eyes to rid myself of the feeling, but the sound came without warning:

Thud-thump. Thud-thump. Thud-thump.

His heartbeat.

My stomach churned, and I fell on my knees and threw up. I coughed, choking on the taste of the tea I had earlier. I rubbed my face and watched the discolored liquid swirl down the drain with the soap. When it was gone, I turned off the water and stood on shaky knees.

I got out, wrapped myself in the towel, and opened my bathroom door. Steam curled against the ceiling, and I ran my hand over my clean hair. My insides felt worse than my body.

"Jessie?"

I was shocked my mother had stayed in my room. "Mom—"

"Are you okay, sweetheart?" she asked.

I walked into my closet before she saw the bruises on my neck. I didn't know how I would explain, so I grabbed a turtleneck and pulled it over my head.

"I'm fine," I lied, stepping out to face her.

She was sitting on my bed, and her fingernails dragged across my sheets. "I heard you puke."

"It was nothing."

"Crystal's mom dropped off your purse this morning," she said, revealing her knowledge. "Lola said Crystal showed up intoxicated without you. I called Robb's phone, but he didn't answer."

His name made my empty stomach lurch. "It's not what you think," I attempted, but she cut me off.

"I'm glad you're okay, Jessie," she said. "But I'm worried. Your father is, too." She was paler than I had ever seen her before. "I know you're a teenager, but this is so unlike you—"

"I know," I managed. "And I'm sorry. I just got caught up, and it won't happen again." It was a promise I knew I would keep, but strangely enough, the reason I wanted to keep it was I promised Eric.

My mom laid her hands in her lap. "What happened, Jessie?"

I didn't know what to tell her, but I knew I couldn't tell her everything. I couldn't even tell myself. "My friend helped me," I explained. "I stayed at his house."

Her eyebrows shot up to her hairline. "His?"

"Eric," I clarified. "Nothing happened."

Her face twisted. "Isn't he that Welborn kid? The one with the Charger—the one who wrecked his Charger?"

"Yeah," I breathed. "It's okay. He put me in a guest room." I couldn't tell her it was his room.

Her eyes lingered on my expression like she already knew, and I prepared myself for her to slip into the protective parent she usually was. Instead, she stood up, crossed the room, and draped her arms around my shoulders. She squeezed me into a hug, and I winced as she brushed my neck.

"I love you, Jessie," she said, holding my shoulders as she stepped back. "You know that your father and I are here for you."

I couldn't believe it.

"I know, Mom."

She touched my hair where it began to curl. "So, you can talk to us when you need to," she continued, tapping her fingertip against my forehead. "But don't think we'll tolerate this a second time."

I had to bite my lip. I didn't want to speak because I was afraid I'd cry. I didn't deserve her help. I had broken her rules, acted recklessly, and lied about it. I wanted to be yelled at. I wanted to be grounded or punished or anything. Just not dismissed as if I hadn't done anything.

"Get some sleep," she said, turning to my door. "It'll help with the hangover."

Before I could thank her, she left and shut my door. I wished she had slammed it. I was shaking and wrapped my arms around my chest to keep my sobs inside, but it didn't work. I couldn't deny the truth any longer. I cried.

35

"**D**OES IT HURT HERE?" THE DOCTOR PRESSED MY CHEST FOR the hundredth time.

"Not at all."

"How about here?" He had barely moved his finger.

"Nope."

His brow furrowed behind his glasses. "Now, don't lie to me, Eric," he pretended to joke, but he failed miserably.

"I'm not lying," I said, and for once, I was telling the truth. The pressure didn't hurt. It was more annoying than anything. "I feel fine." Aside from my senses. They were enhancing as we spoke, and I knew it was because I accepted the fact that I was fully healed. I could turn into a shade whenever I wanted to, and my body yearned for the transition.

The florescent lights stung, and the smells curdled in my lungs. Every time I moved, the sheet beneath me ripped, and I cringed. It was hard enough to ignore the sounds of six other patients in the same hallway as they did the same thing. Service clerks tapped their keyboards, and someone banged on a nearby vending machine. If the customer moved it to the left, the snack would be free.

"Is there any pain here?"

"There's no pain, Doc," I replied, fighting the urge to rub my temples. "I think I'm healed."

The man didn't say anything as he sat down and glanced

over the computer screen that was turned away from me. I kicked my legs back and forth, staring at the photos on the walls—two mountains and one informative piece on STDs. I wished I hadn't tried to distract myself.

"Sir." There was a knocking on the door as it opened, reminding me of how Noah entered my room. "The boy's father is here."

I tensed when he appeared. "You're home early," I said, but he was concentrating on the doctor.

"Hello, Mr. Welborn," the doctor said, shaking my father's hand. "How was your trip?" Apparently, the entire town knew about it, which was exactly what the Dark wanted.

"Tiring, but good," he answered. "Sorry I'm late."

"At least one of us knew you were coming," I spoke up, but, again, they ignored me.

"I would've called, but I don't like using the phone when I'm driving," my father excused. "Wouldn't want to crash." I gritted my teeth as he continued to talk to my doctor. "How are things looking?"

"Eric healed a little earlier than I expected," he said, suddenly switching from his interrogation to agreeing with me. "But that's a sign of a healthy, young man."

"That's nice to hear," I muttered, but neither reacted to my comment.

"My son is a healthy kid," my father remarked.

"We need more healthy youth," the doctor said.

"Eric doesn't play videogames," he said. "He likes exercise."

"And my training," I spoke telepathically for the first time in weeks, and my father's eyes slid to mine. He was not happy.

"Back in my day that's all we did—exercise," the doctor continued.

I winced at the "back-in-my-day" line. Stories always followed, and I was too eager to be free to listen to it. Sure enough, the doctor opened his mouth and babbled about his schooldays. The two men laughed like old buddies, and I rolled my eyes, standing from the table.

"Well, it's been great," I said, folding my arms as I moved

toward the door. "Can I have my papers?"

The doctor blinked, and my father draped his arm around the man. "We'll catch up another time, Kenneth." *Excellent. Now they were on a first name basis.*

"Sounds good, James," he said, ripping off a paper to give me. I snatched it like it was the secret to the prophecy. "Don't let me see you for crashing again."

"Don't worry about that, Doc," I said, straightening my shirt. "My new car barely hits forty when I try to crash it."

The doctor paled.

"Sarcasm," I clarified, but the man didn't laugh.

My father grabbed my sleeve. "Let's go," he mumbled and dragged me from the room. "What are you thinking?"

"It was funny."

"Hardly," he said, but he was smiling. Apparently, I inherited his sense of humor.

We were free from the human hospital in minutes, and when I got to the parking lot, he let me go. I stood on the concrete sidewalk and looked over his face, searching for any sign of contentment. I was waiting for him to say he knew about Jessica, but he remained silent.

"How was your week?" he asked.

I pulled my car keys from my pocket. "Thanks for the car," I said, finally able to show him my appreciation.

"You'll need it," he said, returning to his cold demeanor. "Are you feeling better?"

"I thought that was obvious," I responded telepathically.

"Good." His lip twitched. *"Now, you better start training again."*

"I will tomorrow," I replied aloud.

"Tonight," he corrected. "You will go tonight." *"Urte's waiting for you already."*

Of course he was. "I have school in the morning." *And I had to confront Robb.*

My father pulled his glasses out of his shirt pocket. "That's never stopped you before."

He paid more attention to my actions than I wanted to

believe. "Fine," I said, and he started to walk away. This time, I was the one to grab his shirt. "Wait."

He stared at my grip like it was the first time we had touched. "What do you need?"

I cleared my throat. "Do you know where Jessica's parents are buried?"

"What?" His tone was sharp. "Why would you ask that?"

"I—uh—" I couldn't explain. Not yet. "Just curious."

He straightened out, looming over my height, but he didn't speak. His hand snaked into his back pocket, and he pulled out his wallet. In seconds, he had his business card out, and his fingertips hovered over the back. Scrawling black words appeared beneath his touch.

"You should be able to get there before it gets dark out," he said, handing over the address.

"But training—"

"Go tomorrow," he suggested. "Before training."

I glanced at the address with confusion. I knew the location. "There isn't a cemetery there."

"Trust me." My father's expression slid into a knowledgeable grin. "You'll find it." With that, he turned his back and walked away. I stared, unable to look away as he left, his shoulders bouncing in a slight chuckle.

36

Jessica

THE CLASSROOM BELL SOUNDED MORE LIKE A DEATH SENTENCE than a routine warning to sit down. I hadn't slept the night before, not when I knew I would be facing Robb. Biting my nails, I stared at the clock. One more bell before he would show up—Eric, too.

I shivered at the reminder of my midnight hero. For once, I wished he didn't always show up at the last minute. I wanted him next to me and wasn't even ashamed to admit it

"Jess." Crystal sounded exasperated as she collapsed in Eric's chair. "What happened to you?" she asked, widening her eyes. "I filled up your voicemail trying to reach you—"

"I didn't have my cell phone," I muttered, realizing she was clueless. I was tempted to take off my scarf and show her the bruises Robb had given me.

"Yeah, I know," she exhaled, rolling her eyes. "But you could've made an exception after Robb and you disappeared. He hasn't talked to me either."

"For being a reporter, you're really uninformed." I avoided the explanation since we were surrounded by eavesdropping teens.

"I shouldn't have to ask my best friends what happened to them." She stuck out her bottom lip.

I sighed, knowing I had to find a way to tell her, but I was too late.

"Good morning." The greeting was as sudden as his appearance. Robb McLain. He was standing in front of my desk, and I couldn't bring myself to say a word. Crystal was too busy screeching.

"What happened to your face?" she yelled, and my eyes landed on his black eye.

"Got in a fight with some psycho," Robb dismissed coldly.

"I like the sound of that nickname."

Robb tensed as Eric brushed past him. He dropped his bag on the floor as the final bell rang. The room was silent as the two glared at one another.

Eric was as still as a predator, and Robb mimicked his posture poorly. His arms were folded. "What do you want, Welborn?"

"I don't want anything from you," Eric said, leaning his lower back against the countertop. "But I bet Jessica does."

"Jessica?" Robb repeated my full name with bitterness.

"An apology," Eric clarified, waving his hand toward me. "I'd like to hear it, too."

Robb's face flushed. "Is that your business?"

"I think you made it mine."

"Boys," Ms. Hinkel attempted to interrupt their tension, but they didn't budge. "Take your seats. You, too, Crystal."

She flew to her desk, and Robb stepped backwards, refusing to show his back to Eric. "We'll talk after class," Robb muttered to me before he left.

I shoved my hands under the table to prevent myself from seeing them shake. Eric, however, didn't ignore them as he sat down next to me. "Are you okay?" he whispered the question he asked too many times for me to bear.

"Better now that you're here," I replied, surprised by my honesty. Eric blinked, and I flushed. "How was your doctor's appointment?"

He pointed to his ribs. "All healed." His words relaxed me.

"Good," I whispered, ending our conversation as class began. I was relieved when the teacher put on a documentary, and the class was distracted. I faced forward and lost myself to the film about genetics.

The recessive genes fascinated me the most—the ones that didn't necessarily show up but still retained a significance people couldn't deny. I wondered if my parents were surprised by my blue eyes or worried about disorders they could pass on. I didn't know anything about their health, but my curiosity was returning. I cursed myself for not asking for their records when I had visited Eric in the hospital.

I glanced at him in my peripheral vision. One second, he was a stern outcast, practically begging for trouble, and the next second he was a teasing, crossword champ. He was intelligent and attractive, but didn't seem to care about the effect he had on everyone. He either scared or excited them. To me, he did both.

The lights switched on, and Eric's gaze met mine. I froze, and for a second, he did, too. When he smirked, his previously startled expression seemed like an illusion. "Did you like it?" he asked, and I bit my lip as I nodded. "Me, too."

I wanted to talk to him about it, but he looked behind me, and his eyes slit into a glare. I didn't have to turn around to know who he was looking at.

"Leave me alone, Robb," I said, gathering my things.

"But I wanted to talk to you—"

"That's not a mutual feeling." I stepped around Eric to walk behind the table. I stayed as far away from Robb as I could, and Eric was helping. He sprang up and walked by my side, staying between Robb and I. Crystal was hovering in the doorway with a pale face, and I wondered if he told her.

"You know, I didn't mean it, Jess," Robb said, walking next to Eric. "I was drunk—"

"Most drunks don't choke people," I said.

Eric grabbed my hand, stopping me in the doorway. I could sense students staring, but I didn't want to look. I was too focused on Eric.

"If she doesn't want to talk to you, why don't you leave her alone?" he suggested.

Robb crossed his arms. "How about you do your usual

thing and stay out of it?"

Eric's lips curled into a snarl. "Kind of hard when you're talking through me, don't you think?"

"Then, leave." Robb sounded like he was giving orders, but Eric wasn't about to obey him.

"She doesn't want to talk to you."

"Oh." Robb raised his thick eyebrows. "Now, you're talking for her, too."

"I don't want to talk to you," I said, grabbing Eric's arm to pull him into the hallway, but Robb stepped in front of the door.

"You have to talk to me eventually."

"No, I don't," I argued, stepping under his arm. Crystal latched onto me, and I spun around to see Robb pushing his finger against Eric's chest.

"We have a problem, Welborn," he said.

This time, I was pulling Robb back. "Leave Eric alone," I said.

Robb whipped around, his face reddened. "Eric?" he repeated. "I didn't realize you were so close to him all of a sudden."

"Robb." My voice was rigid, a tone I hadn't heard from myself before. My heart pounded, but my hands weren't shaking. I was steady, because I was preparing for the worst.

Robb threw his hands in the air. "Why are you protecting him?" he shouted so loudly the teacher ran into the hallway.

"Because he's protecting me," I said.

Robb snarled. "Yeah, I'd protect my slut, too."

My racing heart dropped before I comprehended what had happened.

In movements too fast to see, Eric had grabbed Robb's arm, twisted it behind his back, and shoved him against the wall. Robb's face was against the white bricks, and Eric's face reddened with anger.

"Take that back," Eric demanded, pulling Robb's arm up.

"I don't have to," Robb managed.

The teacher stomped her feet on the marble floor. "Mr.

Welborn. Mr. McLain," she screamed, waving her arms through the air. "Office—now!"

Eric ignored her, holding Robb against the wall for seconds that seemed like minutes. Even when he shoved Robb and let him go, the veins on Eric's neck were sticking out. When he turned to Ms. Hinkel, no one breathed. "My favorite place," Eric said, grabbing his bag off the floor. I hadn't even noticed him dropping it.

He put on his headphones and strode away without covering his back. The confidence sent shivers down my spine. Eric didn't care if Robb attacked him again. In fact, he was teasing Robb with the opportunity. He wanted it.

"Office, Mr. McLain." Ms. Hinkel pointed a shaky finger down the hallway.

Robb dropped his face and grumbled as he followed Eric to their punishment. I half-expected him to talk to me, but he didn't. Ms. Hinkel did instead. "Get to class, Ms. Taylor." It sounded like an apology.

I stared at the usually strict woman. "Shouldn't I go with them?" I asked, hoping she would send me.

"You didn't do anything wrong," she dismissed, walking after the boys. I wanted to shout that I had, that I caused the fight with my recklessness over the weekend. Even though she thought I hadn't done anything wrong, I knew I was the problem.

"Jess." Crystal's usually loud voice was quiet. When she touched me, I jumped, and she sprang back.

"I'm sorry," I sighed.

"It's okay," she said. "Robb wrote me a note in class. Explained the whole thing." She cringed, and her eyes drifted over my scarf. I was paranoid she could see my bruises through the thick fabric. "I'm not talking to him either."

"You don't have to do that."

"Yes, I do." She took my bag, steadying her small body between both of our backpacks. "I'm your friend, after all."

37

GETTING SUSPENDED RUINED ANY CHANCE I HAD TO GO TO THE gravesite after school. George Stone had to pick me up, and he drove me straight to the training room. As punishment, Urte was throwing everything he had in my direction.

My sword was weightless in my hands, and my body tingled like the cooling air outside. I was swift, and my concentration was impeccable. I wouldn't use my anger to fight like I had before, even though I had a lot of it from the day. I had learned to control it. When the battle would happen, I didn't know, but I knew one thing: I felt ready.

But I wasn't battling Darthon today. Instead, I was fighting Urte's bickering as he stomped around the room. "Do you know how hard it is to keep you in school?" he lectured. "You've gotten in enough trouble as it is, Eric. With all your backtalk, you should've been expelled."

"You should've let me get kicked out," I retorted, slicing a beam of light in half. "I'd have more time to train."

"And you'd stick out more."

"I think I stick out more when they make exceptions for me," I argued, but Urte wasn't going to continue the argument. He knew as well as I did that I wouldn't give up. I was too stubborn.

"That isn't the point," Urte resigned.

I finished the last of his tests and felt my sword return to my veins, zipping against the very blood that cursed me with the power. "Then, what is?" I asked, picking up the nearest water bottle I could find.

"You got into a fight at school."

"At least I stayed in my human form." I nearly crushed the water bottle in my hand. "I would've killed Robb if I were Shoman."

Urte grabbed his bristled chin. "Don't even joke about something like that."

"I wasn't joking."

"We don't need you to be fighting," Urte said.

The irony of his words made me laugh. "I can handle myself, Urte."

"You already have fractured ribs—"

"Had," I corrected him. "I had broken ribs. They're fine now."

"That doesn't mean you need to find an excuse to break something else," he retorted. "I saw Robb's face. He could've done the same to you."

"That human?" I spat the words. Using his name aloud would be too difficult. "Only cowards hit women."

Urte's demeanor changed. He rushed over, and his wild eyes searched my face. "What are you talking about?"

"What do you think?" I watched the realization spread over his expression. "I told you I had to help Jessica for a reason."

"Eric." Urte's tone was quieter. "When you said that Jess was drunk with another guy, you never said he was beating her."

"He choked her," I corrected as the bones in my hands tightened. "And kissed her."

"I think one is more important."

"I'd say both of them upset me."

Urte put his hands out like he was ready to shake me. "I would've understood the situation better if you told me this," he said. "You have to stop keeping secrets."

"I'm practicing to become an elder," I remarked.

Urte smacked his forehead. "I swear you prepare for these conversations," he grumbled. It was an aggravation I was used to.

"I don't know why I didn't tell you, Urte." I leaned my back against the wall. Now that I could transform, it was strange to be taller than he was. "I thought Camille would've figured it out."

Urte raised his brow. "Why's that?"

"She changed her into my T-shirt." I hoped he already knew that detail. "I was sure she saw the marks."

Urte was silent for a moment. "If Camille did, she didn't say anything to me."

I would have to ask my guard when I saw her next, but I wasn't sure when it would be. She was training on her own. Unlike the other guards, she would fight, and fighting by my side wouldn't be easy.

"Does my father know about this?" I asked, referring to my brawl at school.

Urte nodded. "I think he expected this sort of behavior eventually." My father was the only person I knew who was ahead of me. "He'd be angry if you'd gotten hurt."

"I would've healed."

"Bob wouldn't have."

"Robb," I corrected hastily. "His name is Robb, not Bob."

Urte smirked. "Now, that is something that doesn't matter."

I groaned. The joke couldn't even lighten my attitude, and I was too tired from training to respond. It would only turn into an argument anyway.

Urte laid a hand on my shoulder, and I stared at the hair on his fingers. "You should go home early," he said.

It was the first piece of good news I'd received all day. "Thanks," I said, knowing I couldn't accept the offer. "But I wanted to talk to you about something."

"We haven't talked enough?"

I ran my hand through my hair. It stood up from the sweat. "Is it possible for Jessica's confidence to disappear with her memory?"

Urte was awestruck. "Why would that happen?"

I shrugged, thinking over the series of events that had brought me to the conclusion. "When I first met her, she was a confident person, shade or human."

"That's exactly why your theory doesn't make sense," he pointed out. "She was confident before she knew what she was."

"Was she?" I asked. "We don't know that much about her life before she moved back to Hayworth. I've never heard her mention previous friends, boyfriends, nothing really."

Urte was grinning. "You can't complain about the boyfriend part."

I glared at the man's humor. "Urte."

He chuckled. "I apologize, Shoman, but seriously—" His words lingered between us, "where'd you get such an idea?"

"A few months ago, she would've never acted this way," I said, knowing I'd gotten close enough to Jessica to understand her behavior. "This girl isn't her. Not completely anyway."

"Well, she isn't complete," Urte said, shifting his weight from foot to foot. "I suppose it's possible for her personality to shift, but I'd have to ask Luthicer."

"I don't think that's necessary," I said, deciding I didn't need confirmation. Jessica had lost a part of herself—her Dark self—and that was where she pulled her confidence from. It explained how she was remarkably capable in the first place, able to manage her identities and learn without hesitation. As a human, she didn't like herself. I could see that now.

"It must be weird to be in a constant state of confusion," I said.

"Be careful or you might put me in one." Urte's cocky grin disappeared when he met my stare. I didn't even have to say a word. "Who knew you'd be the one to tell me to take things seriously." His face lit up like the proud second father he was. "You've really grown up, kid," he continued. "I only want you to continue to do so."

"I'll defeat Darthon."

"Forget that for two seconds." It was the last thing I expected to hear from my trainer's mouth. "Remember how far you've come, and you won't have to rely on a destiny for your future. It will come on its own."

38

Jessica

I HUGGED CRYSTAL'S PILLOW TO MY CHEST AS SHE PAINTED HER NAILS, only to repaint them again and again. We had gone to her house the minute school ended, but it didn't make the day easier. The rumors were circulating, and I heard from Jonathon that Eric and Robb were suspended. I wanted to call Eric, but I had forgotten my phone, not to mention I didn't have his number. The best I could do was show up at his house, but I wasn't sure how his father would feel about my presence.

Crystal's phone buzzed. "He's calling again." I didn't have to ask to know it was Robb. "Zac called, too."

"Why didn't you answer?" I asked, thinking Crystal's crush might tempt her.

"He isn't calling for me," she sighed, laying her cheek on her knee. She was moving on to painting her toes. "I think he still likes you."

My throat tightened. "I don't want anything to do with him either."

"Why?" she asked. "He didn't do anything."

Somehow, I felt as if he had. It was a bizarre feeling, considering he wasn't even present, but I wouldn't deny my gut. If I had gone with my instincts in the first place, I wouldn't have gone out drinking, and nothing would've happened. Plus, I promised Eric I would try harder, and that was exactly what I was doing.

"Zac makes me uncomfortable," I admitted.

Crystal exhaled. "You're just shaken up."

"He creeped me out before all of this," I clarified.

Crystal replaced her nail polish cap and slammed the bottle on her table. "Don't tell me he did something, too." Her face was as red as her crimson piercing. "I swear everyone has lost their minds."

I shook my hands. "He didn't," I said, thinking of how he had picked me up after I ran down the street. "Nothing like Robb did anyway."

"Jess." Her tone was sharp. "You better spill."

I wasn't going to tell her about the car ride. "Robb's warning didn't bother you?" I used the only memory I could fathom. "How he told us not to date him?"

She gagged. "Because Robb is the best person to listen to right now."

"He told us that before he went psycho."

Her bleached hair fell into her face. "If you didn't notice, Robb lost it a while ago."

Of course, I had noticed. He was distant, even jumpy, and he was always worse around Zac. It was another reason I didn't like his friend.

"I think his parents might be getting a divorce, but that's hardly an excuse," Crystal continued ranting. Her father had walked out. She wouldn't sympathize with Robb's actions no matter what he told her. "But I never thought he'd do something like this."

Her gaze drifted over my bare neck. My scarf had been off since we got into her bedroom. There was no point in hiding it now. "I'm sorry, Jess," she said.

"It isn't your fault."

"But I'm the one who suggested going out that night," she said. "And I knew you didn't want to. I pushed it—"

"It isn't your fault," I repeated, harsher this time.

Her eyes watered, but she blinked, and the tears were gone. "It isn't your fault either."

My sternum felt like it was breaking. I was surprised I

could still speak. "I know," I whispered, hoping I could accept the words as truth one day.

Crystal grabbed her hair and spun around in her chair. "This is so messed up," she said. "Robb's never been an angry person, let alone a violent drunk, and Eric of all people—why was he even there?"

"I don't know." I wished I had asked him. "But I'm glad he was."

"Me, too," Crystal agreed, staring at her wet nails. The paint had smeared, and she spun to the mirror. It was in her hair. "Great. Just fantastic."

"It'll wash out," I said, getting up to go to her bathroom. I grabbed a towel, ran the water over it, and took it to her.

She scrambled to clean up. "I need to dye my hair again anyway," she dismissed, but her tired tone gave away her true feelings. She was overwhelmed.

"I should tell you something else—" I started, and Crystal met my eyes in the mirror. They looked darker in the reflection.

"I'm guessing it has to do with Welborn."

In the mirror, my shoulders rose, and heat crept across my neck. Crystal gasped and spun around. "I knew it," she exclaimed. "Something happened between you two."

"It's kind of complicated," I said, even though one kiss wasn't.

"This whole thing is complicated." Crystal stood up only to pull me onto her bed. "Just tell me."

"I kissed him."

"You already told me what Robb did," she stated, and I bit my lip, shaking my head from side to side. Crystal's mouth dropped. "Eric?" It was the first time I heard her use his first name without Welborn following it. "You kissed Eric Welborn?" Then, she added it for dramatic effect.

My reflexes took over, and I smacked my hand over her mouth, even though it was impossible for anyone to hear us at her house. "Not so loud," I said, my hand slipping off her face. "And, yes, I kissed him."

"What?" She was in disbelief. "How? When? Where?

Why?" The five key journalist questions. They summarized my anxiety.

I shrugged, unable to explain how I had mistaken him for the dream boy. "He was there, and I was confused," I dismissed. "I don't really know why either."

"So—" Her exaggerated word hung in the air, but her expression startled me. She was smiling.

"So, what?"

"So, are you going to give Welborn a chance?" Crystal asked, bouncing up and down.

"What?" Her excitement startled me. "I thought you hated him."

"It's not like I'm considering dating him."

"I—I'm not talking about this," I stuttered. I only wanted to tell her I kissed him, not contemplate his dating life. "We aren't like that."

"Really?" Crystal didn't believe me.

"Really." I didn't believe myself.

"You kissed him, Jess," she pointed out. "I don't see how you're not like that."

"Because he doesn't date," I said, desperate for any excuse, but Crystal groaned.

"He dated Hannah Blake."

She might as well have pulled the hair out of my head. My mind was screaming. "That was a long time ago."

"Well, he seems better about it," Crystal said, leaning against the wall next to me. "He didn't talk to anyone until you moved here last semester."

The previous months felt like a distant past, something that had happened to someone else in another place entirely, not events I participated in myself.

"I think he likes you," she finished.

My fingers curled, and my nails pressed against my palms. "We just sit next to each other in class."

"Then, why'd you go to his house for the project?" Her high-pitched tone was accusatory.

"For homework."

"And prom?"

My head was spinning again. "What about it?" I talked through the fog.

Crystal giggled and pushed against my arm. "Don't tell me you don't remember dancing with him," she said it like it was a clever pun, but it was true. I didn't remember.

"I—what?" I panicked, jumping to my feet.

Crystal's eyes widened. "You danced with him before you left together." She informed me like the walking gossip column that she was. "You never told me what happened—which reminds me, I want to know."

It was impossible, but my mind was racing. My memories—my life—were gone, and I had no idea why.

"Jess?" Crystal cooed for my attention. "Jess Taylor?"

"What?"

"About Eric?" she teased, but her grin faded. "You really don't remember, do you?"

But I wasn't listening to her questions. I was staring at myself in her mirror. The only piece I recognized was how pale my face had become.

"Jess." Crystal was on her feet, and I watched her get closer to me. "You're freaking me out. What's going on? Did something happen at prom, too?"

Too. Like something had to have happened to me.

"Zac aggravated me at the dance," I decided to lie, knowing his story was my only opportunity. "I wasn't comfortable, so I left."

Crystal's thin eyebrows twitched. "What a shame. Your pink dress was so pretty."

"It was just a dress," I said, moving to walk past her, but she latched onto my arm.

"Jess." Her voice was shaking. "It was black."

My attempted lie failed, all I could say was, "Oh."

Her grip tightened. "What happened to you?"

"I don't know." I dreaded my answer. "I have no idea."

"You need to see someone, a hypnotist or a specialist, maybe—"

"Why would I need to do that?"

"Because you don't remember anything," she said, tapping her own head. "And that slice on your shoulder—"

"What slice on my shoulder?"

She rolled her eyes, grabbed the collar of my shirt and pulled it to the side. She pointed to my shoulder, but I didn't see anything. "You didn't have that scar before prom."

I only saw the smoothness of my skin. No scar. No mark. Nothing that would indicate what Crystal was pointing at.

"You told me you scraped it against a tree branch," Crystal explained, assuming I didn't remember that either. "But I always suspected something else happened—between Welborn and you." Her words were growing my migraine. "Did he hurt you, too, because I'm about to murder all the boys in our grade."

"Eric wouldn't do that," I defended him before my confusion defeated me. "Would he?"

The idea of the same boy who saved me being my problem in the first place shook me. He spoke to me in class, helped me with crossword puzzles, made me tea, and dressed me. He didn't seem like a malicious person, but neither did Robb until he choked me.

"You have to remember something," Crystal prompted. "Anything."

"I think I need to rest," I said, grabbing my jacket.

Automatically, Crystal grabbed her keys. "Just promise me something," she said, using her transportation against me. "Call me if you need anything. Please." Her small smile wasn't the usual beaming one I knew. "I don't want anything to happen to my best friend."

Best friend. The chaos made us closer.

"I will," I promised, hugging her. "But, please keep this between us."

When I pulled back, she looped her arm with mine. "I didn't consider anything else," she said. "Now, let's get you home, so you can sleep."

She dragged me away, but I wasn't going to sleep. I wouldn't be able to. Not until I figured out what happened at prom.

I had to ask Eric if I wanted to learn anything.

39

Eric

WITHOUT CLASSES, MY WEEK WAS AS EMPTY AS THE FIELD IN front of me. The acres stretched to the horizon, and I glanced at the address my father had written down. I was in the right place, about ten miles away from my high school, but I didn't know why he expected me to know where to go. I didn't see a trail of any kind or signs hinting to the gravesite's location. I only saw dying grass spread over a field of dirt.

I grabbed the flimsy wood and hurdled over the fence with ease. The lot was abandoned, obviously unused by whoever owned it. I bet the owner was my father.

I had only taken two steps when my phone rang. I pulled it out of my pocket and stared at my father's picture on the screen. I didn't know why he bothered calling when he could use his telepathy. I flipped the phone open anyway.

"Where are you?"

I continued to walk. "I'm about to go to training, don't worry—"

"There isn't any training today, Eric," he interrupted, but I couldn't believe it. There was always training to be done. "Don't you know what day it is?"

"Uh—" *Was this a test?* "Thursday."

"It's Thanksgiving."

"Oh," I said, recalling we started celebrating it when my

father remarried. The only holiday the Dark had was the Naming. I hardly paid attention to the human ones.

"Mindy's almost finished cooking."

"I'll be home soon," I said, and he chuckled on the other end. "What are you laughing at?"

"Did you figure it out yet?"

I stopped walking and glanced around, half-expecting to see him following me. He knew exactly where I was the moment I told him I wasn't at the shelter. "Not really."

"Look for the light," he said before hanging up.

I stared at the screen, watching his face blink away. This was how he taught me—detached mockery. Unfortunately, I knew I was the same way.

I slid my phone into my pocket and looked around. Aside from the sun, there wasn't a light in sight, and it was too early to transform. The late afternoon sun would be blinding to a shade.

I cringed, preparing myself for the worst as I contorted my vision to the Dark. Normally, the sunlight would be scorching, bright enough to blind any shade, but this time it wasn't.

The sun was purple, the sky was black, and a red light flickered a few yards away. I shifted out of the Dark vision only to slide back into it, just to make sure I wasn't hallucinating. I wasn't. The red light was still there, and I walked toward it.

When I got to the edge of it, the light dissipated, and the grave appeared as if viewable by anyone, but it wasn't. As a human, I saw grass—as a shade, I saw the thick slab of stone decorated by two pictures—her parents' faces.

They were young, smiling as if death hadn't been a worry to them when the photo was taken. But that wasn't the painful part. I could see Jessica's face in theirs. She had her mother's hair and her father's expression of concentration when she was studying the Dark. I had only seen the expression once since she lost her memory, and it was when she watched the genetics documentary in class. She was fascinated. It wasn't until she looked over that I turned back to the film.

I had seen the movie before. The Dark explained more

than history to us. As children, they also taught us the science of our people, and that included our genetics. The Dark gene was beyond dominant—a recessive gene didn't even exist. If it had, I doubted our kind would still be alive. The only fallacy came when we bred with the Light. Their genes didn't mix with ours, and the children of half-breeds would always be human.

When I found that out, I was surprised marriages weren't arranged like they used to be one hundred years ago. Apparently, my great-grandfather had changed that rule. And it was the catalyst for our bloodline's power returning.

I rocked on my heels and looked down at the deceased couple I would never meet, the people who had given life to my only love, my only weakness.

"I don't know how this works," I started, wondering if I had to speak aloud for them to hear me or not. "But I'm here to ask you something."

———◆———

Thanksgiving was awkward. Mindy wanted all of us to share what we were thankful for, and I didn't know what I could say, other than family. Mindy was beaming at that, but I was more guilty than grateful. My nerves were still twisting from the gravesite. I did what I meant to do and didn't regret it, but I worried. Would I ever have a chance to finish what I promised to complete? The fact that she and Noah were putting up the Christmas tree didn't help either. It already had three gifts below it, and I knew they weren't for the holiday. My birthday was two weeks away.

"You're running the water too hot," my father said, cranking the sink's knobs until the rushing water chilled my burning hands. I hadn't noticed the pain. "You don't have to wash the dishes like that."

I laid a cleaned plate on the countertop. "Just helping out."

"Or avoiding the tree." He started scrubbing plates. "Did you do what you wanted to?"

"The spell was different," I replied telepathically.

He didn't twitch as he responded, "*It was designed for only a few people to be able to see.*"

"*Me?*"

He chuckled. "From the beginning, Eric."

I struggled to imagine a time before I existed, before the Dark was preparing for the end of an era—the Light's era. It seemed impossible for shades to live their double lives without worry, and it was hard to imagine what life would be like after the final battle. I was born into chaos. I didn't know what peace felt like.

"Jonathon is here," Noah shouted, and my father looked over the balcony.

"Hey, kid," Jonathon said, rushing to get upstairs. When he met my eyes, I tensed. He didn't have his glasses on, but he wasn't stumbling. He was using his shade vision. "Sorry for interrupting the holiday, Mr. Welborn."

My father didn't care about Thanksgiving any more than I did. "Go to my office," he said. Jonathon was already walking down the hallway. "*I'll distract Mindy.*"

When I caught up to my friend in the office, he was already facing me. "We need to talk."

"We do," I agreed, thinking of the night Robb attacked Jessica. "Why weren't you with Jessica—"

"We have worse problems," Jonathon interrupted, shoving a letter against my chest.

I grabbed it. "What's this about?"

"Open it."

I stared at my best friend as he jumped up and down. "Just do it," he ordered, and I slipped my fingers into the envelope. The letter came out easily, already crumbled by someone else's hands. When I unfolded it, I couldn't breathe. The words consumed me.

It was signed by the Light, and it was a list of five boys' names.

Mine was at the bottom.

40

Jessica

I T WAS HARD TO MOVE THE DAY AFTER THANKSGIVING. I REMAINED full and was glad I was sitting as I handed my mother tools to fix the kitchen sink. "Wrench." She stuck her arm out, I handed it over, and her torso disappeared beneath the counter. As pathetic as it was, I enjoyed the sight.

When it came to stereotypes, my parents had a backwards marriage. My father cooked and cleaned, and my mother fixed everything that broke. I loved that about their parenting style. It was one of the reasons we were close—or used to be close.

"I'm sorry," I muttered, and a bang rattled behind the small door separating us.

"Ouch." She cursed as she ducked out of the cranny and rubbed her head. The blue bandana holding her hair back shifted, and blonde threads poked out. "What are you sorry about?"

"About how I've been acting."

She patted my leg. "You're a teenager." She dismissed it like she had dismissed my drunken escapades. "I know you'll tell me what's bothering you eventually, even if it's when you're thirty."

But I wanted to tell her now. "Mom?"

"What's wrong, Jessie?"

"Where's my prom dress?"

"Your prom dress?" Her forehead crinkled. "Why are you

looking for that old thing?"

"It isn't that old." It had only been seven months.

"But it's destroyed," she said, and I gripped the counter. "I told your father to throw it out, but he insisted on keeping the fabric around the house just in case—you know him, he's such a packrat."

"Where is it?" I asked, but my mother tilted her head at my tone. "I wanted to use the fabric for a school project."

"I can get it for you later."

"It's due tomorrow."

"Jessie." Her lecture would follow soon.

"I'm supposed to meet up with Jonathon later to finish it," I continued the lie, using Jonathon of all people. "We decided to add extra credit."

She returned to the sink. "It's in my closet," she said. "But your father will have to get it. I'm busy."

"I can still help you."

"It's okay, Jessie." Her voice was soft. "Go do what you need to. You know where my car keys are."

I had to force myself to stand up. "Thanks, Mom," I said. "I won't be back late."

I ran upstairs, almost tripping when I stumbled into her bedroom. "Jessie." My father put down his book on a stack of newspapers and magazines. "How's the sink coming along?"

"Great," I said. "Where's my prom dress? I need it for a project."

He lit up. "I told your mother something like this would happen," he said, stretching his arms as he stood up. "But I don't know where she put it in her closet."

"I got it," I said, knowing my mother's closet.

She kept all her favorite clothes—mainly her pajamas—at the front, and she placed all her heels on the shelves. Her pants hung next to her unused business clothes and her winter sweaters. My father's clothes were in a corner. When I twisted around the right-angle leading to the walk-in closet I knew exactly where to look.

At the top of the last countertop, a bag sat on my father's

high school sport jacket. I reached up, pulling it down. I could see the black cloth through the white plastic.

My heart skipped as I clutched it to my chest. I wasn't sure I wanted to see it.

I paused, standing in their closet as if I were contemplating entering a haunted house. I was a girl afraid of her own dress. My fingernails ripped open the plastic, and I sat down, letting it fall into my lap. When I lifted it, I heard myself gasp. It was worse than I was expecting.

The silky designs that once decorated it were torn, showing the thin fabric underneath, and the color had faded. Grass stains littered the bottom, but the worst stain was on top— where the strap of my dress should've been. It was too dark to be water, and I knew Crystal wasn't lying when she said I had a scar on my shoulder. The bloodstain was undeniable, and I ran my fingers over it, hoping to recall a memory from the mysterious night, but nothing came.

There was only one person who could explain it. I threw the dress over my shoulder and ran out of the house. "I'm leaving," I shouted backwards as I ducked out, running to the car. I had to talk to him, and I wasn't going to wait another day to do so.

41

I WAS ONE OF FIVE THE LIGHT SUSPECTED OF BEING SHOMAN, AND I wouldn't be surprised if they would kill all of us just to guarantee their future. But I wasn't as worried as my father was.

"I'll fight him if he shows up," I said, looking at my father from across the kitchen table. He hadn't stopped talking about it since yesterday. In fact, the letter remained in his pocket.

"I don't think you should return to school." This had become his mantra.

"Then they will know, and they'll come here to get me," I pointed out. "I don't want Mindy or Noah to get hurt because of this."

His upper lip twitched. "I thought you didn't care about humans."

I rolled my eyes. "Don't make me admit it out loud," I said. *Of course I cared.* "Either way, they don't deserve to be war victims."

"You're right," he said. "Maybe not just about this."

"What about?"

"Marrying a human."

"Dad." My tone was sharp. "You can't change it now, and you shouldn't want to." I wanted to continue, but the door rattled with an assortment of rushed knocking.

"It's probably Jonathon," my dad said, standing, but I stopped him.

"I got it," I said, walking downstairs to get it myself. My aggravation grew as Jonathon continued to knock. He knew Mindy and Noah wouldn't be home. He could've transported in.

"You don't have to knock—" I stopped talking when I opened the door and saw the person in front of me. Her hand hung in the air, ready to knock again, and her brown hair frizzed around her scowl. "Jessica—"

"We need to talk," she said, barging into my house.

"Wha—what?" She was the last person I needed around me. "You can't be here."

"I don't care," she said, chucking a piece of cloth at me.

If it weren't for my enhanced reflexes, I wouldn't have caught it.

She was pointing at it. "I figured out what was confusing me," she said. "And I need an explanation."

I lifted the cloth up, and the bottom tumbled down, stretching out to reveal what it was. "Your prom dress?" For once, I was the confused one.

"Right."

"So?" I handed it back to her. "What's the point of this?"

She fumed. "You tell me why you can remember this, and I can't."

Her words might as well have been Urte's torture machine. "You—you don't remember prom?"

"Not a second of it." She tugged her shirt collar, revealing her shoulder. "And I can't see an injury everyone else can."

I stared at the bruises Robb gave her. They were fading, but it didn't make my frustration dissipate. "You could see them last week."

"Not the bruises, Eric," she sounded exasperated, pointing at her shoulder. Unlike her bruises, her pink scar hadn't faded. "My shoulder. There's a scar, isn't there?"

My eyes darted between her exposed skin and her expression. I didn't know what to say. I could see it and knew exactly why she couldn't. Luthicer's memory wipe affected more than he had planned.

"I don't know what you want me to say," I managed. "I can take you home if you need me to—" I was too focused on getting her out of my house.

"I'm not going anywhere until you tell me what happened that night," she said. "I know I left with you."

She had left after me, not with me. "I thought you didn't remember anything."

"Crystal told me."

Of course she did.

"Did you hit me?" she asked.

"Hit you?" I stepped backwards, feeling as if she had punched me across the face. "Did I hit you?" My words strained against my throat. "Are you crazy?"

"How else do you explain this?" She was shaking, but so was I.

"I didn't hurt you," I said. Darthon did, but I couldn't tell her that. "I saved you from your own friend. Why would I have done that if I hit you myself?"

The reminder flashed across her face, and she turned away as if I hadn't already seen her expression.

"You know I wouldn't do that," I said, quieter this time. "But I can't tell you what happened."

"Why not?"

"Because I don't know."

Her frustration turned to tears. "Why don't I believe you?"

I had to remind myself that she had a knack for predicting liars. After she got to know me, even I wasn't immune to her talent.

"I'm sorry," I muttered.

She lifted her face, her blue eyes shifting over my expression. In seconds, her confusion fluttered away, and it was replaced with an emptiness I never imagined I would see on her face when she looked at me.

"I hate you," she said it like it was a fact, emotionless and undeniable.

My heart dropping was the only part of me that moved. Jessica, on the other hand, was out the door, leaving like it was the last time I would ever see her. I couldn't allow it to happen.

I ran after her, barely containing my human form as I shot into the darkness. She opened her car door, but I slammed it shut. Breath hissed between her teeth, and I heard the air shift as she lifted her hand to hit me.

I grabbed her wrist in midair, and the blood in her veins shook beneath my grasp. I wrapped my arms around her before she could move again. "I'd never hurt you, Jessica," I whispered. "Never. Even if you hurt me, I'd never consider laying a hand on you."

I loosened my embrace, half-expecting her to smack me, but she curled her fingers against my shirt. "Do you know why I kissed you?" she asked.

It was the last question I was prepared to answer, and my silence grew when she pressed her ear to my chest. "You have this heartbeat—and I know it. I've dreamt about it."

I already knew about her dreams. But I couldn't talk about it. Not now. Not when Darthon was watching me.

"I think you need sleep," I said, barely able to push her away. I had to close my eyes to say the rest. "But you can't come here anymore. Understand me?"

The sound of her holding her breath was worse than her hateful words. I knew what she would do before she even grabbed her car door and opened it. "I wasn't going to come back anyway," she said, climbing inside.

I didn't stop her this time. I had said everything I had to say to keep the secrets that guarded her life. It was the only reason I didn't lose my control when she drove out of my driveway, screeching the tires as she did so. I was no better than the devil in her eyes. She didn't need to know the real Satan was after her until Darthon was dead.

"You should've told her." My father's words didn't faze me as they usually did. "It'd be easier."

"Easier could also lead to the Dark's death," I retorted, but my voice wasn't as confident as I planned to sound.

"Eric—"

"I don't want to talk about this," I said, drifting away into the dark. "I'll be at the shelter."

42

Jessica

I WASN'T SURE WHAT WAS WORSE—REJECTING ERIC, OR THE FACT that he rejected me seconds later.

I was wrong from the beginning, and my guilt was more overwhelming than my confusion. Eric hadn't attacked me, but someone had, and he knew what happened. His tone never sounded stilted when he talked to me. But I didn't know why he would keep anything from me either. I was there for him when he was in the hospital, and he was there for me when Robb was drunk. His sudden shift in personality didn't calculate. And it was the only reason I could stand at his locker and wait for his arrival.

Crystal had told me Robb was back from his suspension, so Eric must have been, too. I had yet to see either one of them, and classes were about to start. I would wait until classes started if that's what it took to apologize to Eric. If I didn't do it now, I was afraid I wouldn't have an opportunity in homeroom.

"What are you doing here?"

I spun around, ready to face the boy I had accused. "Eric—" I stopped when I realized it wasn't him. "Zac?"

"That's what I prefer to be called," he said, glancing from me to the locker I was leaned against. "You waiting for Welborn?"

I didn't want to answer. "What are you doing here?"

His eyes lingered on the lockers. "I asked you that first."

"It's more appropriate for me to ask that question."

He waved a piece of paper in the air. "I'm transferring, re-member?"

I wished I didn't, but I couldn't deny it. Considering Eric's locker was next to the office, Zac's presence made sense, but mine didn't. My locker was two yards away. I was about to excuse myself when his hand landed on the wall, inches from my face.

"Actually," his voice lingered. "I was hoping to run into you."

Zac always said the last thing I wanted to hear.

"Why?"

"I heard what Robb did."

"I don't want to talk to him or you about it," I snapped, but he didn't move away. In fact, he leaned closer.

"I thought you'd want to talk to someone."

I stepped away. "I have Crystal, thanks."

His lips slid into a smirk. "Interesting girl," he said, but his focus remained on me. "I've been talking to her more."

"Good for you." I didn't know what else to say.

"I've gotten closer to her."

He was lying. Crystal was ignoring him, too. "And?"

"And she's your friend," he added.

Crystal was right. Everyone had lost their minds.

"That doesn't mean I know everything about her," I managed, glancing down the hallway, but Zac maneuvered into my vision.

"You seem to know a lot about other people," he said, lowering his face so that his black hair swung in front of his eyes. He lifted his hand and tapped Eric's locker. "Like Welborn."

I crossed my arms, fighting the urge to leave. I wouldn't let Zac scare me out of talking to Eric. I was staying. "He stood up for me—"

"Are you friends?"

I doubted Eric considered me one.

His face was glistening. "More than friends?"

Someone else answered for me. "Definitely not."

I turned around to see Eric standing less than a foot away. His backpack was hanging off one shoulder, and he flipped his keys over his hands.

"Mind if you two have your meeting someplace else?" Eric slid his eyes to me. "Your locker doesn't look occupied."

Zac was between us. "So, you're the guy who hit Robb," he said it like it was a delightful thing.

Eric's shoulders were squared. "Don't tell me he sent someone else to get his revenge."

Zac chuckled, but he rolled up his white sleeves. "I could care less about that," he said, and Eric's stern expression wavered for a millisecond. It was the first time I had seen it happen.

"So, we have nothing to talk about," Eric said, brushing past Zac to his locker.

Zac stepped aside, and I sighed in relief too early. Zac laid a hand on Eric's shoulder, and a burst of static electricity sizzled through the air. Both of them leapt back.

"Ouch." Zac waved his fingers through the air. "Didn't mean to—"

"What?" Eric snapped. "Touch me for no reason?"

Zac was grinning. "Didn't think your bubble would be so small when you're always getting into everyone else's," he said, laying his hand on my shoulder. I shook him off, but Zac didn't seem to care. "Have a good day, Jess."

With that, he was gone, disappearing down the hallway and into the office. When I turned back to Eric, he was staring at me. "Come to yell at me again?" he asked, shoving books into his locker. "Because I was hoping for that."

"It isn't like that—"

"Then, what is it like?" He was more tense than usual. "I come back from fighting one guy only to find another waiting for me." His knuckles were white.

"Zac wasn't waiting for you," I explained quickly. "I was."

My words affected him. His shoulders dropped, and he exhaled sharply. "I already told you what I know."

"I know you're lying, but I don't care," I said, but my voice was shaking. I thought the apology over all night, but it was hard to say it aloud. "I know you wouldn't hurt me, and I'm sorry." It was all I could manage.

Eric held his locker like it was the only thing holding him up. He glanced away, and the side of his jaw popped. He wasn't going to speak. I was rejected again.

I sucked in a breath. I had done everything I could to rebuild what I destroyed, and all that was left to do was walk away. I went straight to my locker, trying to suppress my rapidly beating heart. Only Eric could affect me that way, and I had to ignore it if I were going to function for the remainder of the day.

I put my books away and grabbed my drawing pencils for art class. At least I could distract myself by talking to Jonathon. I wouldn't be completely alone.

"You aren't alone."

I nearly fell over from Eric's voice. He was right next to me. "Wha—what?"

He was smiling. "You were talking out loud."

Heat shot up my spine and crawled across my neck. "I was not."

He ignored me. "If you didn't want to be alone, you could've asked me to walk you to class." He had returned to his usual, smirking self, and I couldn't even bring myself to be irritated.

"Then, walk with me," I said, surprised by myself as I stomped away.

He did exactly what I told him. He bounded up to my side and walked next to me. It took every inch of my confidence to glance over, but he was focused on the hallway, his eyes darting from person to person.

"Are you looking for someone?" I asked.

His face turned so quickly that I was surprised he didn't get whiplash. "Why would you ask that?" His voice was rushed, almost breathless.

"You were glancing around."

"I always do," he said, shifting his backpack higher onto

his shoulders. He was definitely stressed, and I wanted more than anything to help.

"Would you mind if I come over after class?" I asked, hoping to talk to him about whatever was on his mind, but he shook his head as we stopped outside of my classroom.

"I meant it when I said you can't come over anymore." His tone was sharp. "Family stuff."

"Oh."

He laid a hand on top of my head. "Don't worry that curly head of yours." His fingertips brushed across my scalp. "Everything's good between us."

I could barely breathe. "That's good."

He removed his hand only to grab my shoulders. "Now, go to class," he said, spinning me around to face the door. "I'm sure Jonathon is waiting for you." I could feel his words on my neck. "I'll see you later."

His warmth dissipated before I turned around. "But—" He was already walking away, waving over his shoulder like he always expected me to face him again.

43

S HE WAS IMPOSSIBLE TO IGNORE, SO I LEFT SCHOOL EARLY, HOPING to avoid her at least. Teresa—or Camille—joined me as soon as I asked.

"She wasn't talking out loud," I explained to my guard as we strolled down the only shopping street in Hayworth. "I heard her thoughts."

Teresa grimaced. "But that's impossible."

"It should be," I agreed. "She doesn't have any powers."

"Well, obviously she does," Teresa commented, tightening her maroon coat. The color stuck out from the plain, winter clothes everyone seemed to be wearing.

"She doesn't seem to be aware of it," I added, noting how easy it was to convince Jessica that she was talking out loud. She trusted me, even though she had hated me the day before.

Teresa exhaled, and I half-expected to see her breath fog out in front of her. "She needs to know, Eric," she said. "You need to tell her."

"You sound like my father."

"Bracke told me what she said to you," she said, and I wished I hadn't brought Jessica up.

"She meant it, even if it were just for a second," I mumbled.

"And when she gets her memories back, that meaning will disappear," she argued. "The elders know about the list with your name on it. I'm sure Luthicer would take the block down if you talk to him."

I thought of Luthicer's scars. "I don't think we have time for another meeting."

"And we don't have time for your hesitation."

We only had a week until my birthday.

The house was already decorated, and the intensity increased in the air. I had begged my father to take Mindy and Noah away, but he wouldn't. Not when it could expose us more. No matter what we did, every decision felt like the wrong one.

"Her power block would disappear if she got her memories back," Teresa suggested.

"I can't return them on my own." Only Luthicer could.

Teresa shook her head, and her black hair whipped around. "You can get through to her," she said. "If she will listen to anyone, it's you."

I cringed. "I don't know how she'd take all of this at once, especially without proof."

"So, transform in front of her."

"And give her a heart attack?" I couldn't imagine her reaction. "No, thank you."

"At most, she'd faint."

"I don't want that to happen either," I said.

Teresa walked by my side as if we hadn't contemplated taking the Dark's fate into our own hands.

Her sigh ended our debate. "Did anything else happen at school?" she asked, but I knew the real question. She wanted to know if I thought the Light was getting closer.

"No," I confessed. "The only people I saw were Jessica and—Zac." I couldn't say his name without my voice shaking. "I don't like him."

Teresa rolled her eyes. "Because of jealousy."

She was right. "I still don't like him." *And I didn't like how he talked to me.*

"Do you think—" Teresa didn't have to say it.

"He can't be Darthon." I sounded more confident than I felt. "He's all talk, no action. It doesn't fit his profile."

Teresa's head bobbed up and down, but breath escaped in

a hiss. "Personalities can change just as much as the physical transformation."

She was right again. "When did you get so smart?" I joked.

She pushed me with her arm. "You forget how much I've been by your side through this entire mess," she said. But I couldn't forget. I never would. She had witnessed enough that she might as well have been the first descendant. Her life was sacrificed for mine, and mine didn't even belong to me.

As we neared the coffee shop at the end of the street, a question consumed me. "What do you think you'll do when this is all over?"

Her expression was the same one she had when she accepted her guard position. "I'd like to be a therapist," she said, and I realized I didn't know as much about her personal life as she knew about mine. "But I'd come back to Hayworth after school."

The last part astounded me. "Why would you want that?"

Her right shoulder lifted in a half-shrug. "I know," she began. "It's not like my family is around. The Dark raised me. I don't even know where my parents are," she said. "But the Dark is my family. I couldn't leave them."

I didn't think I could either, but I didn't have the choice like she did.

"Do you know what you're going to do?" she asked.

I shook my head. "The war is only a beginning," I repeated the words the elders had said to me. "The Dark will have to adjust to whatever happens afterward."

"They could do that without you."

"I don't think I want them to," I confessed, knowing I wanted to stay, even if I fantasized of leaving.

Teresa didn't say anything after that. She grabbed the door of the coffee shop, and it sprang open before she could pull it. Two girls walked out giggling, only stopping when they met our eyes.

"Jessica," I stumbled over her name before I added a hello.

"Eric." Her cheeks were rosy. "Hey, Teresa."

"You remembered," Teresa chirped, tilting her head. If I

hadn't known better, I would've thought they were acquaintances running into each other on the street. As far as Jessica knew, she had only met Teresa once.

"What are you doing here?" I asked. I left class to avoid her, not to meet her in public. "School is still in."

Jessica fumbled with her purse, but Crystal was the one to respond, "We skipped," she spoke like she deserved an award—which she did. I couldn't fathom how she always got away with it as much as I did. I doubted she was friends with Luthicer.

"Are you taking the day off, too?" Jessica asked, but her voice was quiet.

"Yeah."

"I'm going inside," Teresa said, pretending to shiver, but her eyes were locked with Crystal.

Jessica's friend straightened up. "We're leaving anyway," she said, dragging Jessica behind her. "See you later," she called over her shoulder, and Jessica turned around, her blue eyes as gray as the winter sky. She waved before she turned her back to me and walked down the street with her friend.

When they were out of earshot, Teresa grabbed my arm. "You two really can't stay away from each other, can you?"

I shrugged her off. "It's a coincidence."

"Don't tell me you actually believe that."

"I'm currently convincing myself of it right now," I said.

"It's fate, Eric," she said it like destiny was a factual concept. "She's going to be a part of this war, whether you like it or not."

I didn't like where our conversation was going. "I'd like to have a coffee before I hear another lecture," I said, pushing past her, but her words followed me in.

"*She needs to be able to defend herself,*" Teresa argued in our minds. "*You need to tell her—*"

"*Fine,*" I surrendered. "*I'll tell her.*"

44

Jessica

CRYSTAL CLUTCHED HER STEERING WHEEL AS SHE DROVE THROUGH the outskirts of Hayworth. Her bangs hung above her eyes, and she chewed on her lip ring like it was candy. Driving around town was her new habit, and I was her accomplice.

"Are you stressed out or something?" I asked, wondering if she would continue it for the entirety of winter break.

"What? No." Crystal's tone answered yes. "Why would you ask that?"

"You haven't said anything in a while," I said, wondering how long we had been in the car. It felt like hours.

"So?"

She always had something to talk about, even if it was just petty rumors. "It's unlike you," I stated the obvious, hoping she would confess. But she didn't.

"How are Eric and you doing?" she asked, changing the subject.

My back sank into the passenger seat of her Sedan. "I talked to him about prom."

Crystal's eyes widened. "Is that why it was so awkward running into him?"

I shuddered at the reminder of the coffee shop incident. "He didn't know anything," I said.

"I swear you left to see him."

"So, I didn't leave with him?"

"No," she clarified. "But you danced with him, and you seemed pretty upset when he walked out. I just assumed." She tilted her head. "My hunches are normally right."

I couldn't tell her I believed in her hunch. It was mine, too, but he hadn't talked to me all week. I had endured four days of an awkward silence between us in class. Even though he said we were good, I knew we weren't. "I don't think he likes me."

Crystal groaned and leaned into her steering wheel. "My eyes will be stuck in a permanent roll if you keep talking about him like that."

I giggled, but Crystal turned to me long enough to glare at me.

"The guy practically revolves around you."

I had no idea what she was talking about. "We sit together in class."

"And he got into a fight over you," she argued. "No one does that for fun, not even Welborn."

I cringed, thinking of how protective he was around me, especially with Robb and Zac. I had assumed he was always defensive, but now I wished I could see him when I wasn't around.

"I don't think I could ask him," I managed, unable to tell her the truth—he rejected me, told me to stop coming to his house, and then contradicted himself by walking me to class.

"Well, how do you feel about him?" she asked, and I stared at her, unable to speak. She started giggling. "I guess I don't have to ask that."

"Is it that obvious?" I squeaked, unable to deny my growing emotions. When it started, I didn't know. "I feel like I've known him a long time."

"It's almost been a year since you moved here," she said. "In a way, you have known him a long time."

"I guess I never thought of it that way." I thought about Eric's history—it was filled with death. It was no wonder he rarely smiled. "I just don't think he has an interest in dating me."

"That's not what Zac said."

Her words made my fingers curl into fists. "What?"

"Zac," she repeated. "When I talked to him, he said you were waiting for Eric at his locker. He also said Eric wasn't very happy to see him."

So, Zac hadn't been lying—they were talking.

"Zac shouldn't have gotten in the middle of it," I ranted. "He should've turned in his paperwork and left."

"Paperwork?" Crystal straightened. "He turned that in a long time ago."

"Then, why was he at our school?"

"Hell, if I know," she said. "He didn't say anything to me."

Maybe Eric wasn't wrong to think Zac came to get revenge for Robb. "You don't think—"

My best friend knew me well enough to guess what I was thinking. "He could've been," she said. "Zac's really protective of Robb and Linda. In fact, those three are inseparable," she said it like she was never a part of their clique.

"What about you?"

Her eyes darted around the street. "They've known each other since birth," she said. "I came in later. It's not something I can fix."

I stared at my friend, realizing she was more like me than I thought. She didn't have many friends because of her gossip column. What students didn't know was how loyal Crystal was. Classmates would have had less of a chance of appearing in the newspaper if they talked to her like a normal human being.

"I'm sorry, Crystal," I said. "If I hadn't gotten involved, you wouldn't have to pick a side."

"Sides aren't something that are picked, Jess," she said. "They happen because of our morals, and I was brought up better than they were. Obviously."

I couldn't help but think about her poor relationship with her mother, and Crystal looked at me like she was expecting my reaction.

"I know I complain about Lola," she said. "But I really respect how she raised me singlehandedly."

"Then, why act like you don't?"

She was stifling her laughter. "You are the strangest teenager I know," she said. "You always seem so put together, even when things are happening to you. I'm envious."

She wouldn't have said it if she knew how I had treated Eric.

"I'm not that great," I managed.

"But you are," she argued. "And you get along with your parents—"

"I'm adopted."

My interruption silenced Crystal, and her face flushed.

I sighed, looking up at the ceiling of her car. "Do you remember that car wreck I had you research? The one where the couple died?"

She nodded. "And the baby—"

"That's me."

Her fingers turned white as her grip tightened on the steering wheel. "You were born here?"

It wasn't the question I was expecting. I expected her to demand why I hid it, why I lied, or why I pretended a part of my life wasn't falling apart. Not what she had asked.

"Yeah," I said. "Why is that important?"

"It's not," she said, but her voice was tight. "But I always wondered where you got that gorgeous hair of yours." She was laughing, and I couldn't help but join her. I didn't resemble my adoptive parents, and it felt good to finally admit why.

"Thanks for understanding," I said.

She wagged her finger at me. "Don't think that distracted me from Eric."

I groaned, and she jiggled in her seat. "Don't you see how he looks at you?" she asked, but I couldn't answer. He always looked like he was in pain. "It's pretty obvious how he feels."

"Then, why would he ignore me?"

"Because boys are complicated," Crystal explained.

"I thought girls were the complicated ones," I joked, but Crystal wasn't laughing.

"If I've learned anything from journalism, it's that everyone is complicated," she said.

Seconds Before Sunrise

I looked out the window. The fields on the edge of town reminded me of how isolated the Midwest was compared to Atlanta. When I lived in Georgia, I hadn't known many people despite being in a homeschooling program that introduced me to other teenagers. I felt isolated. I had given up on the concept of friends until I met Crystal and Robb. Out of all the places I could've found friendship, it ended up being in an isolated town.

Crystal's stereo vibrated the car as she zoomed past the last corner of Hayworth. I tensed when a red light flickered past a fence by the road.

"What's that?" I asked.

Crystal turned her stereo down. "What's what?" she asked, peering out the same window.

I blinked, and it was gone. I shook my head, wondering if my lack of sleep was affecting my vision again. "Never mind," I dismissed my question, looking over my shoulder to see the red light again. It wasn't there.

"We could get him a gift," Crystal suggested, and I had to replay our conversation to realize she was still talking about Eric.

"Christmas is weeks away."

"His birthday isn't," she said. "It's in a few days, isn't it?"

"I forget you guys used to be friends," I mumbled, but Crystal ignored me.

"We'll go shopping," she continued, winking. "And then you'll give it to him, and he'll realize how he feels about you."

My stomach twisted. "That's kind of superficial."

"Do you have a better plan?"

I didn't and couldn't deny it.

"Okay," I sighed, forcing my hopes down. I didn't want to get excited if I were only going to be let down again. "But I don't know what to get him." I didn't even know what he liked.

"That's what shopping is for," Crystal said, turning her car toward town. "It'll be fun."

45

W HEN I TRANSPORTED, IT WAS SNOWING. JESSICA'S YARD WAS
silent, and her house was as dark as my midnight
timing. She was probably sleeping, completely un-
aware that my birthday was two days away. She didn't even
know my best friend was guarding her house.

"Shoman," Pierce's grumble appeared before he did. A
black hole stretched across the grass, and he stepped out of
it. "You could've at least been a little more discrete with your
arrival."

His nonchalant attitude confused me.

He chuckled. "Camille already told me the plan."

Of course she did. "So, you'll help me?"

He cracked his neck. "I'll help you until the end," he said,
speaking like there would be one. "I've been scouting the area
since the list."

My eyes darted around the front yard. He was right. Darthon could be waiting. "Any sign of him?"

"None," he said. "Just don't let your guard down."

"But Camille isn't here," I punned, and his cocky demean-
or shifted.

"It's my job to make jokes at times like this," he said, and
we laughed as if we weren't rebelling against the Dark. When
our laughter died, I stared at Jessica's bedroom window.

"Are you actually going to do this?" he whispered, and the

snow shook the nearest tree as if it knew how I was feeling.

"How long do I have?" I asked.

"Five minutes," Pierce said, laying out his hands. The world rippled with green waves of light, expanding and contorting around the house. "Starting now."

And I was gone, transporting into her bedroom before my thoughts could hold me back. The cold air slammed against my chest, cooler than outside, and I gasped as I solidified. I wasn't prepared for it.

"It's you."

I wasn't prepared for that either.

Her startled voice echoed against my eardrums, and I pressed my back against the wall. My eyes locked onto her, sitting up in her bed, fully awake—like she was expecting me.

"You—you're—"

"Real," I finished, unsure of what else to say.

She was barely moving, and the expression on her face wasn't comforting.

"Please, don't scream," I said. "But you're not dreaming—not this time."

Her fingers curled around her blankets. "I won't scream," she said, but her voice shook.

I crossed the room before she could say anything else. I sat on her bed, grabbed her hand, and her fingers shook beneath my touch. "These dreams you're having—"

"They aren't dreams." Her tone suggested she had always known.

It was too late to turn back. "We took your memory away, okay? But you're in trouble, and there's a man after you, and—"

"That explains a few things," she said before she kissed me, and it was unlike any kiss we had ever shared. It was desperate. She wanted it, even without knowing me, and I wanted her more than anything. I had to push her away.

"We can't," I breathed.

Her forehead pressed against mine. "I know."

"Jessica, I came here to tell you what we took from you."

She blinked.

"The Dark—"

"Why'd you take my memory?" she asked.

I stared at her, unsure if I had the time to explain. "It was your plan," I admitted, remembering the moment she proposed the idea in front of everyone, willingly giving me up for the safety of others. "Do you remember anything?" I asked, even though I already knew the answer.

"I don't remember anything," she said. "Should I?"

Camille's theory was wrong. Even I couldn't break the seal on her. I grabbed her hands, pulling her to her feet. "I have to take you to the shelter." I didn't care how much trouble we would get in.

She let me go and stepped back. She wasn't coming.

I turned around, gaping at her. "You need your powers," I said. "And they're the only ones who can return them."

She was glaring. "Then, why wouldn't you do that in the first place?" She wasn't even scared to learn she had powers. It was completely unlike the first time I met her. "You're in trouble because of this." Her guess reminded me of the intuition she always had about the Dark's matters.

"We'll be in more trouble if this Darthon guy knows who we are," I argued, but a glaze slid over her eyes.

"I know it's you, Eric."

Her words stole my breath.

"And I bet they do, too," she said.

I let her go. "I have to go," I said, turning away, but she grabbed my hand.

"Are you going to be okay?"

I couldn't look back at her. She knew as much as the Light did, and she didn't even have to be a supernatural being to figure it out. "You'll be fine."

"I wasn't talking about me," she said. "I was asking about you."

I thought of the war—how Darthon suspected me, how my name was on a list, how Jessica was probably on another list. "If I don't give up, I should be." But I already felt like I was surrendering. Jessica wasn't safe, neither was I, and we couldn't protect one another. We never could.

"Promise me you won't give up," she said, but doom had never felt more inevitable.

"I love you, Jessica," I said.

From behind me, she wrapped her arms around my back, and I stared at her petite hands in the dark. "Please, don't say it like it's a death sentence," she whispered. "Wait until I come back, and say it again."

"Okay," I said, disappearing before I admitted the truth.

I didn't know if I would have the chance to say it again.

46

Jessica

I COULDN'T BREATHE, AND IT DIDN'T MATTER HOW MUCH TIME passed.

After Eric—whatever he was—left, I stayed awake to prove I hadn't been dreaming. He was the same man I dreamt about, and a part of me had known that since I kissed him during my drunken stupor. Kissing him again was the only confirmation I needed, but I didn't know what to do with the information.

The sunrise burned my eyes, but nothing was as painful as the reality my dreams had morphed into. The Dark was real, even if I didn't know what it was, and Eric wasn't human. I had to remind myself that I wasn't either.

I clutched my mug of hot tea, ignoring the heat as it spread over my fingertips. I had powers. What they entailed, I didn't know, but I used to know. I used to know everything, including what happened at prom. I couldn't believe I had given it up to protect people I couldn't even remember, people who were in trouble.

I laid my head in my hands and gripped my scalp, knowing I had literally lost my mind. I wasn't any better than anyone else.

"Jessie?"

I sprang up, hitting my knees on the table, and my tea splashed over the rim. I waved my hand in the air and hissed before my mom walked around me.

207

"Are you okay?" she asked, grabbing a paper towel off the countertop. She handed it to me as I wiped the hot liquid away, but I couldn't look at her. Did she even know who—or what—she adopted?

"Mom," I began as she sat down. "Did I—" I didn't even know how to word it. Did I have powers as a kid? Was I different? How was I supposed to ask something that would possibly put me in an asylum?

"What's bothering you, sweetheart?" she asked, folding her hands on the table. She looked like she had gotten less sleep than I did.

"Why'd you adopt me?" I blurted out the only phrase I could muster.

She smiled like she had heard the question one hundred times. "Your father and I couldn't have kids," she said, reaching over to grab my hand. I knew she could feel my fingers shaking. "It's been a blessing."

She sounded like a Hallmark card. "Was it ever difficult?" I asked. "Was I ever different?"

"Different?" she repeated the word like she didn't know the meaning.

"Did you ever look into my biological parents' health records? Things like that," I tried to justify my question, but she seemed to be slipping further away. If the Dark had taken my memories, I didn't doubt they did it to her, too.

"Are you having problems?" she asked, her eyebrows squeezing together. "You can tell me anything."

Yeah, right. Like explaining how a boy from school had appeared in my bedroom as a totally different person would be accepted.

"No," I sighed, hanging my head and moving my hand away. "I'm okay."

"Having nightmares again?"

I tensed as if I hadn't told her, even though I knew I had. But the meaning had changed—now they were real.

"I had them as a kid, right?" I asked, remembering her talk about it.

"You grew out of them the further we moved away. It was one of the reasons I didn't want to move back," she said, tying her hair up. "There's something not right with this town."

"I don't want to move again," I said it without contemplating the words, but it was the truth. I was meant to be in Hayworth. Every part of me knew it.

"But—"

"I like it here," I said, standing up from the table. "I'm sorry if I worried you." My words sounded forced, but she accepted it. It was as if she had forgotten how to discipline me.

"Don't worry, Jessie," she said. "We aren't planning to leave any time soon."

I knew my next move. "Can I borrow the car?" I asked. "I told Crystal I'd go Christmas shopping today."

"Sure," she said, gesturing to the key ring on the wall. "Take a fifty, too. Get something for yourself."

"Thanks, Mom." I tried not to sound guilty.

There was only one person I wanted to see, and it wasn't Crystal.

I went upstairs, threw on clothes, and grabbed Eric's birthday present. He wanted me to stay away, but I couldn't. I had to confront him, and he was the only thing on my mind as I rushed downstairs.

"Bye," I shouted, knowing my parents were lingering within earshot.

I opened the door and rushed into the cold, stopping short when I reached our front porch.

"I tried calling you," Crystal said, wrapping her arms around her torso as my eyes darted behind her.

Robb and Zac were in my driveway.

"What are they doing here?" I hissed.

Crystal rolled her dark eyes. "Robb wants to make up," she said. "I couldn't stop them, so I came with them." Her frustration grew into a frown. "Trust me, this isn't my idea of a good time."

I tightened my coat as my heart slammed itself against my ribs. If Eric was right, someone was after me, and his name was Darthon. But Eric had looked like a completely different person. I didn't know if Robb and Zac were who they said they were.

"I don't want to make up," I shouted to the boys as I stomped past Crystal. I only wanted to leave, but Robb's Suburban was behind my car. I couldn't leave until they did.

"I told you it was impossible," Robb mumbled, but Zac didn't give up.

"It'll only take a minute."

I dug my boots into the freshly fallen snow. "It should take a lot longer than a minute to make up for what Robb did," I argued.

"So, let's take a couple of hours," Zac suggested. "All of us can get lunch and talk." He was smirking. "Unless you're too tired, of course. You look like you didn't sleep last night."

I had seen myself in the mirror. My lack of sleep wasn't obvious, but I bet my shaking hands were. Zac's eyes were all over them.

"Who's the present for?" he questioned.

I tightened my grip, hoping my fingers would lock in place, and turned to Robb. "I'd appreciate if you got your car out of my driveway," I said.

Robb's eyes widened when I met his gaze. He hadn't been expecting it.

"I'd do anything to make it up to you, Jess," he spoke as if he hadn't heard what I said. "Anything."

"See?" Zac's voice had deepened. "He cares about you."

"And Linda?" I asked, hoping to gain an advantage. "I would think she'd want to be a part of this conversation." I doubted she even knew what Robb did.

"Come on, Jess," Zac coaxed. "Let's focus on the problem here. Robb was drunk and—" His black eyes dipped to my neck, but I knew my bruises were gone. "Robb hit you." His tone made my injuries feel as if they'd returned.

"He choked me," I corrected in a shaky voice.

The darkness in Zac's eyes was suddenly more frightening than what Robb had done. I moved away only for him to reposition himself.

I glared at him. "There's nothing to discuss."

He leaned in. "But haven't you been through worse?"

I froze as Crystal rushed to my side. She grabbed my arm like she was my bodyguard. "She doesn't want to talk about this," she said, but her voice was quieter than usual.

Zac skimmed his hand across her arm. "Friendships shouldn't end so easily, don't you think?"

It wasn't easy, I thought. Crystal didn't argue, and I couldn't speak. Zac knew something, and he had threatened me with it.

"You were both drunk," Zac continued, controlling the debate. "Neither of you knew what you were doing."

Robb sulked over from his Suburban, his hands in his pockets. "I know it isn't forgivable," he said. "But I can try to make it up to you."

"And everyone can use more friends," Zac added. "No one likes to be alone."

His words lingered like his continuous threat. It hadn't even occurred to me that going out alone was dangerous because I was too focused on Eric.

"I'm not alone," I said, gesturing to Crystal, and she straightened up.

"But she wants you two to be friends again," Zac spoke for her, meeting her eyes. "Or is that not what you told me last night?"

I whipped around to face her, and the flush of her cheeks gave away her guilt.

"I thought you were on my side," I said.

"I am," she squeaked, signaling what I was already thinking. She was a completely different person when Zac was around.

"She just wants her friends to get along," Zac said. "Is that so bad?"

He made it sound simple, like Robb and I had argued over what party to go to, but it wasn't. And my life wasn't either. Petty drama couldn't even be compared to what had happened the night before.

"Think of everything Robb's helped you through, Jess," Zac said. "Like your nightmares." He brought up my biggest problem like he could read my mind. "Those stopped, didn't they?"

When I looked at him, he was grinning. Next to me, Crystal looked like she would faint over his smile. Robb folded his arms. I only wanted to get away, but I didn't want to be alone, and I wasn't sure how to trust Crystal. I had a decision to make, and I had to make it quickly.

I turned to Robb. "I can try to forgive you."

His eyebrows shot up. "Really?" His tone was as heightened as when we met. "You mean that, Jess?"

I forced a nod. "But I can't hang out. I need to go somewhere," I said, grabbing Crystal. "And you're coming with me."

"What?" She couldn't comprehend why I wanted her around. She didn't know that I needed her as protection.

"I'm running errands that need your expertise," I said, eyeing her until she agreed. My anger was second to my situation with Eric, so I turned to the boys. "We'll get lunch tomorrow."

"I'm busy tomorrow," Robb spoke before Zac for the first time. "Both of us are."

"Then, next week," I dismissed, moving toward my car. "We'll get together then."

"Okay," Robb agreed, bouncing up with newfound energy. "Thank you, Jess."

"Sure thing," I responded, and Robb ran back to his car, ready to move it.

Zac, however, didn't move. "Mind if I talk to Jess for a minute, Crystal?" he asked her without moving his eyes away from me.

She blinked, and Zac grabbed her arm, pulling her close. He laid a kiss on her lips, and I sucked in a breath. "I'll call you later," he said, and she left like he controlled her.

When she was out of earshot, I folded my arms. "Your relationship sure took off."

He dragged his thumb over his lip. "Jealous?"

Heat spread over my face. "You better be good to her," I warned, but he didn't budge.

"I was wrong about you, Jess," he said, walking past me. "You are capable."

I watched his back, contemplating my own verbal assault until he disappeared into Robb's car. They backed out, and Zac waved before I rushed to my car. I threw Eric's present in the backseat and got behind the wheel, slamming the door behind me.

"Dump him," I said.

Crystal looked like she would cry. "I'm sorry. I wanted to talk to you first, but—"

"You didn't hear me, did you?" I turned my torso to glare at her. "I don't care about you coming over with Robb. Just dump Zac."

She was pale. "I—I can't. I like him."

"He's an asshole," I said, telling her what he said as he left.

Her lip quivered like she couldn't fathom it. "He's sweet to me," she justified. "He's probably still hurt from prom."

"That's not an excuse," I said, and Crystal was quiet. "You can do better, and you know it."

"I'm not like you, Jess," she said, and I reached across the car to shake her shoulders. When I stopped, her eyes were wide.

"You're smart, capable, and pretty," I argued. "You don't need them."

"But you forgave Robb," she said. "Doesn't that mean something?"

I couldn't tell her I only forgave him to get them to leave. I had someone after me, and Zac seemed to know about it. I didn't want to think about how close I came to meeting whoever was after me. "I guess," I surrendered, knowing I needed to keep myself safe before I dealt with my personal life.

I started the engine and backed out of the driveway, trying not to dwell on my emotions. I didn't have time for that.

"Are we dropping off Eric's present?" Crystal asked, knowing what was inside.

"No," I said, unsure of how close I could get to him without risking everything. "We're going Christmas shopping, and you're sleeping over."

47

"**H**APPY BIRTHDAY," MINDY CHEERED AS I LIFTED NEW HEAD-phones out of the box she had wrapped them in. "I hope you like them."

"They're great." I attempted to look excited. "Thank you."

"He'll use them so much he'll need a new pair next year," George joked.

Jonathon tried to grab the glass from his father's hand. "You've had too much to drink," he said, but George pulled away.

"Nonsense." The beer sloshed around. "It's Eric's birthday. We're here to celebrate."

"*Or get so drunk that we can't remember the prophetic battle,*" Jonathon ranted to me.

"*He'll be fine,*" I said, hoping to calm my friend, but we both knew it was a lie. How George would fight drunk was beyond me, but he also had hours until it happened. The sun wouldn't set for a while.

"My present—on the table," George slurred.

"Thanks, George," I said, moving upstairs. Teresa and Jonathon followed me. We sat at the kitchen table, overlooking the living room, and Noah bounced around us.

"What is it?" he asked.

Mindy waved her son away. "Let them talk, Noah," she said, and he obeyed her without a pout. He was continuing to mature, and I wanted to reward him for it.

"Here," I said, handing it to my stepbrother. "You open it."

He grabbed it. "Really?"

"Why not?"

His grin looked like it could break his face in half, and he tore the gift open. "It's a gift card." He sounded disappointed.

"I thought putting it in a big box would be funny," George laughed to himself, turning to my silent father. "What did you get him, Jim?"

"He already gave me a present," I answered for him. Everyone had curious stares but my father. His old, brown eyes lit up, and we nodded to each other, knowing the black box my mother left me was possibly the most important gift I would ever receive. But I didn't want to talk about it.

"I got you another present," my father said, resting against the wall. I wondered if he drank as much as George did. "I just haven't picked it up yet."

My brow rose. "Another one?" "*You didn't need to do that.*"

"*Yes, I did,*" he responded telepathically first. "I'm giving it to you after your birthday," he explained. "I want to make sure you can survive the responsibility of being eighteen before I give it to you."

Everyone laughed like it was a joke, even though mostly everyone knew it wasn't.

I laid my hands in my lap and stared at the table as the adults started their own conversation. Noah ran to his bedroom, and I knew no one would hear us.

Teresa laid a hand on my shoulder. "It's still your birthday," she said. "Try to enjoy what you can. We don't even know if it'll happen tonight."

"It's my birthday," I grumbled. "It's happening tonight."

"If it were that simple, the Light would be knocking on your front door," she argued.

"But they want a war," Jonathon said. "And it's obviously to their advantage."

"They want to wait." Teresa suddenly took our side. "But I don't see why."

"Me neither." I knew the Light had said they wanted to take out as many people with them as possible, but the theory relied solely on their downfall. A war was their surrender, but they weren't acting as if they were giving up. They were still after Jessica and me.

"It didn't work," I said, informing Camille of the situation with Jessica.

"What do you mean it didn't work?"

"I don't think I have to explain it more than I already have," I said. "She doesn't remember, and she doesn't want to."

Teresa's glance shifted between Jonathon and me. "But she needs to defend herself."

"It's too late, Camille." It was useless to hide her Dark name on the day of the battle.

"No," she said, standing up. "It's not."

I grabbed her arm as she attempted to rush away. "What are you thinking?" I hissed, knowing my father was watching.

"I can do everything Luthicer can," she entered my mind, and my stomach twisted. She didn't care if my father could sense it. She was going to force the spell off.

"You could hurt her," I said, refusing to let go of my guard.

She laid her hand on mine and slowly pulled my fingers off her wrist. "And you need to trust me," she said before turning around and walking down the steps.

I followed her, brushing past my family. "I'm walking Teresa out."

"Me, too," Jonathon joined.

We had the front door open before anyone could question us, and we had frozen in the doorway before we realized what was in front of us.

A young girl stood on the driveway. Her hair was as white as the recent snowfall, and her eyes were pools of ink, yet she somehow stared at us. She was a light.

I slammed the door behind me, and Jonathon put up a silence barrier, but we couldn't transform. Not until sunset. And we were hours away. Teresa was the only one capable of protecting my family, and she was Camille before I could order her to transform.

In a second, my guard's hands were wrapped around the girl's hair, and the light's face was shoved into the ground. If I hadn't grabbed Camille's arm, she would've broken her neck.

"I'm on your side," the girl screamed, but Camille didn't let go of the girl's hair. Their resemblance made them look like sisters. "Shoman, I swear—"

Camille stepped on her face. She didn't need a weapon to silence the child.

"Let her speak," I ordered my guard, but Camille refused to look away from the enemy.

"She's an intruder," Camille said, but she didn't kill her. "You can't trust anything she says."

"I'll decide that," I said, and Camille's foot moved to the girl's back. She wasn't letting her get up.

The light whimpered, and I knelt down to meet her eyes. "You're safe," I said, knowing my words were debatable.

"Thank you, Shoman," the girl squeaked, and I tensed, knowing my identity was gone. She tried to push herself up, but I grabbed her shoulder.

"I don't control her," I said, pointing to my guard. "Stay on the ground."

The child's eyes were filled with tears. "Promise me a life, and I'll guarantee your survival at the battle."

"He's destined to win," Camille said, grinding her foot into the girl's back. "He doesn't have to promise you anything."

"I promise," I said, ignoring my guard.

The girl wriggled. "Let me up."

"She's asking for too much," Camille said, but I glared at her, and she moved off the light.

The girl squirmed to her knees before she made it to her feet. "I'm not like them, the other lights," she began.

Camille interrupted her. "So, stop babbling and tell us why you're here."

The girl shivered, stepping away from my guard. "Stop protecting the third descendant," she said. "Can't you see that's what the Light wants?"

I couldn't breathe.

"What are you saying, light?" Jonathon was in-between us, and the girl was panicking.

"Darthon can't survive without the third descendant," she said. "All your protection does is give them a chance at winning," she ranted. "If she dies, he dies. It's that simple—"

Jonathon stopped her. "We won't kill the third descendant."

The girl turned her face and focused on me. Her cheeks were pale. "You're actually in love with her?"

It was the last thing she would ever say.

A beam of light blew out of her eyes, and her mouth hung open, releasing a gasp. Her ribs folded in on one another, a cracking sound splitting the air, and she crumbled to the driveway. She was a human, and she was dead.

Jonathon stumbled back, falling into me, and I grabbed him, unable to look away from Camille. Her fingertips were shaking, and her hair was spiked up, hinting at her powers. She had killed her, and did it without touching the girl. I was reminded of what Luthicer said about half-breeds struggling with their conscience. For the first time, Camille didn't seem to have one.

"There are other ways to kill lights," she mumbled, falling back into her human form with ease. It was enough to know she had killed before. "You didn't need to listen to that."

The girl's warning was echoing inside of me. "Jessica's safe," I said, knowing Darthon wouldn't kill her. "She's been safe this entire time."

"Then, why would she warn us?" Teresa spat. "It's probably the opposite, Eric, and that girl was trying to convince you to kill someone to guarantee their survival."

"I would never kill Jessica."

"She obviously didn't think it through," Teresa said. "But Darthon will if it means you'll die along with her."

Teresa was convinced it was the opposite, that I would die instead of Darthon, but the look in the girl's eyes had been too convincing. I'd even promised her life, and it hadn't happened.

"If they know who you are, they are going after her right now," Teresa continued. "She needs to be able to defend herself."

"You can't go to her now," Jonathon said.

"And why not?"

"Because she's with Crystal—"

"You're Jessica's guard, and as a guard, your duty is to protect her first," Camille said. "Not her human friend."

Jonathon didn't have an argument.

"Where is she right now?"

Jonathon grabbed Camille's hand, and a spark flickered between them. Teresa's blue eyes were black pits for only a millisecond, and I knew Jonathon had transferred his tracking. "You should know now," he said.

"Thank you," she said, turning to me. "You need to prepare yourself. This is about to get ugly." She transported away as the front door opened, and a golden light spread over the girl's body.

The door shut. "What happened here?" my father asked, rushing forward, and Jonathon divulged everything with impressive speed.

"What do we do?" Jonathon asked, and my father picked up the girl's body.

"I'll take care of this," he said it like he had picked up the trash. "You two go with George to the shelter until sunset." The directions sounded far away. "There's a war waiting for us."

48

Jessica

CRYSTAL HAD SLEPT OVER, AND I PROMISED HER A COFFEE FOR staying. We were sitting in the coffee shop, only silent because her obsession with pumpkin flavoring kept her lips on her mug. I didn't mind if it meant avoiding the topic of Robb and Zac. She had already apologized too many times for me to handle.

"Are you seeing him today?" Crystal asked, breaking away from her drink.

I was barely listening. "Who?"

"Eric," she said, sipping once more. "It's his birthday, remember?"

I knew it was, but I wasn't sure if I could get close to him. The more time that passed since his visit, the more I believed I couldn't help him. "I'm not seeing him."

She pouted. "Why not?"

"He's busy." I acted as if I had spoken to him. I wanted to avoid talking about Eric as much I wanted to avoid talking about the other boys.

"Seems everyone is busy today," she said, glancing around the shop. For a weekend, it was unusually empty. We were the only customers, and Crystal had no problem pointing directly at the owner. "I think he's closing up early."

I glanced over my shoulder and watched him as he cleaned up. "Sorry, girls," he said, shrugging one shoulder. "I'm closing in fifteen."

I groaned, turning back to Crystal. "Looks like it."

She wasn't nearly as upset as I was. In fact, her eyes lit up with curiosity. "Is something going on?" she asked the owner, but he didn't respond. She lowered her head and whispered, "I wonder what's gotten into everyone. All the hotels in town are booked. Even Zac and Robb are busy."

She mentioned everything I didn't want to think about, and my stomach twisted with nausea. Whatever was going on had to do with Eric's visit, and I hated to dwell on something I couldn't fix. I wanted to talk to Crystal more than ever, but I bit my lip to stay silent.

"I am sorry—" she started, but I stopped her before we could repeat the same conversation again.

"It's fine."

"But it doesn't feel fine," she whined. "And I don't want to go home feeling like that."

A panic rose in my chest. "When are you going home?"

"My mom is coming to pick me up."

I sighed, laying my head on my hands. I couldn't be mad even though I wanted to be. She couldn't stay with me forever, and I would be alone before I knew it. "Can your mom pick you up at my house?"

"She's already on her way."

Of course she was.

"I texted her when I saw he was closing," she said. Her mom would be here within minutes.

"It's okay."

"Listen, Jess," Crystal said, touching my arm. "If something's going on, you can tell me."

But I couldn't. Not without looking crazy. Even if I could tell her, I doubted I would. It was hard to trust her since she was dating Zac. I could only hope she would take my advice and get rid of him.

"Nothing's going on," I said, and she accepted it without an argument.

Her phone buzzed on the table, signaling the end of our

conversation. "Lola's here," she said, standing up. "I'll see you later?"

"Sure," I managed.

She left, and the soft music seemed louder than before. It stopped, and I turned my chair around to face the owner. "Mind if I stay for a minute?"

"Only ten more," he said, continuing to clean. "I have to be somewhere."

"Thanks," I said, watching the clock as time inched forward and wondering if I would have to face whoever was after me the second I left alone.

49

FOOTSTEPS ECHOED OFF THE UNDERGROUND WALLS OF THE SHELter, but no one spoke. Shades rushed around, avoiding eye contact, and suited up, dressing in lavish garbs as if they were going to a fancy party instead of a death match.

Boys and girls wore thick, leather pants, and they braided their long hair down their backs. The youngest fighters had taken the opportunity to paint their faces with the colors of their powers—emerald-greens, midnight-blues, and moonlight-silvers. I yearned to see the royal purple Jessica's powers had, but she was the only one I knew of with that color, and she wasn't here.

"Put these on." Urte—the previously drunk George—spoke without a slur to his tone and threw us heavy clothes without swaying. "We'll leave soon."

"You sobered up quickly," Pierce muttered, throwing on the bigger jacket.

"Alcohol doesn't affect my shade self," his father said without explaining if it was exclusive to him.

Pierce got dressed instead of asking. "These are surprisingly comfortable," he said, squaring his shoulders as he shook his arms out. The sleeves fit him perfectly.

I sulked into mine. "I don't see why these are necessary," I said, even though I did. It was added protection, but I didn't want to admit that I needed it. Not when the battle was close enough to taste in the air.

"You'll be fine," Pierce said, jumping up and down. "Are you ready?" I half-expected him to punch me in the arm like we were preparing for a sporting event.

I didn't answer as Urte walked around the crowded room. Everyone was awaiting his orders, knowing we had to obey the second he spoke them. One man vomited in the corner while another pulled him to his feet. A woman, perhaps his sister or girlfriend, ignored his nausea in shame. I wanted to tell him it wasn't shameful, but the crowd stared at me.

I was their descendant, and my actions would dictate how long the war lasted. There would be death before daylight, but we didn't have to wait for daylight to end it. The quicker I killed Darthon, the less of a massacre there would be. But I couldn't afford to think about my people if I were going to stay focused. They knew it as much as I despised it.

"We're going," Urte spoke as his eyes flashed. "To the hill," he ordered, and the room filled with the smoke of those who transported first.

I followed before I could see if anyone lingered.

When I reformed, I was standing on my favorite place in Hayworth. The grass was blanketed with a thin layer of snow, but the willow tree swayed like it was summer. A leaf brushed my shoulder before my heart even had a chance to pound.

The sun was setting, and the small slit of sunlight burned my vision. I could only see the field in front of us, littered with an array of shades, young and old, but I didn't see the slightest trace of the Light.

"Where are they?" I asked to no one in particular.

"They're here," Urte answered, standing in front of his son. "They're just hiding."

The hill looked odd with dozens of black-haired, light-eyed people walking from side to side. Snow shifted beneath them, turning into misty rivers, but the weather was to their disadvantage. Our dark hair would stand out in the moonlit reflection of the snow.

I glanced from face to face, trying not to think about

which ones would die. "Where's Camille?" I asked, wondering how long it had been since she went after Jessica.

"I don't know," Pierce admitted.

I tried to send out a telepathic message, but it crackled out.

"I already tried," Pierce said, knowing what I had done.

My gut twisted, and I distracted my worries with a checklist. My father was present. He was with Luthicer, and Eu hovered nearby. I glanced around, wondering which woman was his wife, Ida, and I regrettably remembered their daughters, too young to fight, too old to be oblivious. The amount of families who would lose someone in the battle shook me.

"Where are they keeping the kids?" I asked Pierce.

"Not at the shelter," he said. "Too dangerous."

I thought of his brother, knowing he didn't have anyone to look after him tonight. "Where's Brenthan?"

"Home," he answered without a flinch. "I only hope he stays there."

Brenthan was only thirteen, but he had a warrior's heart. He wasn't the only kid who might show up despite the laws against it.

I opened my mouth to keep talking—why, I didn't know—but I stopped myself when the sun dipped beneath the horizon. I took one breath before the edge of the valley, covered by trees, shifted.

A light crawled out on her hands and knees, her hipbone jutting out. Her limbs contorted as they outstretched, and she stood. Her short hair spiked up, blending in with the falling snow, and her dark skin glittered.

Every shade faced the singular woman as she marched forward. She only stopped when she reached the middle of the field. She paid no attention to us as she dusted twigs off her thin clothes, not even bothering with armor. When she finally looked up, the forest was shaking, and more lights—dozens of them—crawled out to join her. She was soon lost to the crowd.

The lights were a collection of creatures I couldn't have imagined on my own. Some had three arms. Others had weapons that looked impossible to carry. Their fingernails outstretched like blades, and their flushed faces suggested they were waiting longer than I thought.

"They aren't human," Pierce muttered, tensing.

I smirked, fighting the urge to correct him. None of us were.

"Don't forget, they can use illusions," I said. Their extra limbs and heavy weapons were probably fake, designed to shake us. I wouldn't let their tactics invoke fear.

Pierce nodded, but I doubted he heard me. "When do we attack?"

I waited, studying the crowd as they spread out. They were standing still, refusing to begin the battle. "Darthon isn't here," I said, but I was, and the lights were pointing at me. They knew my face.

"Should we wait just because they are?" he asked.

"There's no point in starting something without the end in sight," I said.

He dug his toes into the snow. "What if that light wasn't lying?" Pierce asked the last question I wanted to hear.

The little girl's death was the first of many, but her words were worse.

"Do you think she was?" I managed.

"No," Pierce admitted.

"Me neither."

"But—"

I met Pierce's green eyes with a glare. "I'll choose Jessica over the Dark," I said, knowing the Dark would expect me to kill her if they knew the truth.

Pierce was grimacing. "You won't have to."

"You heard her—"

"And, apparently, you didn't," he argued. "She didn't say Jess must die for Darthon to. She only said her death would kill Darthon." He gestured to my hands. "You can still kill him with those."

I stared at my palms, stretching my fingers to the cold. Pierce was right. I was the only one who could kill Darthon.

We figured that out the moment Jessica broke his neck and he resurrected.

"But I suggest keeping your decision to choose Jessica over the Dark a secret," Pierce said.

When I looked up he was smiling, and I laid a hand on his shoulder, knowing he wouldn't tell. "I haven't thanked any of you enough."

"Don't start your eulogy yet," he muttered, suddenly freezing in his stance. "It's only the beginning," he finished.

I followed his gaze to the field.

In the middle of Darthon's people, a beam of light spread out, and it shattered like glass. A man stepped out of the remnants, and he lifted his chin toward the hill. Even with his hollow eyes, I knew he was looking at me when his lip curled. Without a word, he lifted his hand, the lights roared, and the field exploded.

50

Jessica

I LEFT WITH THE OWNER AND WATCHED AS HE LOCKED UP THE SHOP behind us. The street was eerily dark, and I shivered, wishing I had worn a heavier coat. The snow had started up again, and I shoved my hands in my pockets instead of getting my car keys ready. I wanted to ask the man to walk me to my car, but he was sweating profusely.

"Are you okay?" I asked.

He swung his keys around his fingers. "Get home safely," he croaked, ignoring my question. "This weather can get nasty—"

As he spoke, the ground shook, and I grabbed the brick wall to prevent myself from falling. The lantern hanging over the door fell and shattered at my feet, and I jumped back. When I met eyes with the owner, his were wide.

"What was that?" My voice shook as much as the ground.

"I'm late," he said, turning to run away. He didn't get far.

A hand grabbed the side of his face, slamming his head into the wall. His unconscious body crumbled to the ground, and a woman stood in his place.

It was Teresa.

"What did you do?" I screeched.

She rushed forward to grab my shoulders. "You need to calm down, okay?" Her voice fogged out in a rush. "I'm with Eric."

His name consumed my racing heart, but I still pulled away. "I don't know what you're talking about," I said, trying to leave, but she gripped my hand.

"I'm not Darthon," she said, somehow knowing the conversation Eric and I had shared.

"I—I—" I couldn't tear my eyes away from the helpless man.

"It was necessary," she said. "He could've hurt you."

"He was leaving."

"To fight Eric," she said, and my body ached. Everyone knew what was happening but me.

"Leave me alone," I said, but she wouldn't.

She clutched my arm, and her pupils stretched over her blue eyes. I lurched away, kicking at her shins, but she wouldn't let go. "Calm down or this is going to hurt," she ordered, but I didn't listen.

Her fingernails scratched across my face, and I reeled away. She pressed her body against mine to hold me against the wall. Her hand brushed my neck, and everything Robb had done flooded back in a panic.

I fell forward, expecting her to catch my weight. But she jerked backward, hands gripping her violently from behind. The hands belonged to a man I had never seen before.

He was tall and lanky, and his mismatched eyes bore into mine. He looked human, but his limbs moved in a way that humans couldn't.

Teresa's short, black hair became long and translucent, and her boney shoulders shifted as she punched him across the face. He stumbled back, and she was in front of me before I even realized there was another woman next to us. Everyone was moving too fast.

"I see you didn't take our weasel's advice," the woman said, staring at Teresa. They could've been twins.

"Like I'd fall for your tricks, Fudicia," Teresa spat.

Fudicia rolled up her see-through sleeves. "It wasn't a trick," she said, and a light spread from Fudicia to the floor to my feet. My body warmed, nearly paralyzing my legs, and

I grabbed for Teresa as she turned. But my hands fell through her.

"What—" I began, shaking my numbing limbs.

Fudicia ignored my panic, continuing to talk to Teresa. "It's too late for you to kill her now," she said, and I disappeared.

51

Eric

THE EXPLOSION WAS HOTTER THAN ANY LIGHT POWER I HAD FELT. It scorched my exposed skin, and the smell of ash filled my burning nose. In the cloud of debris, I blinked, wondering what direction I was looking in. I wasn't on my back, but I wasn't standing either. My knees were in the snow, and my heavy clothes kept me there. They were fireproof.

"Shoman," Pierce's voice split the fog. "Get up," he ordered, and a hand wrapped around my jacket's shoulder. He lifted me to my feet, and we stumbled against the tree. When I grabbed it for support, the bark crumbled into my fingers. It had taken most of the blow.

"You boys all right?" Urte asked, appearing as the cloud dissipated.

Pierce answered for us as I gaped at the scene in front of us. Aside from a couple of dead shades, the field was empty, and I spun around, searching the area. Shades were the only people I saw, but that didn't mean the lights were gone.

My sword ripped out of my hand before I even thought of mustering it up. "Stop cowering behind your protection, Darthon," I shouted, demanding him to remove whatever illusion he was using.

As if waiting for my order, the air shifted, and a knife collided with the tree, bouncing off the trunk. I spun around, and my sword struck Darthon's. He leapt back, and my eyes swept over the crowd behind him. They had waited in the school's outside lunchroom. I wondered how long my back had faced them, exposed to their weapons.

"Being uphill isn't always an advantage," Darthon said, the tip of his sword swaying from side to side.

I didn't respond to him. I hadn't come to talk. I came to kill him, and I wouldn't hesitate.

I leapt forward, but Pierce latched onto my shoulder. "Wait," he growled as if he were my trainer instead of his father.

"*For what?*"

"*For them,*" Pierce's voice rumbled in my mind as the shades, the ones I was raised around my entire life, rushed to my side. They waited for my orders and no one else's.

I eyed them in my peripherals as Darthon's gaze lit up. "Someone seems to be missing," he said, and I knew he was talking about Camille. "I would've liked to watch her die, but knowing she will is enough."

My grip twisted around my sword's hilt.

"Even half-breeds can't survive in the Light realm for long," he continued, his lip curling. "And I can't say what'll happen to Jess when I die and the realm collapses."

As if on cue, the spaces next to him sizzled, and Fudicia appeared with the half-breed I'd seen before. She was already celebrating their victory. "They're secure," she said, knowing Darthon had already told me.

Their words collided with my body, worse than any attack they were capable of.

"Hesitation, Shoman?" Darthon wouldn't use my human name. "That's odd coming from you."

I ignored his taunts. "Camille is stronger than you'd ever imagine," I said, knowing it was the truth. If he wasn't lying, and I didn't think he was, Camille would get Jessica out of there. My guard said I had to trust her, and I did. I was relying on her.

Darthon's expression twisted when he realized I wasn't as fazed as he hoped. "But is Jess strong enough?"

I didn't get a chance to respond. Pierce flew forward, and

Fudicia met him. At the first blow, the lights rushed forward, and the shades responded, colliding around us. I jumped to the side as three lights fell from out of the tree, pushing the elders back.

My heightened hearing attached itself to every scream of agony, every sickening sound of a knife splitting skin, every threat, and every last breath. In milliseconds, I heard a body, then two, hit the ground, but I couldn't look to see if they were on my side or his.

I dug my feet in the ground as Darthon attacked, ramming his weapon against mine. Sparks scattered into my face, but I kept my burning eyes open. Our gaze locked and he pushed me back. I stumbled. If it weren't for the hand that pulled me away, I would've fallen.

Pierce's breath skimmed my neck as I realized who had prevented it, and Darthon laughed, refusing to look away from me. "You need to have someone watch your back?" he mocked as Fudicia and the half-breed attacked my friend at once.

He flew backwards and leapt to his feet. "I can handle it." He moved between the two before I could stop him.

"The half-breed was supposed to fight your guard," Darthon talked like battle was a first date. "But he obviously won't get the chance."

This time, I was the first one to strike, and the blue light from my blade scorched Darthon's cheek. He gritted his teeth, and the smell of his burning flesh filled my nose. Our faces were inches apart, and I slammed my foot on his.

He jumped, kicking my shin, and we broke apart as the world spun around us. "This battle is between you and me, Shoman," Darthon said.

"Between you and me," I repeated, chuckling at his attempt to threaten me. "Just like it was supposed to be."

52

Jessica

THE STONE FLOOR WAS COLD AGAINST MY PALMS, AND I SHIVERED as I pushed myself up on shaky legs. The room was red—as crimson as Fudicia's sadistic grin—and the walls were embedded with shimmering gold. Four sets of black horns stuck out of the floor, and a heatless fire roared inches away.

I didn't recognize any of the ancient furniture or the eerie statues that lined the room. I had never seen the place before, yet I was strangely comfortable, like I was dreaming all over again.

"Jess." Her screech shattered the room before she fell from the ceiling, smacking against the floor.

I rushed to Teresa's side as she flickered between her human self and the white-haired woman she'd been before. "Teresa," I gasped, grabbing her shoulders. When she looked at me, blood trickled from her eye.

She wiped it away. "I'm fine," she breathed, but her pupils rolled around. "You're not hurt."

I shook my head, and she stared at me like I was a ghost, someone who shouldn't be alive. I ignored it and panicked at her injured state. "We need to get you to a hospital."

"Those don't exist here."

"What—"

"Relax," she said, solidifying into a supernatural being. She laid her hand, hot and humid, on my face, and her fingers

235

pressed against my temples. This time, I obeyed, and darkness suffocating my conscience into emptiness. The hollow state didn't last long.

People—faces, voices, touches, and smells—spun by too fast to comprehend. When it slowed, I recognized the smell of the river first. I touched the guardrail beneath my fingers. I heard his footsteps. I saw him, his straight hair settling around his pale face and iced-over eyes. He moved through the shadows, his hands disappearing and reappearing, and then he was touching me.

Everything rushed out of him—the night we flew, filled with sparks of blue and purple, and the first time his lips pressed against mine, thirsty with desperation. Bats soared across the morning sky, and I remembered Fudicia's golden hair as she threw my body away. My heart crushed as Shoman left me and reformed before Darthon's knife sliced against my shoulder. And Camille was there, clutching me to take me to the Dark.

I recalled everything, and the world shattered, revealing the woman who brought everything back.

I dug my nails into Camille's arm, knowing she was Teresa all along. We were in the Light's realm, and I should've been in pain. I should've been dying. But I wasn't, even though Camille was suffering.

"We have to get out of here," I managed, trying to stand up, but she yanked me to the ground.

"Do you remember everything?"

"Eric is in trouble." It was my only response.

Camille, on the other hand, was gaping. "You're not in pain?"

"No," I ranted. "But we need to find a way out of here—" *Before we die.*

"Only lights can control this place," Camille said, and I knew I couldn't leave on my own. Still, she smiled. "Good thing I'm half of one."

I grabbed her arm. It felt like she was thinning with every second. "You can't," I said. "You're hurt."

"That's what Darthon's counting on," she muttered, refusing to surrender. "That's what separates us from them. We realize sacrifice is a must."

She said it like she wasn't leaving with me.

"What will happen to you?"

"This isn't about me." She avoided a direct answer.

"Camille!"

"Tell Eric the girl was right," she instructed, steadying her fingers on my face. "He'll understand."

"You'll die if you stay," I argued.

She looked away, her black eyes reflecting the flames from the heatless fire. "Shoman loves you, Jess," she stated. "He needs you, and you need him. If you die, he will, too."

"He wouldn't want you to die for me."

"He wouldn't want us both to die either," she retorted, turning back to me. "It's one or the other."

"Both of us can get out."

"No, we can't," she said, and warmth flooded my veins like a relaxant. "I've already bestowed my energy to you," she explained, and I knew her Light powers were inside of me.

Her form dissipated, and a side of Teresa I had never seen before looked back at me. She was sickly, thinning as if her blood had been drained from her body. She was dying in front of me. "Saving the Dark is worth dying for." Not life. Not love. Only duty.

I sniffled, rubbing the tears from my face as they ran down my cheek. "I don't want you to die."

"For what it's worth, I've always seen you as one of us," she stuttered, barely able to breathe. "Remember that when you're fighting."

I tried to hold onto her as a bright light engulfed me, and a willowing structure appeared in the mist. "Goodbye, Jess," she said just as I joined the battle.

53

THE HILLSIDE LOOKED LIKE A YIN-YANG SYMBOL, QUAVERING AND swirling together in the ironic imbalance that created it. Blood mixed with my sweat as it trickled down my forehead, and the liquid left the tips of my hair crusted together. My brow was slit, and my right arm was slashed from my shoulder to my elbow. Darthon's sword had only struck me once, but the injury was numbing my limb. I would've been at a disadvantage if I hadn't gashed his leg at the same time he struck me.

I panted, glancing at the field that once had been covered in snow. It was now pink with diluted blood, and the slaughterhouse waved as if it would take us down at any moment.

"How much longer can you handle me?" Darthon spat as our swords collided again.

"As long as you can stay alive." I shoved him back, and my muscle tore further. I grit my teeth as he laughed, but he didn't attack.

He wiped his face, revealing a slit cheek I hadn't even realized I had given him. I took advantage of his break and spit out the tangy blood that had collected in my mouth. My lip was cut.

"How's your leg?" I asked, hoping to deter his confidence.

"Better than your arm."

I shifted my sword to my left hand. Urte had trained me

to be ambidextrous. "You're the one hesitating now," I said, even though I was relieved by the break.

"I don't want this battle to end so quickly." He smiled, but it crumbled from his face when the slit on his cheek stretched. "I want to enjoy my victory."

"That's going to be hard when you're dead."

He lunged forward, and we fought, my back pressed against the willow tree. "You won't kill me," he wheezed, his nose inches from mine. "Not when it would collapse the realm on Jess."

My heart dropped, my adrenaline rose, and I made a decision. I absorbed my sword, ducking beneath his blade, and his dagger stuck in the bark. He didn't have time to react. I slammed my hand against his chest, and he soared backwards, skimming across the ice like he was no more than a ragdoll discarded by a malicious child.

My footsteps shook the ground as I trudged toward him, slamming my foot on his wrist. His black eyes flashed as his weapon disappeared, and I brought mine back, placing it next to his throat. "Bring them back," I ordered, my voice tearing. "Now."

"Or what? You'll kill me?" he croaked. "I'm taking them with me."

I flicked my wrist, and my blade sliced across his chest. He screamed, and I dug the toe of my boot into his hand. "Want to answer that again?"

He wouldn't budge as a groan escaped him.

"Bring them back before I kill you."

"Kill me and win this prophetic battle of yours," he screamed back. Even he knew I was in control of his end.

"Not without Jessica."

"Your Jessica is gone," he spat.

I raised my sword, slamming my foot against his throat as I brought my weapon down for the kill. Inches away, a woman's scream interrupted my actions before her attack did.

My left side was struck with fire, and I crumbled over, filled with a pain I'd never felt before. It filled my insides as if my organs and muscles were tearing apart. My powers were suffocating, and my sword was gone. When I opened my eyes, a fog of snow exploded into the air, reacting to my collision, and it glittered against the night sky like a hundred new stars. A stifled moan came out of my lungs before it drifted away.

"Darthon," the woman continued to scream as she fell on her knees at his side. It was Fudicia who attacked me. "Are you okay?"

Darthon stood up, ranting, but his words melted together. All my senses were blending. I couldn't speak, feel, or think clearly. Anything was everything. There was no singularity.

I saw Pierce, holding the half-breed against the ground, and then I heard the war. There was a shout, and Pierce's green eyes glowed through the darkness. But I couldn't react. I already felt as if I had died.

Darthon's voice was the first one to bring my focus back. "You're pathetic," he said, and I realized we'd switched positions. He was on top of me, and his sword was against my throat, burning my thinning skin. "You're weak enough to fall from Fudicia's hand—"

"I thought this war was between you and me," I used his words against him. "What happened to our war?"

"Our war is over," he bellowed. "Our war is my victory."

"It's Fudicia's victory," I retorted, and he faltered, moving his blade away. I took a breath as he stepped back.

"Get up," he demanded.

I didn't give him a chance to change his mind. I pushed myself to my feet as quickly as I was able to. Behind my enemy, Fudicia gaped. "You aren't going to kill him?" she screeched, her white hair spiking around her snarl.

He pushed the woman who just saved his life. "Not with you in the way," he growled.

"She won't get in the way again," a boy said, and I looked over my shoulder to see Pierce, covered in blood that wasn't his. When my eyes traveled past him, the hill seemed darker than before, blanketed with shades instead of lights. They were losing.

"I thought I got rid of you," Fudicia glowered, but her voice was shaking.

"Not quite," Pierce said, and then he was fighting her, directing her backwards with every blow.

"*Be careful,*" I spoke to him, but I regretted my lack of concentration instantly.

Darthon's hand wrapped around my throat, and he pinned me against the tree. It was a simple mistake, but it was big enough to end my life. He was in control again, and no one had intervened but me.

"Looks like the first descendant will also be the first to fall." His breath was musty as it brushed my face.

I managed to get my sword out, but he was too close. The pressure of heat scorched my gut, and I knew my own blade would slice me open if I didn't get back.

I leaned away, but he repositioned, and my shoulder blades dug into the willow tree's bark. Out of all the places to die, this had to be the most ironic.

It didn't matter if my people were winning. I couldn't kill Darthon if it meant Camille and Jessica would die in his realm, and I couldn't force him to bring them back. I'd die from exhaustion before I would kill him. Even with destiny on my side, I was too weak to win everything I had prepared myself for. But Jessica would be alive.

At least, she would have a chance.

I let go of my sword, and it disappeared before hitting the ground. "Looks like you win," I said, but Darthon didn't cut me in half.

He held back, waiting for my people to witness my fall. The sounds of clashing weapons shifted into the cheers of the Light and the cries of the Dark. "Don't give up, Shoman," one screeched, and I wondered what my father was shouting. "Fight back."

But I couldn't fight anymore. People were dying in my name, and others were murdering in Darthon's. Until one of us was dead, more would fall. My death would save more people than my life would save. Fighting was pointless—absurd even—and I had already made up my mind. It was my night to die.

Darthon swung his sword backwards, and I stared at his face, knowing he would be the last person I would ever see. I wanted to hear the blade strike me, but the only sound I could hear was my heartbeat, thundering quietly as if it were preparing to fade away. The air shifted as he brought it down, but it wasn't cold. It was hot, and it was exploding.

I wasn't standing upright anymore. I couldn't see the stars or hear the shouts of my people. I only felt the snow beneath my hands. My palms thumped with my blood-filled veins, and I stared at my shaking fingertips. I was alive, but I couldn't make sense of anything.

"Get up." Her voice shattered my decision to die, but her presence froze my life.

I couldn't believe what my mind was telling me, and the silence suggested the crowd couldn't either. She'd appeared from Darthon's sword, and she hadn't hesitated to blast him away from me. He was yards away, struggling to stand, and I was saved by a purple-eyed girl.

"Jessica." I never thought I would be able to speak again.

"Get up," she repeated, grabbing my shoulder before she yanked me to my feet. She was beyond alive. She was fighting, and I couldn't stop her.

54

Jessica

I SPIRALED AT HIM, SOARING THROUGH THE AIR WITH MORE POWER than I recalled having. Even my sword was larger, piercing the sky with a brightness never seen. I handled it like it was an extension of my body and aimed it at Darthon's chest. He stumbled to the side.

When my feet hit the ground, I was panting, and I didn't leave my back to face him. I turned around, expecting an attack, but he held his hands up.

"How'd you know that you could get out?" he asked, his voice rushing over me.

"I didn't," I said, lifting my hand to mirror his. "Camille did." A light blasted out of my palm too strongly. It shot my body backwards, and I skidded in the snow. It flew up in a mist, blocking my vision, but I turned around, sensing her.

Fudicia was behind me, and I grabbed her wrist, flipping her body over my head. She slammed into the frozen grass, and I exhaled, finally achieving the revenge I wanted on her since she threw me months ago.

The mist cleared as she leapt out, readying to strike me, but I put my arm up, hoping to block it. She never struck me, and I peered out to see Darthon pulling her back.

"Don't," he ordered, and she obeyed, using her hand to wipe the blood off her mouth.

I didn't like it. I wanted to fight her, if only Eric would

fight Darthon, and he wasn't near us. I had seen his injuries before I had even transported in. He was losing, and I solidified in the last minute. I couldn't afford to give them any more time. We had to end it—together.

"He already gave up," Darthon said, and I ignored him, kicking Fudicia as I sliced at his face. The two flung away from each other, and I struck Darthon.

He fell over, and I stood on him, watching as his dislocated jaw popped back in place. Every injury I gave him healed. "You can't kill me," he mocked, but I stabbed him anyway.

His body recoiled, and he rolled away, tearing open his abdomen. I could see his insides, but his skin closed before he stood up, perfectly fine. "You're fighting a useless battle."

"I may not be able to kill you," I said, shaking with the warming power Camille gifted me. "But I can bring you pain, and that's enough for me."

His slit brow rose. "Revenge for the pain you feel?"

Camille. She was dead, and I would've struck him again if his eyes hadn't shifted behind me. I used my peripherals to see Eric—barely able to hold his form as Shoman together. Pierce was next to him, and behind them was an army of all those who had sworn to fight for us.

"It's over, Darthon," Shoman said.

Darthon didn't agree. "She didn't tell you, did she?" he asked, his eyes sliding back to me.

Camille's last order echoed inside of me. *The girl had been right.* That's all she had said.

Darthon was focused on me. "If you die, I die," he said, and my stomach twisted, knowing every shade had heard his words. "Who's your enemy now?"

55

Eric

"THAT'S NOT TRUE," JESSICA SAID LIKE IT WAS FACTUAL. Darthon reeled back as if she had punched him, and I glanced at the shades behind me. They teetered, leaning on their tiptoes in two directions. Some faced Darthon, but more faced Jessica. They would have a better chance at killing her than him, and they would take the opportunity out of desperation.

"It's true," he insisted.

She stepped back to stand at my side. She didn't even bother protecting her back from her kind.

"You wouldn't have killed Hannah then," she pointed out, remembering my first girlfriend before I did. Her returned memory was stronger than mine, and she had to be right. The Light had thought Hannah Blake was the third descendant, and they murdered her. They wouldn't have done that if it meant Darthon dying.

"We knew she wasn't you," Darthon snapped, wild-eyed. "We only wanted them to believe your life was worth protecting. Why do you think we chose a war?" he ranted, rushed and desperate. His people were retreating. "It gave them another reason to protect you."

The debate was fickle, and the Dark wouldn't accept it. They were no longer facing her, and Darthon's eyes slid over my army. His desperation was his greatest weapon, and I saw it before he used it.

"Get out of here," I shouted back at my people, preventing more of their deaths. "Now."

Many of them disappeared without hesitation. The ones that stayed were elders— people I had fought as much as I had fought the Light—and they were willing to die. It was too late to stop them.

I grabbed Jessica as he lifted his hand, and snow shot off the ground, soaring into the sky. Bodies followed it, defying gravity, and I relied on my heavy clothes to keep us down. Through the chaos, a light engulfed the man, and it spread over the land, burning any part of me that hadn't been burned before. At any second, he would burn us all, evaporating our bodies into hell.

"Shoman," Jessica shouted, grabbing my hand, and I gaped at her unscarred flesh. She wasn't burning. "You have to kill him."

But I couldn't even conjure my sword. I was too weak, and the power would kill me if I used it.

"We can't," the man said as he laid a hand on my shoulder. His blue gaze was the only thing I could see through my watering eyes. "We have to go—"

"We can't retreat," Jessica said, filled with horror.

"He retreated once," my father argued. "It's our turn."

"But it's supposed to happen tonight."

"If it happens tonight, he won't be the one dying," my father said, and I knew it was true. We were burning alive, and we couldn't get close to him even if we turned to ashes while doing it. But ignoring the battle was impossible.

I was supposed to leave with Darthon dead at my feet. I was supposed to be victorious. I was supposed to save the Dark. There weren't any instructions for after the battle because he was supposed to be dead. Now, he wouldn't be. He would be alive, and there wouldn't be a battle to end the torment he would cause. All because I hesitated for my one weakness.

"The prophecy—" I started, but my father's hand tightened on my wrist. I could see the bones of his fingers.

"I don't care about that," he said. "I care about getting my son back alive."

Jessica was looking at me, and I grabbed her hand, unsure of every decision I had made. I wanted to tell her to leave me, to escape, but I didn't get the chance.

"Let's go," she agreed with my father, and we were gone.

56

I MOVED MY ARM UP AND DOWN, TESTING URTE'S STITCHING ABILI-
ties. My skin was hardened, nearly impossible to work with,
but my trainer had managed for the time being. I volunteered for the threads when I realized they didn't have enough
dissolvable stitches for everyone injured. After all, there
weren't any spells imbedded in my injury, and my shade form
would heal within a couple of hours. I could endure the pain
until then.

"They look good to me," my father said, and I glanced over
at his healing face. Half of his burns were gone.

"They feel great," I admitted, feeling as if I could return to
battle and end it, but it was too late. It was over, and there was
no victory.

"I'm surprised," Urte said, sitting next to me. "I've never
stitched someone up before."

"I'm flattered to be your guinea pig," I joked, and he chuckled.

Luthicer cleared his throat to drown the laughter out, and
I stared at the half-breed elder. He was the least injured out of
all of us, but he hadn't spoken since we'd returned. His dark
eyes closed, eyelashes shadowing his cheeks, and I wondered
if this was how lights cried.

Eu hadn't returned, but no one mentioned him. Even
then, I doubted Eu was the reason behind Luthicer's mourn-

ing. He was thinking about Camille, my guard and his prodigy. She was a daughter to him, and she was gone. Jessica could hardly tell us she was so upset.

"Why don't you check on Jess?" my father suggested it as if we shared a mind.

I leapt off the table and walked into the hallway bustling with shades healing other shades. I wondered how many people we actually lost or how we would explain it to the human population. It was a mess and wasn't even resolved. It was a relief to leave the hallway and dip into the room I knew Jessica was hiding out in.

I stopped in the doorway when I saw her. She was human already, completely unharmed, and holding Jonathon's hand. "You're both human," I said, closing the door behind me as I tried to ignore my jealousy. It was irrational. He was her guard.

"Thought it'd be more comfortable," Jonathon said, but it didn't make sense. He was injured, and he would feel more pain as a person. "*For Jess,*" he clarified, and I walked across the room.

She let go of Jonathon's hand to grab mine. "Are you all right?"

"I'm alive if that counts for anything."

"That counts for everything," she said, tugging on my hand lightly. She didn't want to hurt my stitches, but she wanted me to kiss her, and I didn't know if I could. I had just lost everything. I didn't feel like I deserved to have her.

When I didn't move, her eyes became misty. "I'm sorry," she blurted out, and I didn't have to ask to know what she was talking about.

"Don't be," I said, kneeling down to touch her face. Her skin sizzled with all the energy Camille left behind. "I'm just glad you're okay."

"But Camille—"

"She knew what she was doing," I pointed out before she could dwell on something none of us could change.

"That doesn't make it any better," she argued stubbornly.

"No, it doesn't," I agreed. "But she died doing what she

thought was right, and for that, we have to respect it."

Jessica blinked her tears away. "You won't mourn her?"

"Of course I will." *I already am.* "But there has been enough death tonight. We need rest."

"I agree," Jonathon said, looking directly at Jessica. "It'd probably be best if you stayed away from the shelter for a while."

His words almost started a new kind of fight. "So she can be an easy target?" I asked, using my words instead of my fists.

"She's an easy target here," he said and we knew what he meant. If one shade believed Darthon would die if Jessica did, she was in trouble.

"I can defend myself," Jessica interrupted, placing a hand on my chest.

I looked at her like she had agreed to kill Pierce if need be.

"If I have to," she clarified, and I turned away, knowing I couldn't argue. She wasn't safe anywhere—not from our kind—and the only one who could protect her was the man I should've killed tonight.

"Then, she stays," Jonathon changed his mind, silencing as he stood up. No one wanted to discuss it.

We didn't talk again until the door opened, and my father stepped inside. "How are you kids holding up?"

"I'm not in pieces yet," Jonathon joked, but no one laughed. He rubbed the back of his head and stared at the wall. I knew what he was thinking. Camille would've slapped him for making fun of a serious situation.

"We should get everyone out of here," my father continued, ignoring Jonathon's reaction. "And I'd prefer if you stayed at our house tonight, Jess—until we are positive Darthon's given up."

"Yes, sir," she mumbled, knowing her parents would have an illusion spell put on them if it hadn't happened already.

"Do you have enough power to transport?" my father asked, and I shook my head.

"I do," Jessica said. Despite being in the Light realm, she hadn't suffered physically at all. It was her emotional pain I worried about.

"Come in five minutes," my father instructed, slowly disappearing. "I have to talk to Mindy." When he was fully gone, I wondered if my stepmother would be placed under a spell, too.

"Are you going to be okay, Jonathon?" Jessica asked, and I wished I knew when he had exposed his identity to her.

"I'll be fine," he promised. "Brenthan stayed home," he said to me.

"Good," I said, feeling my first bit of relief, even though I knew three girls who wouldn't be getting their father back. I could only hope Ida had survived. "Let's go now," I said to Jessica, not wanting to voice my thoughts.

She nodded, and we were in my house before I realized she had done it. I hadn't even seen smoke or felt the transport. It was too smooth.

I gaped at her as her shoulders lifted in a half-shrug. "I think my powers are enhanced," she whispered just as my bedroom door flew open.

Mindy was in tears. "You're okay," she said, crossing the room to embrace us both. I struggled beneath her hold and froze when I saw my father in the doorway. He was still a shade.

"What—"

"I've always had a feeling something wasn't right," she explained, pulling back as she wiped tears away. "It's okay now."

But it wasn't. It was too easy, and I was looking from my father to her, wanting a better explanation. "How could you accept this so easily?" I asked.

Mindy tilted her face to the side. "I love you guys," she said it like she was actually my mother, and I hated to admit that I wished she was.

"I have more explaining to do," my father muttered, falling into his human form. Mindy's eyes got big, and she giggled like she was experiencing magic instead of everything that caused her family pain.

"I'll have to adjust to that," she said.

My father took her hand. "Let's leave them alone," he said, and she waved as he directed her out.

My knees buckled beneath me, and Jessica grabbing me

was the only reason I didn't fall. She sat me on my bed and crawled up next to me. "It's okay," she said, and I realized I was crying—sobbing like the child I had never been allowed to be.

"She's human," I gasped, and Jessica's fingertips brushed across my cheek. "Humans exist." And it felt unfair that I would never be one.

"Look at yourself," Jessica said, only grabbing my hand to lift it. The skin was burnt on one, and the other one was still bleeding. "You're human, too, and you're a brave one."

The tears stopped. "I gave up," I admitted, thinking of how easily my life could've been taken. "I gave up."

"What do you mean—?"

"I gave up because you were going to die if I killed him." I knew it was wrong even when I did it. "There was no reason to live after that."

She slapped the back of my head. "What are you talking about?" she asked. "The Dark needs you—"

"And I need you," I interrupted, turning my torso to meet her eyes—the girl I had always loved, who finally remembered me. "You don't know how hard it was without you here."

She was silent, and it was the last sound I wanted to hear.

"I have something for you," I said, jumping to my feet to cross the room. I could feel her eyes on me as I opened up my dresser drawer and pulled out the black box my father gifted me. My legs shook as I sat down next to her. I opened it before I could stop myself.

Inside was the one thing my mother had left behind—her wedding ring. It was silver and glittered without light. The sides twinkled as they spun out like two wings, curling down the ends. Between the twists, two sapphires intertwined as if they were one jewel, and a single diamond sat above them.

She scooted away. "Eric—"

"It's not an engagement ring if you don't want it to be," I explained before she could deny it. "It can be more like a promise if you want."

She wasn't breathing, and I was about to hyperventilate.

"I know this is a lot to be asking, but—" I grabbed her

hands and put the box in her palms. She was shaking. "I knew I had to do this—even months ago, I knew I wanted this," I explained, wanting to make sure she understood I wasn't doing it as a reaction of the night. "Life is short, and I want to spend it with you."

Her fingers skimmed the jewels, but she was looking at me. "You're serious, aren't you?"

"Very."

She stared at it for the first time, and I swore I could see the sapphires reflecting in her gaze.

"It was my mother's," I managed, and she squeaked. "She left it for me because she knew I'd find you."

"I—I—" She wasn't answering, and she dropped the box in her lap, so she could rub her forehead. "I'm really tired, Eric," she said, but I didn't give up. I wasn't capable of giving up on her.

"Did I do something wrong?" I asked, touching her arm.

She leaned into me, placing her head on my shoulder, and I half-expected her to pass out.

"If this is too soon—"

"You didn't do anything wrong," she whispered, and I laid my arm around her torso. "It's perfect. It's just—" She hesitated.

I pushed her back to lift her chin up. I wanted to look at her. "What is it?" I asked. "Just tell me."

"I don't deserve this." Her insecurity broke me more than her rejection. "Not right now."

"You've always deserved it," I argued, grabbing the box from her lap. She didn't even fight me. "I'll prove it to you," I said, and she started to speak, but I kissed her to prevent it. When we broke apart, I asked one last question, "Can I take you somewhere tomorrow?"

I leaned over to put the ring on my desk before she nodded. "I'm sorry—" she started, but I lifted the blankets on my bed.

"I don't like it when you say that," I said.

She bit her lip.

"Get in," I instructed, pointing to the covers.

She crawled in without arguing. I only followed her when she stopped squirming. Her nervous movements were oddly endearing, and I wrapped my arm around her side, surprised that her hair still smelled like shampoo.

"Goodnight, Jessica."

"Do you believe him?" she asked.

I had practically proposed to her, and she was still focused on Darthon. I sighed, more upset at myself than her hesitation.

"Do you?" she repeated, and I knew she was wondering about her death bringing his.

"I'd never hurt you," I answered, and she tensed. It was an indirect response, but it said everything she asked to hear. I believed him. "What do you believe?" I asked.

"I don't know."

I threaded my fingers through her curls. "Can I say one last thing?"

She flipped around, and her forehead pressed against mine. "I can't really stop you."

"I love you," I said.

She smiled for the first time that evening. "I love you, too," she said, and for once, I felt like I had won everything—all because we were able to express our love without being forced to stop it.

57

Jessica

I WOKE UP BEFORE HIM AND MANAGED TO GET OUT OF HIS BED WITH-
out waking him. It felt like a bigger accomplishment than
being alive, but I didn't feel very alive. My entire body felt
drained, and I struggled to walk down the hallway to the
kitchen.

"Morning, Jess." His father was chipper, and Mindy
bounced around like she hadn't just learned of another world's
existence. I stared, unable to comprehend their nonchalant at-
titudes. They only looked up when I didn't respond.

"Are you okay?" Mindy asked, crossing the room.

I waved, hoping she would keep her distance. "Still shook
up," I admitted.

Eric's father put a mug of steaming liquid on the table.
"Hot tea," he said, and I thanked the older version of Eric. I
wondered if all biological kids resembled their parents as
much as Eric did.

I took a sip as Noah bounced down the hallway. "What's
going on in here?" he asked, rubbing his eyes, and I wondered
if he would be told about the Dark one day, too. When he saw
me, he stopped. "What are you doing here?"

"Noah," Mindy's tone a harsh warning, and he
straightened up. "Your breakfast is almost ready." This time,
she sounded kind, and I was startled by how quickly she could
change it.

"Thanks, Mom," he mumbled, crawling into the nearest chair. I stared at Eric's stepbrother, taking in the changes he had gone through. He was growing, and the sudden change was startling. "How have you been?" he asked, eyeing me as if I had checked him out.

"Good," I said.

He opened his mouth as Eric's bedroom door shot open. The wood cracked against the wall, splitting the conversation.

"Where's—" He stopped when his tired eyes landed on me. "Jessica. You're still here."

"Of course I am," I squeaked.

He sighed and laid a hand on his chest as if the night before had slammed into him.

"Why don't we all sit down and—"

"Jessica and I have to go somewhere," he said, but his father held up a hand.

"Relax, Eric," he said, looking from his son to me. He knew something happened. "Get some good food in you first."

"Fine." He plopped into a seat at the table. "But then we're leaving."

Noah's nose scrunched up. "You might want to shower first," he said, and Eric's eyes darted to his stepbrother. "You smell like hell."

"Sorry, kid," Eric said, laying his hand on Noah's head. "I got in a fight with it last night."

Noah pushed him away, but he was smiling. "You're weird," he said, and Eric shrugged as Mindy dropped breakfast on the table.

"Eat up," she said. "You'll need your strength."

———◆———

Eric's father cleaned up the dishes as Eric showered. Noah disappeared to his room, and Mindy eyed the sweater she let me borrow. I shifted beneath the scratchy wool and wondered how she always wore things like it.

"It's a little big," she said, and I wrapped my arms around

my torso. "But it should keep you warm."

"Thank you," I said, knowing she didn't have to give me clothes to wear. Mine weren't even ruined, but I doubted I could ever wear them again. The memory of the battle would be too much.

"I can check to see if I have a coat," she said, and I didn't bother stopping her. She wouldn't listen anyway.

"She has a big heart," Mr. Welborn said, but he had broken a law by telling a human about the Dark. He had also done what was necessary. He needed to know who—or what—she was, now that our identities were revealed.

"Where's Eric taking you?" he asked.

"I don't know," I admitted.

The shower turned off in the hallway bathroom. Eric would be out any minute, and I expected his father to ask me something else—anything really—but he didn't.

"Here, Jess," Mindy said, rushing back in the room. She had me turned around and wrapped me in a fluffy coat before I could even respond. "It's cold out today."

"And it will be all winter," Eric's father said.

Mindy laughed as if he had actually said a joke. "This fits perfectly," she continued, and my body heat escalated. I would get too hot if I didn't get outside soon.

"Hey, Mindy—" Eric started talking as he opened the door, drying his hair with a towel. When he looked up, he stopped to look at me. "Oh, good. You're already dressed."

"Yeah." I tried to keep my eyes off his chest. He wasn't dressed. He was only in a towel.

"We probably won't be back for a while," Eric spoke over his shoulder as he went to his room. "I'll take my phone, but I always have this." He leaned out, pointed to his head, and then ducked back in his room.

His father rolled his eyes as Mindy's brow rose. "Why wouldn't he have his head?" she asked.

"Telepathy," his father said. "Remember?"

She slapped her forehead. "I should take notes."

"Don't do that."

"Don't write anything down," she repeated an apparent rule he had given her. "I remember now." Mindy beamed as Eric came out. "You two have fun," she said.

Eric stopped next to me. I waited for him to touch me, but he didn't. "Bye," he said, but his father sat his mug of tea on the table.

"Wait," he said. "There's something I wanted to discuss with you two."

Eric's shoulders rose at his tone. "About?"

"Just be safe."

"We will be," I said.

"Not about Darthon." His father groaned. "About, you know, what teenagers do."

"Dad," Eric's voice was sharp. "You can stop now."

"We don't need a pregnancy on top of all of this," his father continued anyway, and my face burned. "I know it's fun and all, but you two have responsibilities."

"We aren't sleeping together," Eric responded because I couldn't.

"But—" His father couldn't believe it. "You two are acting weird. I figured—"

"Nothing happened," he said, grabbing my arm as he dragged me downstairs.

His father's confusion turned into a chuckle. "Wait."

Eric grabbed the doorknob but turned his torso around. "We're leaving."

"You're forgetting something," his father said, reaching into his shirt pocket. He pulled out a set of keys and tossed it across the room. "Have fun."

58

Jessica

WE STOOD IN THE DRIVEWAY AND STARED AT ERIC'S PRESENT. A black car—just like the one Eric had crashed—was parked in front of us, somehow untouched by the snow.

"That man is unbelievable," Eric muttered.

"You have a really good dad," I admitted, unsure of when Eric's father had morphed from an uncaring parent to an involved one.

"I know," Eric agreed, glancing over at me. "Your hair looks black when it's wet."

I touched my hair, knowing it curled and frizzed as it dried. "I didn't have a blow-dryer."

"Noah broke Mindy's doing a project last week," he said, reaching inside his jacket. He pulled out a beanie, stepped forward, and tugged it over my head. "Ready?"

"Yeah," I managed, and we got in his car.

He backed out of the driveway. We were silent as the car flew through town. News vans littered the streets, and I had to hold myself back from asking him what the Dark's excuse was. I didn't think he would know anyway.

We drove past them, and I pressed my head against the cold glass of the passenger window. The streets turned to fields, and the fields stretched for longer than I had expected. I only recognized it because Crystal had driven me through it.

"We're here," he said, shifting his car into park. He got out before I could even open the door. When I got out, he was halfway over the fence, and I let him help me over even though I didn't need it.

"What's here?" I asked.

Eric stopped. "Don't you see it?" he asked, and I followed his gaze to the horizon.

At first, it was a field—an ordinary piece of land—and then there was a red light, and everything shifted. I gasped. It was the same light I had seen when Crystal was driving.

He grabbed my hand. "Come on." He pulled me forward, and I let him.

We were across the ground, and the light disappeared. Before I could ask him what we were looking at, I realized what was on the ground—my parents' graves.

"How'd you find this?" I asked, kneeling on the wet ground. "I couldn't find a record of this anywhere."

"Because there isn't." He sat down next to me. He didn't have to explain. The Dark had protected them.

I touched their faces, studying the pictures I had never seen before. They were different from the only article I had of them and even more beautiful.

"I stopped looking for them," I admitted, knowing I had given up as much as Eric had. "When I lost my memory, I lost more than you."

"I know."

I glanced over at him. With my restored memory, I regretted most of my recent actions. "I never hated you."

"You didn't know," he said like he had already forgiven me. "And I shouldn't have believed it, even for a second."

I couldn't tear my eyes from him. His green eyes could see past any façade I put up, and I knew he actually saw me, even when I couldn't. He had forgiven me. My problem stemmed from not forgiving myself.

"My plan didn't really work, did it?" I managed.

He grabbed my hand. "It was everyone's plan," he said every word I needed to hear before I knew I needed to hear it.

"The circumstances were out of our control."

Chaos within destiny. It was the definition of our love.

"Why'd you find this?" I asked, touching their graves.

His teeth grinded. He didn't want to make it about him.

"Please, tell me."

"I wanted to ask them for your hand," he said, and my heart twisted, thinking of the night before.

"Did they respond?" I asked, even though it was impossible.

"I think they did."

I held my breath.

He shifted his weight from knee to knee. "Asking them gave me the confidence to ask you."

I touched his arm, so he would look up. "Do you still have it?"

"The ring?" he asked, and I nodded.

He dug into his pocket and pulled it out. He had been carrying it the entire time, and this time, his hand wasn't shaking when he opened it.

The jewelry was beautiful, breathtaking even, and it was exactly how I felt when I looked at him. "Is it too late?" I asked.

He chuckled, leaning over to touch my face. "You really are ridiculous sometimes," he said.

I giggled before he pulled me into his lap and kissed me. Without a word, he pulled the ring out and slipped it over my finger.

I stared at it, feeling every emotion we shared. "Don't you need one?" I asked, and he cocked an eyebrow.

"I take that as a 'yes' then," he said, and I nodded. "I have my father's at home," he explained. "I only took it out of the box so you could see yours."

"Can I have yours?" I asked, and he leaned back. "I want to give it to you," I clarified.

His cheeks flushed. Even Eric Welborn could get nervous.

"Please."

"When we get back," he said.

"Promise?"

His eyes landed on my ringed finger. "It's beyond a promise," he said, and I grabbed his hand. He looked at our entwined fingers, but a frown escaped him. "I won't ever be able to give you a normal life," he said.

I tightened my grip. "Good thing I don't want one," I said, but he looked at the sky, and it occurred to me that he might want one.

"I will kill Darthon, and this will end," he said.

I pulled him to his feet. "Don't spoil the moment by talking about another man," I joked, and he laughed, shaking his head from side to side. "I believe in you," I added.

He kissed me.

When he pulled back, he didn't say anything, but he didn't have to. His gaze told me everything I needed to know. He believed in me, too.

ACKNOWLEDGEMENTS

And we're here—at the end of the second novel. Seconds Before Sunrise is where it all began. In fact, I wrote this novel first before I realized it needed a novel before it, a.k.a. Minutes Before Sunset, but as many of you know, The Timely Death Trilogy was based off of a series of terrifying dreams I had as a teenager. You saw many of those dreams in this novel, and the person I dedicated this novel to, Calone, was the name of the boy I used to dream of. He is also the inspiration behind Shoman and Eric. He showed me the light in the darkest time of my life, but even though he's ceased to exist, my readers have shown me an even brighter life.

The Timely Death Trilogy is more than a story. It is my connection with my magnificent readers, my most cherished friends, my witty book bloggers, my honest helpers. There are no words to express the amount of love I have for you, but I hope you've enjoyed the trilogy so far, and I hope you look at the Dark in a new way, in the way Calone taught me to, without fear and with love. Without those dreams, this story wouldn't have existed, but without the support and dreams of my readers, this story would've ceased to exist. The Dark is alive because of you, and I thank you from the bottom of my writer's heart for every page you've turned.

A special thanks goes out to my dedicated and squirrel-loving team at Clean Teen Publishing. Another one goes out to my hilarious cover artist Marya Heiman, and an additional one is for my faithful editors, Kelly A. Risser and Cynthia Shepp. Lastly, I would like to thank my father, brother, and friends who've supported and accepted me, even though I still believe in fairytales and things that go bump in the night.

Stay Dark,
Shannon A. Thompson
Join the Dark and visit www.ShannonAThompson.com

ABOUT THE AUTHOR

Shannon A. Thompson is a twenty-three-year-old author, avid reader, and habitual chatterbox. She was merely sixteen when she was first published, and a lot has happened since then. Thompson's work has appeared in numerous poetry collections and anthologies, and her first installment of The Timely Death Trilogy became Goodreads' Book of the Month. As a novelist, poet, and blogger, Thompson spends her free time writing and sharing ideas with her black cat named after her favorite actor, Humphrey Bogart. Between writing and befriending cats, she graduated from the University of Kansas with a bachelor's degree in English, and she travels whenever the road calls her.

Visit her blog for writers and readers at
www.shannonathompson.com

CPSIA information can be obtained at www.ICGtesting.com
Printed in the USA
LVOW06s0004270715

447677LV00002B/91/P